ABOUT THE AUTHORS

USA TODAY bestselling author **Kimberly Raye** has always been an incurable romantic. While she enjoys reading all types of fiction, her favorites, the books that touch her soul, are romance novels. From sexy to thrilling, sweet to humorous, she likes them all. But what she really loves is writing romance—the hotter the better! Kim lives deep in the heart of the Texas Hill Country with her very own cowboy, Curt, and their young children. You can visit her online at www.kimberlyraye.com or at www.myspace.com/kimberlyrayebooks.

Leslie Kelly is an award-winning author of more than thirty books for Harlequin Blaze, Harlequin Temptation and HQN Books. Leslie resides in Maryland with her husband of twenty-two years and their five girls: three human and two fuzzy and yappy. (Okay, they're all yappy....) Please visit Leslie at her Web site www.lesliekelly.com, or hang out in the "jungle" where she blogs with pals Carly Phillips, Janelle Denison and Julie Leto: www.plotmonkeys.com.

Waldenbooks bestselling author, past RITA® Award nominee and *Romantic Times BOOKreviews* Reviewers' Choice nominee **Rhonda Nelson** writes hot romantic comedy for Harlequin Blaze and other Harlequin imprints. In addition to a writing career, she has a husband, two adorable kids, a black Lab and a beautiful bichon frise who dogs her every step. She and her family make their chaotic but happy home in a small town in northern Alabama. She loves to hear from her readers, so be sure to check her out at www.readRhondaNelson.com or visit her group blog at www.soapboxqueens.com.

Kimberly Raye
Leslie Kelly, Rhonda Nelson

Blazing Bedtime Stories

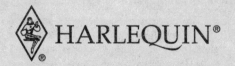

HARLEQUIN®

TORONTO • NEW YORK • LONDON
AMSTERDAM • PARIS • SYDNEY • HAMBURG
STOCKHOLM • ATHENS • TOKYO • MILAN • MADRID
PRAGUE • WARSAW • BUDAPEST • AUCKLAND

Recycling programs
for this product may
not exist in your area.

ISBN-13: 978-0-373-79451-5
ISBN-10:   0-373-79451-7

BLAZING BEDTIME STORIES
Copyright © 2009 by Harlequin Books S.A.

The publisher acknowledges the copyright holders of the individual works as follows:

ONCE UPON A BITE
Copyright © 2009 by Kimberly Raye Groff.

MY, WHAT A BIG...YOU HAVE!
Copyright © 2009 by Leslie Kelly.

SEXILY EVER AFTER
Copyright © 2009 by Rhonda Nelson.

CONTENTS

ONCE UPON A BITE
Kimberly Raye

For all my *Love at First Bite* fans,
your e-mails and letters have meant
the world to me!
Thanks, and here we go again…

And for Rhonda and Leslie,
I'm so thrilled to be included with two
of my all-time-favorite Blaze Babes!

Prologue

"THERE ARE ONE HUNDRED and seventy million, seven hundred and fifty-nine thousand, one hundred and twenty-three people having sex at this exact moment," Burt reported.

Burt was a short, bald guy, who fidgeted as he stood in the middle of LB Patterson's office. The man wore his usual blue leisure suit, a dozen chains around his neck and a look that said *How's it hanging, baby?* "That's not counting several thousand ménage à trois, a few hundred group orgies and a woman up in Jersey getting up close and personal with an authentic African python named Daisy. Needless to say, I've got animal control on stand-by," he added.

"Not bad." LB—known affectionately as Lover Boy and officially as Cupid—punched a few buttons on his state-of-the-art computer and pulled up a spreadsheet. Based on last year's statistics, the sex was up by over a million. A grin tugged at his lips. "We're definitely doing something right."

"I wouldn't pop open the champagne yet," Burt continued. "The number of people doing *it* is definitely on the rise, but less than one third are actually *in* love. Except the Jersey lady. She's definitely head-over-heels for Daisy."

LB's gaze swiveled to the Love category and a bolt of panic went through him. When it came to *amore*, he was the head honcho. The big cheese. The MIC. "But that's down by half."

"I told you not to crack open the bottle. Then again, you could probably use a drink right about now. Venus isn't going to be too happy."

Venus headed the Interaction division for Humans, Inc., a world-wide conglomerate that micromanaged the human race. She was just one of a handful of upper-tier management, but she was no one to mess with. There was also Jupiter, CEO and mega control freak.

Mars was in charge of war and domestic conflicts. Vesta ran morality. Juno monitored reality TV (rumor had it that her two-timing hubby, Jupiter, had a thing for the newest *Bachelorette* and she was determined to catch him screwing around). Bacchus handled addiction. Mercury headed up postal workers. And then there were a half dozen others who managed various aspects of human existence.

LB stared at the numbers again and the Starbucks special blend he'd sucked down earlier started to churn in his stomach.

Contrary to popular myth, Venus wasn't warm or elegant or Miss Touchy-Feely. She was cold, stuck-up and a certifiable ball-buster when she didn't get her way. And her way was dominating the top statistical tier of the organization.

Even more, she wasn't just LB's boss. She was the woman who'd endured hours and hours of labor, a fat backside and swollen ankles—all on his behalf.

"Holy shit," LB muttered. "Mom's going to fry my ass faster than I can say 'till death do us part.'"

Literally.

In addition to being blessed with ethereal beauty, Venus was notorious for borrowing Jupiter's lightning bolt. She also had a black belt in guilt. If the fire didn't end his miserable existence, the mega-dose of "I can't believe my own son is stabbing me in the back and making me the laughingstock of the company" was sure to do the trick.

"Nice knowing you, buddy." Burt shrugged. His gold chains caught the early-morning light that pushed through the wall-to-wall windows. Light danced across the ceiling. "Listen, do you think you might put in a good word for me before she smokes you?" He glanced at the window. "I'm the only sex manager in history who isn't a member of the mile high club because I'm afraid to fly." He glanced at the window that overlooked Chicago (it was a far cry from Rome and an up-close view of the Colosseum, but hey, we're talking the twenty-first century). "This isn't the top floor, but I could make it work."

"Get out."

He shrugged. "You need some quiet time to reflect before you bite the bullet. I understand. Think about the office. I could hook you up with that cute little receptionist down in addiction. She's been wanting to do you for ages."

"*Out.*"

The door closed and LB shifted his attention to the numbers scrolling across his computer screen.

Sex? Way, way up.

Conversation? Not as sky-high, but still higher than last year.

Internet chat? Always on the rise.

Hell, even cuddling was holding its own.

But his baby, his pride and joy, his *livelihood*, had taken a nose-dive straight to the bottom of the list. And he was responsible.

People just didn't believe anymore, and he couldn't say he blamed them. They lived in an era of instant, effortless gratification. From food to shopping, applying for a mortgage to sex. It was all just a mouse-click away. A person could order a pizza, buy the latest bestseller, pay bills and jack off, all without leaving his or her chair.

Love was different. Love required time. Energy. Effort. Even more, love required faith.

That was the real problem. People just didn't believe. They were disheartened, disillusioned and just plain pissed. Which explained the newest *What the hell is this?* memo he'd received yesterday from his dear mother.

He keyed in the Web address referenced on the note. His screen shimmered and flashed as the Web site loaded.

A split-second later, kissmyasscupid.com blazed in black letters across the header, along with a flashing red heart. "Love Stinks" started to play and the heart cracked in two.

Ouch.

He scrolled down to the three video finalists for the site's current anti-Valentine's Day contest. They featured three women—the worst of the worst when it came to non-believers—who despised V-day. They bashed. They scoffed. They bitched about bad dates and loser boyfriends and meaningless one night stands. One even pitched a few handfuls of spaghetti and some gonzo meatballs at the guy doing the video.

They were a prime example of why his numbers were way down.

And…the fastest way to convince Venus to give him a second chance.

The moment the idea waltzed into his head, he should have

pushed it back out. Really. It was hard enough helping out the ones who actually wanted to find the big L.

At the same time, if he could work his magic with this trio of die-hard disbelievers and give them their very own happily-ever-afters, then he could prove his worth to the company. Even more, he could convince his mother that the apple didn't fall *that* far from the tree. Then maybe, just maybe, he wouldn't have to pop a valium before the next Sunday dinner.

If not?

LB forced the thought aside. His numbers might be down, but his faith wasn't. While 99.99 percent of the world categorized love as the stuff of fairy tales and cheesy chick flicks, he knew better. Love was real. Powerful. *Magical.*

Love *did* make the world go round. And it was high time the contest entrants at kissmyasscupid.com learned that firsthand.

1

"I'M GIVING UP SEX FOR GOOD." The declaration came from Shay Briggs, beauty consultant and owner of Skin Deep, the one and only full-service spa in Skull Creek, Texas. "Out of the game, on the wagon, end of story," she vowed as she smoothed the cucumber facial onto the woman stretched out on the table in front of her.

Sue Ann Peters licked at the green glob near the corner of her mouth. "Yum. What's in this?"

"Cucumbers, aloe and my secret ingredient."

"Edible?"

"Only if you want chest hair and an Adam's apple." Sue Ann sputtered and floundered for a nearby water bottle, and Shay smiled. "It has a special testosterone supplement that stimulates phero-mones which are rumored to help shrink pores."

The young woman sucked down several long sips. "Testoster-one can do that?"

"Not all by itself. But mixed with cucumbers, aloe and a few other ingredients, it's a definite maybe. I'm featuring it in next week's column." In addition to running Skin Deep, Shay contrib-uted beauty tidbits for the *Skull Creek Gazette*.

It was a far cry from the stories she'd written as a kid—wild, fantastic stories of love and romance and adventure—and not half as interesting, but at least she was still writing. It was her only con-solation during those rare moments when she became convinced that her life totally sucked.

Like now.

Shay fought down a sudden surge of self-pity and tried to focus on the positive. "I do still have a column, don't I?" she went on. "You're not handing me a pink slip because of the Bobby Barnes incident."

"Of course not." Sue Ann was Shay's best friend and editor at the *Gazette*. "Our readers love Beauty Bites. It's one of our prime features. Second only to Lazarus Buckner's column. No one beats Buckner in the numbers." Lazarus was a retired gastrointestinal specialist who did a weekly report called "People Pipes." "The retirement home ordered an extra fifty papers last week just for the 'Our Friend, Flatulence' piece."

"Any extras sold because of my 'Trick that Trunk' article?"

"No, but I'm sure every woman in town is slathering on the Crisco for a smoother, softer tush."

If only.

After the past two days, Shay seriously doubted that the women of Skull Creek would ever take her beauty advice again. She'd lost their faith, and all because of Bobby.

The low-down, dirty, son of a snake.

Shay gave herself a great big mental kick in the butt and blinked away the sudden burning in her eyes. What the hell was wrong with her? She didn't cry over a man. She didn't cry, period. Her mother had taught her that a long time ago.

"Never let 'em see you weep, dear. Smile and bat your eyes and make them regret ever walking away."

Which is exactly what her mother had done. Five times now, to be exact, and all because she'd fallen for the wrong men. Bad boy types who'd oozed sex appeal and charm. Men who'd been more interested in the night rather than the morning after.

Men like Bobby Dean Barnes.

Bobby was tall, dark and handsome and the latest on Shay's ever-growing list of failed relationships. Instead of sticking around for breakfast the next morning, he'd written a cryptic *We're done, gotta run* in red lipstick on the bedroom mirror.

"My life is a total train wreck."

"I'll give you train wreck. Erwin and Eunice Mcclusky are getting a divorce."

"But they've been married over sixty years."

"Sixty-three, to be exact. It seems Eunice decided that she's tired of faking it. She wants a man who can satisfy her, at least that's what she told Maudette Cranberry. Ever since Erwin had his hip replacement, he just hasn't been able to hit the spot like he used to. So she's dumping him. Which means that my front page article featuring

Skull Creek's oldest lovebirds is a crock. I have exactly six days to come up with a new piece for the Valentine's Day issue. Something sweet and sexy and romantic." Sue Ann sighed. "Now that's a train wreck. You're just experiencing some minor derailment."

Shay stiffened and gathered her determination. "You're right. Sure, my bank account is empty and my appointment book is empty, and my favorite shirt has a tomato sauce stain the size of Texas… But it isn't the end of the world. Things could be worse." Much worse, she reminded herself. She could be starving in a third world country or enslaved by some Colombian drug lord or trapped in a freezer full of Ben & Jerry's.

"Did you try the club soda and lemon juice?" Sue Ann's voice killed her rampant imagination.

"I've tried everything. It won't budge. Next time I'll save my meltdown for the monthly weenie roast instead of the VFW's annual spaghetti dinner."

"Trust me, it wouldn't have been half as interesting. Seeing that jackass Bobby Dean get his ass kicked with a handful of mega-sized meatballs was priceless. A weenie doesn't pack near the punch. He's got a black eye *and* a concussion. Boy, when you reared back and nailed him—"

"Can we skip the details, please?" Especially when each one was already branded into Shay's memory. It was a reoccurring play-by-play sequence of the lowest moment of her life. Second only to crawling into bed with Bobby Dean in the first place. "I never should have slept with him. Everything was perfect until then." They'd dated for two months. They'd gone on picnics and caught every movie at the Paladium. They'd had romantic dinners and long walks in the park. Which had all led her to one conclusion—that Bobby Dean Barnes was more than a bad boy. He had a heart underneath his good looks and the sex appeal, and he actually *liked* her.

She'd given in, slept with him, and he'd broken up with her.

Because Shay Briggs—once-upon-a-time homecoming queen and prom princess, three-time winner of Skull Creek's infamous Miss Pumpkin and Miss Cattle Guard pageants, *and* the only contestant to ever win Travis County Rodeo Darling *twice*—was the absolute worst in bed.

It wouldn't have been a big deal if Bobby Dean Barnes had been interested in more than sex. If he'd been a nice guy rather than the proverbial bad boy. But he'd wanted sex and the big S had never been her strong suit. She'd spent her lifetime holding out for Mr. Right instead of an endless string of Mr. Right Nows and so she'd never really had a lot of practice.

She remembered the red lipstick note on her bathroom mirror and a lump formed in her throat. She'd been so hurt and humiliated that morning and, unfortunately, booked solid at work. Unable to lick her wounds, she'd gone in for a busy Friday filled with people primping for the annual spaghetti dinner later that night.

She'd been preoccupied. And one wax job later, her professional life had joined her personal one in the Totally Screwed category.

"I can't believe I yanked off one of Diane Hardberger's eyebrows." The moment flashed full-color in her head, along with sound effects—the *rrrrippppp* of the wax strip and the horrified scream when the council woman had gotten a good look in the mirror.

"At least you weren't doing a bikini wax."

"You're not making me feel any better."

"So you slipped with the wax and then assaulted someone with several pounds of meatballs? We all have our moments."

But not everyone had their absolute worst "moment" caught on tape courtesy of old man Wintergreen. He'd been documenting the domino tournament being held simultaneously with the dinner and had quickly traded a pair of sixes in favor of a public display of humiliation, name-calling and major ass kicking.

Bobby Dean had shown up with the newly crowned Miss Pumpkin and the truth had been obvious—he'd dumped Shay for someone younger and prettier. Someone who reeked of sex. Miss Pumpkin was twenty-one, with boobs out to there and legs up to here and an ass that could crack walnuts.

Shay, herself, wasn't exactly over the hill at twenty-nine, but she was well on her way up. She'd started to find a few stray grays mixed in with her long blonde hair. Her once-toned body was getting soft in all the wrong places. And the biggee? She'd put on seventeen extra pounds (twenty if you counted the flip-flops and the sweats she'd had on at the last weigh-in). As for cracking walnuts… She'd be lucky to crush a fruit loop.

She dieted and she exercised. She even wrapped herself in plastic wrap once a week. But the upscale spa treatment that had always helped her shed at least five pounds right before every pageant wasn't touching the Stubborn Seventeen.

"Your looks are all you've got, dear. Don't ever forget that."

Her mother's voice echoed in her head. Marlene Briggs had been beautiful, herself, and she'd used that beauty to get what she'd wanted in life, from an endless string of jobs—everything from waitress to nail technician—to husbands one through four—a bull rider, a stock car racer, a professional cowboy and a stunt man. All wild, bad boy types who'd cheated on her even though she'd been Miss Skull Creek six years in a row.

She'd finally found her happily ever after with number five— an accountant named Fred.

Shay didn't want to travel the same bumpy road as her mother, either personally or professionally. She'd gotten her cosmetician's license and a business degree from a nearby community college. Even more, she'd made up her mind at sixteen (after seeing her mother smile and bat her eyes through divorce number three) to skip the hot, unreliable men and go straight for the accountant.

Her head knew that. If only her damned hormones would stick with her mental GPS and stop making detours.

"I'm glad Bobby dumped me," Shay declared. "I'm through with temporary, sex-crazed men."

"Atta girl."

"I want a forever guy. Someone stable. Reliable. Loyal."

"You just described my blue heeler."

"I mean it. This is a good thing." She gathered her resolve and focused on the one positive aspect—she hadn't made the mistake of marrying Bobby Dean. "The best thing that ever happened to me."

"And how. That Kissmyasscupid Web site is awarding a trip to Hawaii for first place. You should at least get honorable mention and a weekend in Vegas for being the most creative." Sue Ann smiled at the memory. "You didn't just morph into a major bee-yotch and flip off men the world over. You morphed and flipped and took out two hundred pounds of spaghetti at the same time."

"He deserved it." Shay shrugged. "And there's no use crying over spilled spaghetti."

"Exactly. Besides, you barely made the front page of the *Gazette,* and even then, you only got a tag line."

Shay glanced at the newspaper spread open a few feet away on the front counter. Her gaze snagged on the black typeface in the bottom right-hand corner.

Shay Briggs and the deadly meatball…see page 7.

"The fact that you would even print the story makes me question the quality of our friendship."

"Don't be so sensitive." Sue Ann shrugged. "News is news. At least you didn't get caught streaking through town in your birthday suit." Sue Ann motioned to the headline that blazed at the top of the front page, along with a picture of a hunky male body, the tush blurred so as not to offend the delicate sensibilities of *Gazette* readers. "I swear, if I were Matt Keller, I'd go into permanent hiding. That or get a job as a male stripper." She let loose a whistle. "The guy is on fire."

"Matt Keller? The new guy?"

"Yeah, He just moved into the old Hinkle cabin outside of town. Rumor has it he used to be a sheriff up in Washington and now he's on the run from some criminal. He's hiding out here, keeping a low profile. At least that's what Emmaline Sugarbaker told Marty Hanson who told the waitress over at the diner who served me my morning espresso."

Shay's gaze snagged on the dark black hair that flowed well past a pair of broad shoulders. "But I thought he had short hair? In fact, I *know* he had short hair. I saw him Friday at the Piggly Wiggly."

Shay had been climbing out of her car while he'd been climbing into his truck. She'd seen him only a moment, but it had been long enough for all of the important points to register—new guy in town, hot guy in town, hot new guy in town.

Every alarm bell in her head had gone off because as much as she'd wanted to walk up to him and offer to show him around Skull Creek, she'd put on the brakes. Matt Keller had B-A-D written all over him, and Shay had given up the big B, along with French fries, Doritos and her beloved Ben & Jerry's Chunky Monkey.

She leaned closer to the picture. "When was this taken?"

"Friday night."

"No way."

"The date was on the film."

"But that's impossible."

"Not really. Maybe he's a cross-dresser and it's just a wig. At least that's what the members of the chess club are voting for." When Shay arched an eyebrow, Sue Ann added, "The newspaper decided to milk the story and take a poll. The Ladies auxiliary is convinced he's taking some really potent vitamins and the domino group over at the diner thinks he's on steroids."

"I heard it was some sort of special mineral wash that promotes hair growth," came the deep voice from the doorway. "Talk about an infomercial waiting to happen."

Shay turned to look at the man who'd pushed through the front glass doors. He was medium in height and a tiny bit overweight with short, spiky blonde hair. A silver earring dangled from one ear and a smile creased his tanned face.

"Can I help you?" she asked.

"The name's Luckyday. Ulysses Randolph Luckyday. I'm the new photographer over at the *Gazette*."

"Ulysses took the picture of Matt Keller," Sue Ann added.

"What happened to Mel?"

"He's on vacation," Sue Ann said. "He won some sort of Valentine's trip to Palm Springs through one of those Internet travel sites and begged me to let him go. I said yes and put in for a replacement. The bigwigs at corporate office flew Ulysses down to fill in."

"I'm from Chicago," Ulysses offered. "Home sweet home when I'm not on assignment. So what about it?" He winked and motioned toward the picture of Matt Keller. "Can you hook me up with whatever he's using? I've been trying to grow my hair out forever."

Shay shook her head. "This picture can't be for real."

"Oh, it's real, all right. I snapped it myself my first day in town.

Shay arched an eyebrow at the man. "You touched it up, didn't you?"

"I never touch up my photos. Unless I'm doing tabloid work, that is. They pay big bucks for me to spray on celebrity pounds." He wiggled his blond brows. "So how much?"

"How much for what?"

"Your super sonic hair tonic."

"I haven't branched out into hair treatments." She'd never had to because her facials, body wraps and waxes had been plenty to keep her schedule full.

Until now.

"My bad. I thought you were the one responsible." He shrugged and glanced around. "Then again, if you had a treatment like that, this place wouldn't be so empty, would it?"

Amen.

He started to turn and Shay's determination fired to life. She'd already lost enough of her clientele. "How about a facial?" She indicated the list of services on the wall.

"A facial?"

"The best in five counties," Shay added.

He eyed the menu for a long moment. "I *could* use better pores." He motioned to her number five special. "Go on and hook me up with one of those orange citrus cleansers. And if you manage to figure out his secret, let me know." He indicated Matt's pic and the hair.

It had to be a wig.

That's what Shay told herself as she finished up Sue Ann's facial and started on Ulysses.

She slathered an orange and mango mixture onto the photographer's face and tried to keep her mind on the task at hand. But she couldn't shake the mental image of Matt Keller with his hot, hunky bod and his long, vivacious hair.

Ugh.

Had she just used *hunky* and *vivacious* in the same sentence? The two just didn't go together, which was the point in a nutshell.

Keller didn't seem like the kind of guy who catered to his feminine side. The one and only time she'd seen him, he'd oozed macho the way Irma Klondike reeked of hairspray and cheap perfume.

He'd worn faded jeans, a plain black T-shirt and worn boots. A straw Resistol had sat low on his forehead, shielding an incredible pair of bright green eyes. Eyes that had peeled away every strip of her clothing at first glance. He'd oozed way too much raw sex appeal to even have a feminine side. That and she happened to know for a fact that he wore regulation white cotton briefs instead of a lace-trimmed thong or cheeky hipsters.

That little tidbit had come from Myrtle Kantor, who'd been in for a sea salt facial and upper lip wax the day of the eyebrow annihilation. The old woman had accidentally gotten a pair of his underwear mixed in with her girdles at the Laundromat on the previous Wednesday. Before the running naked with the vivacious hair incident, which had happened on Saturday night—the same night that old Mr. Wintergreen shot the spaghetti dinner video and Shay's life had turned into the next Titanic.

Then again, what did she know about cross-dressers? About as much as she knew about supersonic hair growth tonics.

She finished spreading on the citrus mask, wrapped a warm towel over the photographer's face and then turned to wash her hands. She set the timer, snagged the newspaper and eyeballed the pic.

Maybe it wasn't a wig.

Maybe he really *had* stumbled on to some sort of miraculous treatment. Or maybe he was washing his hair in spring water jampacked with a high-powered mix of minerals. Or maybe he was taking some heavy duty vitamins or steroids or *something* that had jump-started his hair growth and taken him from short and cropped to long and flowing in less than twelve hours.

She didn't know for sure, but she intended to find out.

She'd be back in business with a vengeance if it turned out to be the real deal. Which meant she was paying a visit to one Matt Keller just as soon as she closed up shop.

In the meantime…

She set the paper aside, ignored the urge to dive into the pint of Cherry Garcia stashed in her portable fridge in the back, and turned to her one and only paying customer for the day.

She gave Ulysses her most persuasive smile. "How'd you like a paraffin foot wax to go with that facial?"

2

MATT KELLER HAD SEEN some freaky shit in his lifetime. Particularly at midnight during a full moon. But this was early in the evening, weeks away from the big M.

He stared down at the huge hard-on and blinked, half-expecting the sucker to whither right before his eyes. Instead, it twitched and throbbed. He shook his head.

Not that he'd never had a hard-on before, or one as sizeable as the ten solid inches staring back at him. Damn straight he'd had one. Plenty, in fact. He loved women, and they certainly loved him. They couldn't help themselves. It was Darwin's theory at its most basic.

As a werewolf, he was the quintessential alpha male. Strong, virile, primitive. Women sensed all three and flocked to him. It was the one and only saving grace in an otherwise cursed life.

Or it had been.

But at thirty years old, Matt had grown tired of the endless stream of women. He was sick of one-night stands. Tired of the constant variety. He wanted a real relationship.

He wanted a mate.

That's why he'd come to Skull Creek in the first place. Because he'd met Viviana Darland while investigating a murder case up in Washington state, and he'd known in his gut that she was more than an ordinary human.

She'd been more, all right. She'd been a vampire.

He touched the two prickpoints at his neck. He still couldn't believe it. A *vampire*. Talk about *freaky*.

Then again, he sprouted a snout and fur at that certain time of the month and so he wasn't one to argue impossibilities.

He closed his eyes as the past few weeks closed in on him. A week ago, he'd left his position as sheriff of a small Washington town to chase Viv all the way to Texas. He'd been convinced she was The One his parents—both full blooded werewolves—had told him about when he'd turned twenty-one. He could still hear his father's voice.

"For every male of our kind, there is a female. It's just a matter of finding her, son. The minute you do, you'll know it."

"That's right," his mother had added. *"She'll fill your head. Your heart. And just like that, you'll know. You'll forget every other woman but her."*

At the time of the revelation, he'd been young and horny and more interested in having a good time than finding his one and only. But over the years, he'd started to feel the loneliness of being "different." A few years ago, he'd finally grown tired of the nameless faces. The constant variety. The meaningless one-nighters. He'd been looking for his mate ever since.

And then he'd met Viv.

He'd known at first glance that she was different. He just hadn't realized how different until he'd stumbled on a handful of vampires and a world of trouble. Vampire Viv, it turned out, had been fleeing two vengeful bloodsuckers, and Matt had found himself caught in the middle of their struggle. He'd been bitten by one of Viv's attackers.

He closed his eyes, remembering the feel of fangs piercing his neck, the draw on his vein and then the nothingness as he'd collapsed onto the motel room floor.

Unconscious, but not dead.

Not even close.

He'd opened his eyes a short while later to find the struggle over. Viv and Garret—the vampire in love with her—had defeated the enemy vamps. They were both alive and well, and so was Matt. Despite passing out, he'd felt as strong as ever. Stronger, in fact. Alive. And hard.

That had been six days ago. One hundred forty-four hours, twenty-eight minutes and counting. And he was still hard.

He'd checked out of the motel and leased a two-story log cabin just outside of town. The house sat atop a large hill surrounded by sixty-three acres of trees and rolling pasture. It wasn't anywhere close to his spread up in Washington—a five-hundred-acre mountain ranch he'd inherited from his folks when they'd died in a Cessna crash two years ago—but it would afford him enough privacy to sort things out and come to terms with what had happened to him before he resumed his search for his mate.

He glanced down at his erection. Correction—with what was *now* happening to him.

He threw his legs over the side of the bed and headed for the bathroom. A few minutes later, he stepped into an ice-cold shower. His skin shriveled, but the Incredible Hulk didn't lose an inch of temper.

Ditto when he opened the refrigerator door a half hour later and let the cold air blast over his naked body. His teeth chattered. His nipples puckered. Even his toes shrank.

· But his dick? Nothing. Not even a friggin' shiver.

Desperation rolled through him and he rummaged under the sink for a large mixing bowl. Retrieving several trays from the freezer, he dumped ice cubes into the container. Mustering his courage, he shoved his throbbing cock inside. The tender skin around his penis froze on contact, his balls pulled back and he ground his teeth together.

Holymotherfriggin'sonofagoddamnbitch—

He yanked free and relief swamped him. A feeling that lasted all of two seconds. Until he glanced down to see Super Cock.

He stroked the rigid skin from root to tip and a burst of need went through him. Hunger stirred, urging him on and it was all he could do to pull away. But he did because he knew no amount of jacking off would help.

Been there. Done that.

He'd spent the past six days eating, sleeping and jacking off.

And streaking buck-naked through town.

He closed his eyes and tried to remember exactly what had happened Friday night. One minute he'd been laying in bed, fantasizing about a hot little blonde he'd spotted in town that day, and the next, he'd been buck naked, hairy and sprinting down main street. Luckily it had been midnight in a map-dot that rolled up the sidewalks at sundown.

Or so he'd thought.

But then he'd opened the local paper the next morning to discover that someone with a camera had been burning the midnight oil. Matt had made the front page, along with the caption *Wolfman? Pervert? Or is Halloween Starting Early This Year?*

He was sure most people would vote for the pervert or Halloween possibilities. Nobody in their right mind would suspect the real truth—that he was a normal, sane, self-respecting werewolf who'd had his world rocked by a vampire bite. They would think the new guy in town was playing some sort of practical joke. At least for a little while. Long enough for him to come up with a plausible explanation, something like "he was president of the National Society of Transvestite Streakers" or "he'd ordered a super-charged hair growth shampoo off the QVC."

Until then, it was a matter of getting his damned body back under control.

Anxiety rushed through him and he was just about to go for another ice dunk when he heard a car engine and caught the faint scent of exhaust. He moved at the speed of light, pulling on a pair of jeans and hauling open the front door.

But there was nothing there. No car coming up his drive. No townspeople coming to lynch him. Nothing but the quarter moon suspended in a star-studded sky. A cluster of surrounding trees. And the sounds.

The buzz of crickets. The flutter of an owl's wings. The faint scrape of deer antlers on a distant tree. The rustle of a raccoon as it dug through the trash.

In the nearest trash can, which was a full mile up the road.

His senses, already unusually heightened because of his DNA, were jacked up even more. He sniffed and the sweet smell of warm peach pie spiraled through his head. His stomach grumbled and he drank in another deep breath. And another.

Tires squealed and gravel crunched and he knew someone was coming. He moved toward the trees and faded into the surrounding forest as lights flashed and a car pulled into view.

His view, that is. He saw the sprinkle of lights through the trees and heard the sounds even though the car was still a good distance away. A full minute ticked by and the sounds magnified, along with the glimmer of lights, the scent of peach pie and the smell of something else.

Something much more rich and potent.

Something infinitely female.

He sniffed, drinking in the scent as a faded BMW came to a

rolling stop in front of the cabin. The lights dimmed. The door creaked and pushed open and out stepped his fantasy woman.

It was her, all right. Same long, thick hair and voluptuous breasts barely contained beneath a white T-shirt that read *Booty Call*.

He blinked. Wait a second. Make that *Beauty* Call.

He shifted his stance. His erection strained against the denim and his gut ached. The warm scent of peach pie grew stronger. His nostrils flared and his mouth watered. It was all he could do to keep his distance. He'd spent a lot of time fantasizing about her, since he'd first spotted her, in fact.

Not because he felt drawn to her on an emotional level, as his father had predicted. She was human and, therefore, out of the running for mate-of-the-year.

It was purely physical.

He'd been celibate for the past year since vowing to find his mate and she was sexier than hell. And so it had simply been lust at first sight.

He held his ground as the crunch of grass echoed in his head. She was heading for his front porch, her curvaceous ass outlined by a snug pair of jeans. Her bottom swayed slightly as she walked, an enticing motion that made him swallow. Hard.

A faint *clink* and a softly muttered "darn it" pushed past the frantic pounding of his heart as she dropped her keys. A strong, sharp aroma joined the warm, sweet smell of peaches.

She was nervous. Scared, even.

Desperate.

That truth became evident as she retrieved her keys, pulled back her shoulders and mounted the porch steps even though it was obvious she didn't want to be there. Still, she balled her fist and knocked on the door. Once. Twice. A third time.

Finally, she turned, her gaze scanning the trees that surrounded the clearing. She stopped when she reached him, as if she could see through the darkness to the place where he stood watching her.

She couldn't. He knew that. Yet, as he stared at her, into her aqua colored eyes, he felt as if she saw him as clearly, as distinctly as he saw her.

What the hell?

The question echoed in his head along with her stats. Her name was Shay Briggs and she needed his help. He wasn't sure how he knew, he just did. She ran the local spa specializing in facials and innovative beauty treatments. She was a once-upon-a-time pageant winner who'd recently been humiliated by her asshole of a boyfriend. She was still hurt, but she'd channeled the pain into something productive. Anger. Determination. Which was why she'd made the drive from town.

She'd seen the front page news like everyone else. But instead of writing him off as a practical joker or, worse, a lunatic, she'd taken the picture seriously. She'd bought into the sudden hair growth and now she wanted his help.

She turned back to the door, killing the endless string of information he'd picked up from her gaze.

He closed his eyes and tried to digest this newest revelation. He'd read her thoughts. He'd read her friggin' *thoughts*.

Sure, he'd always been able to sense things. He was a werewolf, for Christ's sake. He could smell fear. Taste despair. Pick up on the tiniest rush of excitement.

When he'd spotted her in town, he'd sensed her longing right away. He'd seen the glimmer of excitement in her gaze when she'd looked at him. Felt the push-pull when she'd forced herself to turn away because she obviously hadn't wanted to be attracted to him anymore than he'd wanted to be attracted to her. He'd even smelled her disappointment, as potent as his own, as she'd climbed into her car and driven away.

But those were emotions, not thoughts. He'd never been able to read anyone's *mind*.

Before he could dwell on the notion, Shay knocked on his door again. Her ass swayed ever so slightly, drawing his full and undivided attention.

An image popped into his head. The two of them on the front porch. His hands on her bottom and her legs up around his waist. His cock plunging fast and sure and deep into her hot, voluptuous body.

His groin throbbed mercilessly and he knew then that no amount of cold showers or hand-jobs would get him out of this stiff fix. He needed a real woman for that.

The woman standing on his front porch.

The thought struck and another visual rushed at him—the two of them on the king-sized bed inside. Her legs spread and his hips pumping between them. Her arms around his neck and his mouth on her breast. Her nipple straining against his tongue and her body arching into him. His fangs sinking deep and her blood rushing into his mouth—

Wait a second.

Wait just a friggin' *second*.

Blood?

He was a *werewolf.* He howled at the full moon, ordered his steaks rare and, once upon a time, he'd had wild, primitive sex with whichever hottie had vied for his attention. But he'd never sank his teeth into any of them. Sure, the smell of blood turned him on and stirred his baser instincts, but he'd never *drank* the stuff.

The world seemed to fall away in those next few seconds. The normal night sounds faded and his super-charged vision narrowed until the only thing he became aware of was the female standing on his porch.

An awareness that went deeper than her lush body.

The beat of her heart thundered through his head. His gaze fixated on the thrum of her pulse at the base of her neck. The scent of her blood—so warm and ripe and musky—teased his nostrils. A shudder ripped through him.

What the *hell* was happening to him?

Even as the question struck, he knew.

The vampire bite.

That's why he was so hard, so lusty, so *hungry*—for sex and more.

Luckily, they were cravings he could easily satisfy. She was right there, filling up his vision, consuming his senses. And she needed him. Just as much as he needed her.

3

"Matt?" Shay called out as she rapped on the door again. "Matt Keller? Are you in there?"

"Actually—" the deep seductive voice slid into her ears and brought her whirling around "—I'm out here."

"Geez, you scared the pants off me." She drew in a deep, calming breath and tried to steady the sudden pounding of her heart.

A useless effort, she quickly realized, as her gaze drank in the man standing behind her.

He had bright green eyes fringed with thick black lashes, strong cheekbones and a scar that zig-zagged its way across his left temple. Stubble shadowed his prominent jaw and surrounded his sensuous mouth. A corded, muscular neck led to a pair of broad shoulders. An intricate slave band tattoo encircled one massive biceps, making him seem even more primitive. Dark, silky hair sprinkled his muscular chest from one flat brown nipple to the next before funneling to a narrow line that bisected his six-pack abs. The top button of his jeans hung undone, the faded denim cupping his crotch and hugging his sinewy thighs. A frayed hem brushed the tops of his long, bare feet.

"Liar, liar," he murmured, his deep voice drawing her attention back to his face. His green eyes glittered hot and bright and her hormones snapped to immediate attention.

"Excuse me?"

"Your pants, sugar. They're still present and accounted for." His mouth crooked into a grin. "A real shame."

Her nipples tingled and awareness zipped up and down her spine. "What are you doing out here?" she blurted, eager to ignore the sexual energy that radiated from his hot, hunky body.

"Shouldn't I be the one asking that question?"

"My name is Shay Briggs. I own Skin Deep. It's a full-service salon specializing in facials and full body beauty treatments. I, um—" she licked her bottom lip and tried to ignore the way his mouth seemed to follow the motion "—saw the paper and I was hoping that you might help me out." Her gaze touched on his short, dark hair and her small balloon of hope went *popppp!* "I should have known it was a bogus picture. You were wearing a wig, weren't you?"

Indecision flashed in his gaze a split-second before it faded into pure, sparkling green. "No wig."

"It had to be."

"Why is that?"

"Because your hair is short now."

He shrugged. "Maybe I cut it."

"It was short on the day of the picture. There's no way you could have grown ten inches in less than ten hours."

"Trust me, sugar. I can grow ten inches in less than ten seconds." The sexy crook of his mouth sent tiny butterflies dancing in her stomach.

"I'm talking about hair."

"What makes you think I'm not?" His grin widened and her thighs trembled. She'd wanted men before, but her reaction had never been this fast or this fierce.

Because he's different.

The moment the thought landed in her head, she drop-kicked it back out. Matt Keller was every man she'd ever fallen for in the past—tall, dark, dangerously good-looking and with one thing on his mind.

She stiffened and gathered her control. "I'm sorry I bothered you." She went to move past him. "I'll just get out of here—"

"It was real."

She whirled. "What?"

Yeah *what?* The thought echoed through Matt's head as the words tumbled from his lips. "My hair. It was the real deal. One minute it was short and the next thing I knew, it was long."

"But how is that possible?"

Because I'm a werewolf. The truth was there, so close to the surface that it surprised him. He'd never before had the urge to tell his secret. And he'd certainly never had the urge to confess to a stranger.

"And just like that, you'll know."

His father's voice echoed in his head, but he ignored it. His old man had been talking about a female werewolf, not a human.

The trembling in his hands, the tightening in his chest, the excitement zipping up and down his spine… It was nothing but pure lust.

All the more reason for him to give her a load of BS and get rid of her.

That's what he meant to do. But with her eyes so wide, so desperate and imploring, he couldn't quite bring himself to lie. "It happens every once in a while," he heard himself say. "Usually without warning."

"Really?" Excitement fueled her expression as he nodded and a strange warmth shot through him. "Maybe it's something you're eating. Or drinking." She seemed to think. "Maybe it's the shampoo or conditioner that you're using. Or maybe a combination of everything. I'm sure we can figure it out—"

"And this matters to you because?" he cut in.

"Are you kidding me? Figuring this out would be my dream come true. I could feature it in my column first, then offer exclusives at my salon."

"The newspaper?" When she nodded, he added, "I knew I'd seen your name somewhere before." He stared deep into her eyes and an image flashed. Shay, her hands full of spaghetti and meatballs, and a lowly sonofabitch trying to dodge a pretty impressive right arm. "Wait a second. Are you—"

"—the one featured on kissmyasscupid.com? Unfortunately. Trust me, he had it coming." A strange glimmer lit her eyes for a split-second. If he hadn't known better, he would have sworn that Shay Briggs wanted to cry.

She wouldn't. He saw that as clearly as he saw her determination fire to life. She wasn't going to let some low-life player ruin her life. She was taking back her power and *doing* something.

A rush of admiration went through him and his damned dick throbbed even harder. "I don't know about the Internet, but I've seen you before. Outside of the Piggly Wiggly."

"That was you?" She tried to play it cool, but he knew she remembered. He could see it in the sudden darkening of her eyes, realizing then that she'd been fantasizing about him, too. "No wonder you look familiar. So what about it?" She pulled back her shoulders and tried to shift the conversation back to the matter at hand. "You up for a little business arrangement?"

Boy, was he ever. His groin gave an answering throb and he stiffened. "That depends."

She'd been *fantasizing* about him.

The realization made him want to touch her that much more.

"I'm willing to give you full credit and compensation," she added. Her gaze met his and determination sparked in the translucent aqua depths. "Five percent of every treatment I do."

But Matt Keller had something different in mind.

Something much more *intimate.*

Not that he was going to suggest such a thing. *Hell*, no. He didn't proposition women for sex. He'd never had to. Even more, he didn't want to. He'd given up gratuitous sex when he'd vowed to find his mate. *No.* "I really like my privacy," he heard himself say instead. "That's why I moved out here."

"Ten percent."

"You write the beauty column in the local paper, right?" he asked, desperate to distract himself from the idea taking shape in his head.

"That's just a hobby. My business is my bread and butter. Fifteen percent," she added. When he shook his head, she added, "Look, I'll do anything. Just tell me what you want."

He didn't usually proposition women for sex. At the same time, this wasn't the usual situation. He was in a bad way. And it wasn't as if he was taking advantage of her. He fully intended to share a few secrets with her in return for a little relief. Not *the* secret—that he was a bonafide, howl-at-the-moon werewolf—but he had several others he'd picked up over the years, particularly in high school.

Puberty for a male werewolf had been tough and uncontrollable. From the random sprouting of hair to the sudden appearance of his fangs, he'd endured it all before he'd come of age and managed to get his inner beast under control. Thanks to the Internet, he'd come up with several explanations to keep his true identity a secret.

Like the time he'd explained a sudden patch of hair on his right forearm by telling the school nurse he'd spilled a bottle of castor oil—the stuff had long been a home remedy for baldness. Or the time he'd convinced his gym teacher that a square of hair in the middle of his back was the result of his mom using lavender oil in the laundry to get the smell out of his gym shirt.

If she wanted hair-growth secrets, he knew at least a dozen different home remedies that he could share with her.

And what about your promise? No sex until you find The One?

At the rate he was going, he would die from sexual deprivation long before he found his mate. No, he needed to blow off some steam, to ease the hard-on wreaking havoc on his judgment.

That was the only reason he'd felt the instantaneous attraction to Shay Briggs when he'd first spotted her in town. The only reason he hadn't been able to get her out of his head since. It was lust, pure and simple. Once he burned off a little of that, he would stop thinking about her. Fantasizing. Wanting.

He focused on her sparkling eyes and her full, kissable mouth, and the heat spiking in his groin. "I want you," he murmured, and then he kissed her.

HE HAD STRONG LIPS.

That was the first thought that rushed through Shay's head when Matt Keller pressed his mouth against hers. The second? No way in heaven, hell or the in-between, was she going to kiss him back.

Even if he did sweep his tongue across her bottom lip, back and forth, in a mesmerizing stroke that turned her knees to jelly. She fought the urge to slide her arms around his neck and tried not to think about how good he tasted. Like mint toothpaste and pure, raw sensuality.

His fingers dove beneath her hair and his hand cupped the base of her skull. He tilted her head just so and deepened the kiss. He held her as if she were the most precious thing in the world and she had the insane thought that despite his bad boy persona, Matt Keller was interested in more than sex. That, maybe, he wanted to hold her as much as he wanted to plunge deep inside her.

Yeah, right.

Any man that kissed this good…this fast… Trouble. Big, *big* trouble.

She stiffened and jerked away. Her gaze collided with his. There was no mistaking the hot desire simmering in his eyes. Her heart stalled.

He wanted sex, all right.

A zing of excitement went through her, followed by a wave of disappointment.

Because Shay Briggs had sworn off men like Matt Keller.

"Let me get this straight, you'll give me your secret formula if I sleep with you?"

"We won't be doing much sleeping." His grin made her tummy tingle. She swallowed.

"You don't seem like the kind of guy who has trouble getting a date."

"I don't want a date." His gaze locked with hers. "I want *you*." He said the words with such conviction that if she hadn't known better, she would have sworn he was talking about more than sex.

From this day forward, forever and ever, 'til death do us part.

Just as the notion struck, she stiffened. The man was propositioning her for *sex,* not a relationship. Proof in and of itself that he was exactly the sort she'd sworn off of when she'd nailed what's his name with a handful of meatballs.

Girl, please. It's not like you want to spend forever with this guy. This is a business agreement. You want something from him and he wants something from you. It's a win/win.

It was, she realized. She didn't have to worry about him possibly taking a hike after she disappointed him in the sack. After all, she knew he was going to take a hike regardless. And besides, it didn't matter. She didn't have any time or energy invested in him. Other than a few erotic thoughts since she'd spotted him in town, she had no preconceived notions when it came to Matt Keller. No visions of the two of them falling madly in love or walking down the aisle.

Okay, so maybe she'd had one itty bitty vision. Last night. But that had been her revenge fantasy. She and Matt had said yes and pledged their undying devotion with the entire town, including What's his name and Miss Pumpkin, looking on. They'd embraced and kissed and ahhhh…

Shay shook away the crazy warmth that stole through her. This wasn't about falling in love. It was business.

"Let me make sure I'm clear on this. We have sex and then you tell me your secret?" He nodded and her hormones gave an excited *hell, yeah,* followed by a tiny niggle of disappointment.

Not because she wanted more than one night. Hardly. She was bummed about having to wait an entire half-hour or so to learn the secret that would save her business.

"What are we waiting for? Let's get to it."

4

"Can you turn off the light?" Shay asked, once she'd followed him inside the cabin. "I like it dark."

"Suit yourself."

She caught a glimpse of an overstuffed leather couch and a rustic pine table before he hit the light switch and plunged them into complete darkness. Drapes covered the windows and shut out the faint sliver of moonlight.

She blinked and tried to adjust her eyes to the sudden change. Her gaze focused and she made out his large shape standing only inches away. The in and out of her own breaths echoed in her head.

He reached for her, but she inched backward.

"I think we should forego the preliminaries and just get right to it. This is business, after all."

The last thing she needed was a slow warm-up. Time to focus on the frantic beat of her heart and the anticipation bubbling inside her. And the warmth... A strange sensation that spread through her chest when he murmured, "You smell really good. Like warm peaches and sugar."

"Peach Pie Perfection—it's this new facial I'm working on. It tightens the face and smoothes wrinkles."

"You don't have any wrinkles."

"You haven't seen me in a three-way mirror with floodlights." And he never would. Because a man only interested in sex wouldn't be the least bit turned on by the Stubborn Seventeen.

She'd learned her lesson once before. No getting naked in front of the wrong man. From here on out, she was saving the slow strip-tease for her future accountant.

"Take off your clothes," he said as if reading her thoughts.

"You might want to stand back," she told him, fighting down a wave of self-consciousness as she gripped the edge of her T-shirt. "This could get ugly."

"How's that?"

"I'm wearing a girdle."

He grinned, a slash of white in the thick darkness that stalled her heart for several beats. "Don't worry about me, sugar. I like to live on the edge." He stepped closer and Shay forced herself not to turn and bolt for the door.

"Don't say I didn't warn you." She kicked off her shoes and shed her jeans. Fingering one strap of the black undergarment, she wiggled one finger beneath and worked the elastic down one arm and then the other. Grabbing the edge just under her arms, she shoved the top portion down and freed her breasts. She ignored the cool rush of air over her bare skin and nipples and started to push the rest of the material down. She pulled and tugged and made about an inch or progress.

"Let me—"

"I've got this. Really." She twisted away. While he couldn't see her in the blasted thing, feeling her in it would be just as bad.

And it matters because?

It didn't. Tomorrow, Matt Keller would be history. She had absolutely no reason to care one way or the other what he thought about her body.

She did.

Not because she liked him, she reminded herself for the countless time. Or because he made her feel warm inside when he smiled. Or because he liked the way that she smelled when no other man had ever even noticed. It was pure vanity. What straight, single, flesh-and-blood woman wouldn't want the resident hottie to find her wildly irresistible?

She squirmed and shimmied, ignoring the strange sensation that he was actually watching her. Matt Keller might be staring into the darkness, hoping his eyes adjusted enough for a glimpse, but no way could he actually see anything.

Thankfully.

Finally, the black material sagged at her ankles. She shoved the tight thing off to the side and faced him.

"Okay. I'm ready."

"No, you're not." His voice came from behind and she whirled.

"If you were ready," he continued, his voice hitting her from the left this time, "you wouldn't be nervous. You'd be wet."

"How do you know I'm not?" she challenged.

"Because I smell fear, darlin'. Not desire."

She summoned a laugh. "Sorry to bust your bubble, but I'm not afraid of you."

"No." The word was little more than a sigh that slid into her right ear and stirred her nerve endings. "You're afraid of you." The words hung between them for a long moment and she barely resisted the urge to forget the entire thing.

She was trading sex for a great big *maybe*—maybe he had a bonafide secret and maybe it was some crazy hair technique combined with his DNA, which meant that it wouldn't work on anyone else. Talk about a longshot.

At the same time, she was out of options and incredibly turned on despite her self-consciousness. The air between them crackled with electricity and she could feel the heat rolling off his body, wrapping around her.

"I think you're beautiful," his deep voice slid into her ears.

A rush of warmth went through her, a feeling that had nothing to do with the chemistry sizzling between them and everything to do with the sincerity in his voice.

As if he really and truly meant it.

As if it mattered one way or another even if he did.

She stiffened. This wasn't about falling into *like* with him. It wasn't about falling, period. It was a one-night stand. Sex.

"You're obviously horny as hell and can't see a thing," she blurted, eager to kill the strange flicker of hope in the pit of her stomach. "I could be Big Foot for all you care."

"Maybe." His warm breath teased the back of her neck. "Maybe not."

She turned and caught the dark shape of his shadow directly behind her. She had a split-second of confusion because just a heartbeat before he'd been directly in front of her.

But then his fingertip touched her shoulder blade and desire sliced hot and potent through her. She caught a gasp and barely resisted the sudden urge to flip on the light so that *she* could see *him*.

The fierce gleam in his eyes.

His sensuous lips.

His determined expression.

But if she could see him, he could see her. And that would put a stop to things before they could get really interesting.

"Do you?" his deep voice sizzled across her nerve endings.

"Do I what?"

"Have big feet?"

Actually, her feet were the only part of her that hadn't been affected by the Stubborn Seventeen, but she wasn't about to enlighten him on that. "I'd say they're average."

"Sugar, nothing about you is average." Conviction fueled the words and her chest hitched before she could remind herself that she was undoubtedly reading more into his words than he meant.

Wishful thinking got her every time, but not now. No, now she knew full well what to expect—nothing.

No expectations. No disappointments.

She held tight to the last thought; her breath paused, as he stepped up behind her.

She felt the tickle of his chest hair against her shoulder blades as he slid his hands around her rib cage and cupped the underside of her breasts. His thumbs flicked her nipples and she caught her bottom lip.

"Nice," he murmured and desire spiraled through her.

He rolled the tender peaks until they were hard and throbbing. His hands fell to her thighs, burning into her flesh as his fingers slid up the inside until he touched her sex. His fingers parted the silky folds to tease and explore.

Her breath caught as he slid one finger deep inside. Instinctively, she tightened around him and he groaned.

"You're not afraid anymore." His lips moved against her ear, his tongue tracing the outline to dip inside. "That's good. Really good."

"I was never afraid—" Her breath caught as he slid another finger into her.

"You're wet now," he continued, the words little more than a satisfied groan. "And tight."

His body trembled, as if the realization shook his control. He worked her then, moving inside her, stroking and plunging. She half-expected him to shove her up against the nearest wall and get to it. That's what any other man would have done.

Matt pushed his fingers deep until the air lodged in her throat and her senses flooded with sensation. Just when she didn't think she could take anymore, he withdrew, just enough to let her catch her breath, and then the delicious act started all over again.

He pleasured her over and over, bringing her to the brink only to prolong the sensation. As if they had all the time in the world. As if he was more concerned with giving her pleasure than taking his own.

As if.

"Please…" The word was a ragged gasp of air as her hands clawed at his forearms. As delicious as the feelings were, she wanted more.

Another deft movement of his fingers and she came apart. Shudders vibrated through her body and skimmed her ragged senses in wave after wave of sweet sensation. She slumped back against him, weak and damp, her breath raspy, her heartbeat a frenzied rhythm in her ears.

He caught a drop of perspiration at her temple with the seductive glide of his tongue. But it wasn't the contact that stalled the air in her lungs. It was his voice.

"You're so beautiful, Shay."

A rush of pleasure sparked deep inside her and before she could remind herself that he couldn't see her period, much less tell whether or not she was beautiful, she grabbed his hand and touched his palm to her lips.

Matt felt the sensuous press of her full mouth and his heart stalled. He felt her gratitude and joy, and a burst of anger went through him because he knew he was the only one who'd ever told her such a thing and truly meant it.

And then he felt an uncontrollable wave of possessiveness because he wanted to remain the only one who'd ever told her such a thing and truly meant it.

Now and forever.

You'll know it.

It was just sex, he reminded himself as he touched her bottom lip with the pad of his finger. She drew him into her mouth and suckled him and all the soft feelings faded into a rush of desire.

Need hit him like a solid punch to the stomach and he closed his eyes. He groaned, his arousal throbbing, pressing between her buttocks, hot and desperate for entry.

"Wait—" she cried, but he was already pulling away from her. He reached his jeans in record time, retrieved a condom and slid it onto his rock-hard length. He drew back the curtains on one massive window.

Shay started to protest, but he took her hand, urged her up against the glass and stepped up behind her so fast that she'd barely managed a breathless "I really like it dark," before he pressed his erection between her ass cheeks and rubbed.

Her protest ended on a sharp gasp. Her bottom lifted in sweet invitation as she leaned forward and planted her palms flat on the glass.

"It's plenty dark," he reassured her. He rubbed against her, once, twice, and felt the moisture slide around his cock. Pleasure splintered through him and a groan rumbled from his throat. He caught his reflection in the window. Two pinpoints of neon blue light gleamed back at him, a frantic change from the fierce predatory red typical of a werewolf.

He blinked, frantically trying to force the light away, but he couldn't. Years of controlling what he was slipped away in the next few seconds as his primitive instincts took over.

Before she could blink, he swept her into his arms and headed for the bedroom. He urged her forward onto the mattress until she was on all fours, her bottom raised in undeniable invitation.

He stroked her, his fingertips trailing over the wet heat between her legs. She shivered and rotated her hips. He locked his arm around her, anchoring her for a full upward thrust until he was buried to the hilt.

The blood drummed so loudly in his ears, he barely heard her gasp of pleasure. Her body was warm and ripe, milking him even though they were both standing so perfectly still. For several deep, shallow breaths, he poised behind her, not moving or breathing. Simply relishing the sensation.

It was unlike anything he'd ever felt before. The pulsing warmth. The stirring energy. He could feel it bubbling deep inside her and he had the sudden urge to stoke the fire until she exploded.

This was crazy. It was all about *his* pleasure. *His* release. *His* explosion.

Shay gasped, her body drawing him deliciously deeper as she arched back against him.

He felt the sharp graze of his teeth against his tongue and he chanced a glance in the dresser mirror to see the white gleam of fangs and the fierce purple of his eyes—

Holy shit! He had *fangs!*

Sure, he had fangs during the full moon. And a snout. And a body full of hair. But this… This was different.

He closed his eyes and remembered the feel of a similar pair of fangs sinking into his neck. He knew then that he hadn't just been attacked by that vampire. He'd been changed—the eyes, the fangs, the perpetual hard-on, the sex.

Sex had always been great for him. But what he was experiencing with Shay gave new meaning to the word. It was hotter. Wetter. Wilder.

"She'll fill your head. Your heart."

The words echoed in his head a split second before Shay moved again and desperation rolled through him. Suddenly he couldn't get deep enough, fast enough. He thrust into her, over and over, until he hovered on the brink of explosion.

She came quickly, crying his name as violent tremors racked her body. Heat rippled through him, feeding the hunger inside him even though he hadn't had his own climax.

Ecstasy drenched him, sucking him under and holding him prisoner for several long moments. But then he wanted more. He pushed into her again, once, twice, *there*. His heart gave a wild *ka-pow* and his own climax hit him hard and fast.

A growl rumbled from his throat and she stiffened in his arms.

"What was that—" she started to ask, the question catching on a gasp as he whirled her around and kissed her long and slow and deep.

He urged her back down into the mattress and eased down beside her. Folding her body close to his own, he closed his eyes. He needed to think. To make some sense out of what he'd just experienced.

The change in his eye color. The fangs. The damned hunger.

Even now, it waged a tug-o-war inside of him, demanding more than the sex.

His gaze hooked on the throb of her pulse and it was all he could do not to taste her.

Even crazier were the damned feelings churning inside him.

As much as he wanted to bite Shay, he wanted to hold her close. To tell her how beautiful she was. To kill any and every man who'd ever hurt her. To never let her go.

The vampire bite.

He knew that was to blame for the wild changes he was going through—emotionally and physically—and he fully intended to prove it. As soon as Shay dozed off, he was heading into town to talk to a certain pair of vampires.

In the meantime, he was going to do his damndest to keep from sinking his fangs or his cock into the woman falling fast asleep in his arms.

5
_____

"YOU LOOK TERRIBLE," Viviana Darland told him the minute he walked into the business office of Skull Creek Choppers later that night.

The custom motorcycle shop was owned by the town's three resident male vampires—Garret Sawyer, Jake McCann and Dillon Cash. Garret handled the actual build. Jake took care of the design. And Dillon dealt with the high-tech computer software blazing on the various computer screens throughout the monstrous fabrication shop.

"I feel terrible," Matt said as he sank into one of the chairs. Viviana signaled Garret through the wall-to-wall window that separated the office from the actual production area. A few seconds later, he walked through the door. He gave Viv a long, lingering kiss before turning his attention to Matt.

"What's up, guy?"

Matt ran a hand over his face and tried to ignore the scent of Shay on his hands and his skin. In his head. "Something's happening to me." When Garret arched an eyebrow, he added, "Something other than the usual werewolf stuff."

"We saw the pic," Viv winked. "Nice tush."

"I'm not talking about the streaking." He shook his head. "Well, yes I am." He leveled a stare at her. "The full moon triggers everything for me. I know it. I can anticipate it. But this happened during a quarter moon. One minute I'm out at my place and the next I'm standing in the middle of town square. I was hairy and horny. That vampire bite did something to me." He pushed to his feet and started to pace in the small area. "I'm having these urges." He shook his head. "I'm horny as hell. And I'm hungry." His gaze locked with Garret's. "For more than a thick, juicy steak." His gaze shifted to Viv's. "Do you think I'm turning into a vampire?"

"You can't be," Viv told him. "To fully turn, you have to drink the blood of a vampire while you're dying. You breathe your last breath, your humanity slips away and then the vamp blood kicks in and you open your eyes to a new life—the afterlife." She shook her head. "A nonfatal bite isn't enough."

"For the average human," Garret spoke then. "But Matt isn't anywhere close, babe. His DNA is different. Which means—" his gaze zeroed in on Matt "—anything is possible."

"I suppose." Viv eyed him. "What did you do today?"

Matt shrugged. "I spent the afternoon clearing the area around the cabin."

"Outside, right?"

"Yeah."

Viv exchanged glances with Garret. "Vampires can't tolerate the sunlight."

"*We* can't tolerate the sunlight," Garret said, slipping an arm around her. "Matt's something different." His gaze collided with Matt's. "You're still a werewolf, right?"

"I don't know. I mean, I did grow the hair, which is standard operating procedure for werewolves. But I didn't actually morph into a wolf, which is what usually happens once a month. First the hair, then the change. But only during the full moon. When I was younger, I used to sprout hair every now and then, but that's because my hormones were raging. I never sprout hair now unless I'm supposed to."

"Vampires don't grow hair," Viv pointed out.

"But we do crave sex," Garret countered before shifting his attention back to Matt. "It's part of what we are. We can sate the bloodlust with sexual energy. It helps us go longer so that we don't have to feed off the red stuff as often. Let me guess, you tried jacking off and it didn't work."

Matt shook his head. "It made me want it more." He remembered climbing from the bed after Shay had fallen asleep. He'd taken one look at her and he'd been hard all over again. Desperate. Hungry. "Shit," he muttered, sinking down on the edge of the couch. "Shit, shit, *shit*." He shook his head. "So you really think I'm turning into a vampire?" he asked Garret.

"I think that the vamp blood mingling with yours sparked some sort of transition. How far it will go, I don't know. Will you lose the werewolf and become a full-fledged vampire? That remains to be seen."

"So what do I do?"

"You feed," Viv told him. She walked over to a nearby mini-fridge and pulled out a plastic bag of blood. A few seconds later, she'd poured the contents into a wine glass and handed it to him. "The more you feed the beast, the more in control you'll feel."

"Where did you get this?"

"Garret's got connections at a blood bank in Austin. We bag it as much as we can. The rest we take from each other."

"Only each other," Garret added.

"You can do that?" His gaze went from one vampire to the other.

Viv smiled at her significant other. "It's worked so far. But you'll need to supplement with sex."

"Lots of sex," Garret added, sliding an arm around Viv. "But no sex and blood at the same time. It forges an unbreakable bond that can be more trouble than it's worth."

"If it's with the wrong person," Viv added. "But if it's the right person…" She let her sentence trail off as she smiled at Garret.

He pulled her even closer. "If it's the right person, you're one lucky sonofabitch." He lifted his gaze to Matt. "Stick with variety for now while you're figuring things out. Maybe check out a few of the bars out on the interstate. There's plenty of women there who can help you until you get a handle on this."

"And we'll help, too." Viv pulled away from Garret to retrieve another bag from the fridge. "You can have dinner with us so you don't have to worry about draining anyone."

"I would never do that."

"You'd be surprised what you're capable of doing when the hunger gets to you."

He thought of Shay and her voluptuous body. Her pulse echoed in his head and he saw her creamy white throat, her lifeblood pumping just below the surface of her pale, translucent skin. He'd wanted so badly to sink his fangs into her, to feel her heat filling his mouth the way her silky wet warmth had milked his body. His groin tightened, hunger sliced through him and he reached for the glass.

He downed a long gulp. The liquid was salty and sweet at the same

time, and his taste buds came alive. Several more gulps and he finished
off the glass. Still, it wasn't enough to sate the beast that now lived
and breathed inside of him. Nor was it enough to kill the image of
Shay spread out on his bed, waiting for him. So warm and sweet and—

"Can I have another?" he blurted, cutting off the dangerous train
of thought.

"Another glass?"

"Another bag." He needed all the sustenance he could get before
he headed back to the cabin to deal with Shay Briggs.

Deal as in finishing up their bargain by sharing a few of the crazy
hair growth treatments he'd learned over the years. She'd kept her
end of the agreement, and now he had to keep his.

No way was he going to head back home, crawl into bed with
her, and have sex with her all over again. Or drink from her. Or both.
Christ, he had enough problems. He didn't need to be mentally
linked to a woman he hardly knew. Even if there was something
about her that drew him.

Her scent. Her feel. Her.

"You'll know it."

He fought the truth and focused on Garret while Viv emptied a
bag into his now empty glass. "How often will I have to feed?"

"You're new at this, so I'd say every few days. Older vampires
can go longer."

"So this will cut the craving for a little while?" He held up the
glass she handed him.

"Not by itself. But if you have sex, you should be good for a few
days at least."

"What if I already had sex?"

Garret winked. "Then you're good to go for at least forty-
eight hours."

Long enough for Matt to fulfill his end of the bargain with
Shay—without falling into bed with her again. Then he would call
it quits. She would go back to her life and he would go back to
looking for his mate, and all would be right with the world.

If only the notion didn't depress him even more than the possibility that he was turning into a full-fledged vampire.

6

HE WAS GONE.

Shay stared at the empty bed and tried to stifle her disappointment. *Gone* was a good thing. Dawn had already crept over the horizon and pushed its way inside the bedroom. The shadows hovered in the corners, too far away to afford her any decent cover once she threw back the sheets and sprinted for the bathroom.

She strained her ears for some evidence that Matt Keller hadn't jumped ship like every other man in her life. The familiar sounds whispered through her head. The hum of the air conditioner. The chirp of birds. The buzz of crickets.

There was nothing else. No rush of water in the bathroom. No early morning news coming from the living room TV. No *swish* of newspapers. No *glug* of orange juice.

The rat bastard.

Not because she'd fallen for him or anything ridiculous like that. Sure, he was a bad boy and the sex had been phenomenal. But she hardly knew him. No, she felt like crying because he'd bailed *before* sharing his hair secrets.

She blinked away the burning in her eyes and steeled herself. She would hunt him down if she had to. No way was she going home empty-handed.

She kicked the sheets to her ankles and climbed from the bed. She'd just leaned over to scoop up her undies when she felt the whisper of awareness up her spine. Her fingers brushed lace just as Matt's sexy voice echoed in her ears.

"And here I thought the view from the porch was pretty incredible."

Hope rushed through her, followed by a burst of *uh, oh*. She made a mad grab for the sheet, tucking it up under her arms as she whirled. The moment her gaze collided with his, her stomach hollowed out and her heart seemed to pause.

There was just something about the way he looked at her—as if he *wanted* to look—that made her want to let go of the sheet and her inhibitions.

Never again.

She summoned her irritation and nailed him with a glare. "You should try knocking next time."

"It's my bedroom, sugar." His green eyes sparkled.

"Last I heard, possession was nine-tenths of the law."

She meant to piss him off, but the comment drew a flash of admiration and a grin. "Good comeback."

"I do my best work when I'm half-naked."

His gaze dropped to the sheet and his grin faded into an almost wistful expression. "Get dressed. I'll be in the kitchen." And then he turned and walked away.

Once he was out of sight, she inched forward and shut the bedroom door. Throwing the lock on the knob, she snatched up her clothes and ditched the sheet. His scent clung to her T-shirt as she slid it over her head and her thighs trembled. She had half a mind to toss the clothes aside and meet him in the kitchen wearing nothing but a smile.

No, her conscience reminded her. *No more chances. No more heartache. No more getting wild and crazy with the wrong men.*

She finished dressing, then unlocked the door and went out. She found Matt standing near the counter, an open carton of eggs next to him. Bacon sizzled in a nearby frying pan and the smell of coffee curled through the air.

"Have a seat."

Warmth curled around her and filled the small space as she folded herself into a nearby chair.

"I like my eggs over-easy," she blurted, eager to distract herself from the crazy thoughts dancing in her head.

Like how sexy he looked with a frying pan in his hands and how she wouldn't mind seeing him like this each and every morning.

He grinned at her as strong, tanned fingers closed around one of the delicate white eggs. "You're not eating them, sugar." He added a few teaspoons of flour to the mixture and whipped it into a thick paste. "You're wearing them." He picked up the bowl and stepped toward her.

"Excuse me?"

"The hair shaft is made up of protein," he told her matter-of-factly. "An egg is protein which feeds the follicle and promotes hair growth." He set the bowl on the table in front of her. "You spread the paste over your head, wrap it in a warm towel and leave it on for thirty minutes."

"How many times do you have to do it?"

"Two to three times a week for six weeks is usually enough to see some pretty incredible results. But you'll see minimal results in as little as a few treatments."

"This is the secret?" She took a whiff of the egg paste and her nose wrinkled.

"Listen, I know you're after one ground-breaking cause, but I don't think it's any one thing. I do lots of things that promote hair growth," he said as he came around her, setting the bowl in front of her.

She became acutely aware of his strong, powerful body directly behind her and her nipples tightened.

"Such as?" she managed to say, her lips trembling around the words.

"Sit-ups on a bar."

"And this helps how?"

"Hanging upside down sends a rush of blood to the brain. Blood stimulates growth." He swept her hair off her shoulders and every nerve in her body went on instant alert. "Eucalyptus leaves and mint oil work, too. Mix it. Warm it. Rub it on your scalp and wait fifteen minutes." He scooped some of the paste into his hand.

At the first touch of his fingertips on her scalp, goose bumps chased up and down her arms. He smoothed the mixture onto her hair and worked the stuff into her strands with a steady, kneading massage.

Her nipples tingled and her mouth went dry. It was all she could do not to melt right there at his fingertips.

"Not only does the protein recharge each strand," he murmured after several minutes, "but the massage relaxes you at the same time."

Yeah, right. Her skin tingled. Her nipples quivered. Her clitoris throbbed.

"Your hair's really soft." His deep voice rumbled in her ear. His fingers brushed her neck and shivers chased up and down her spine.

"Thanks." She wasn't sure how she managed the one word, except that she wanted—no, needed—to say something. Anything to break the seductive spell gripping her senses.

"There," he finally announced after a few more strokes. "Let me get a warm towel out of the dryer and we'll wrap it up." He disappeared and Shay did her best not to follow him.

She wanted so much to hop up on the dryer and toss her legs around his waist. Instead, she hopped up from the chair and busied herself taking the bacon from the frying pan and setting it on a nearby plate lined with a paper towel. "What do we do with this? Crush it into another paste?"

"This," he said, coming up next to her and snagging a piece. "We eat." He popped the bacon into his mouth and started to chew.

"Oh." Her cheeks fired, more from his nearness than embarrassment. "I thought it was part of the hair growth regime."

"Actually, it is. Diet plays a huge role in hair growth. Bacon contains iron and protein, both of which make for healthy hair. I eat a lot of the stuff, so I'm sure it has something to do with what happened."

"I don't do bacon." A wave of self-consciousness rolled through her. "Actually, I do do bacon. That's the problem. It goes straight to my hips."

"Your hips look just fine to me," he said. Then he frowned as if none too pleased with the fact that he'd just made the statement.

Because the initial infatuation was now over. Where he couldn't think beyond the sex, now he was noticing the details. The imperfections.

"How long does this stay on for?" she blurted, eager to distract herself from a sudden rush of disappointment.

"Thirty minutes," he told her as she rummaged in her purse for a pad and pen.

"Got it." She scribbled the information along with a step-by-step recipe for the egg paste.

She wasn't disappointed. She was relieved. She wasn't any more interested in him than he was in her. She didn't want him to rip her clothes off and make love to her again any more than she wanted to rip her clothes off and make love to him.

Really.

"Eucalyptus and what?" she asked as he dropped into a chair opposite her.

"Mint oil. You can get it at any health food store."

"Not in Skull Creek. The closest we get to health food is a jar of Flintstones Chewables over at the Piggly Wiggly. The drawback of living in a small town."

"Skull Creek is nothing compared to Jamison."

She wasn't going to ask. The less she knew about him, the better. "Is that where you're from?" she heard herself say anyway.

"I was born and raised in Seattle, but I've spent the past ten years in Jamison. It's a small town in upstate Washington."

"Do they have a McDonalds?"

"If you're talking old man McDonald who owned the local pharmacy, then yes, we had one. If you're talking fries and Big Macs, I'm afraid not."

Shay let loose a whistle. "Even Skull Creek has a McDonalds. I mean, it's not actually in town. It's fifteen miles out on the interstate, but still. So what did you do in the desperately small town of Jamison?" Not that she was interested. But the more he talked, the less she thought about him doing other, sexier things with his sensuous mouth.

"I was a private detective at first. Most of my cases came from Seattle, but I lived in Jamison because that's where I grew up. I eventually ran for sheriff after I inherited my folks' place. They passed away three years ago."

She barely resisted the urge to rest her hand over his and chase the suddenly bleak look from his eyes. She balled her fingers and settled for "What happened?"

He shrugged. "They were flying a small Cessna, on their way back from Niagara Falls when their plane hit a tree. They crashed and burned in a matter of minutes."

"I lost my dad in a trucking accident," she heard herself say. "I was only two, so I don't really remember him."

"What about your mom?"

"Alive and well and happily married to an accountant named Fred. Finally." When he arched an eyebrow, she added, "Fred's a good guy, but she hasn't always been so lucky. She has a bad habit of falling for the wrong men."

"How many men?"

"Fred is number five. But that's not the Briggs record. My grandma was married six times. She's widowed now and lives in a retirement home in Austin. The last time I talked to her, she was working on wrong man number seven. A retired air force pilot who's been married almost as many times as she has."

"What about you? Are you carrying on the family tradition?"

"I've never been married, if that's what you're asking. But I've gone cold turkey as far as the wrong men are concerned. I want more than a little bump and grind. I want bacon and eggs." When he grinned, she added, "Eggs that you can actually eat. Not that there's anything wrong with bumping and grinding. I'm sure you live your life looking for the next B & G, but I want more. I'm through with players. I want a nice guy. The right guy, you know?"

Boy, did he ever. Matt had spent the past three years searching for the right woman. For his woman. His mate.

Someone he could have hot, wild sex with *and* talk to.

The way he was talking with Shay Briggs right now.

He nixed the last thought. He wasn't *talking* to Shay. It wasn't real talk, the deep, meaningful kind shared between two people who were friends, as well as lovers. He and Shay were nowhere near that close. He hardly knew her and she hardly knew him. Even more, she never would.

"That probably sounds lame to a guy like you."

"A guy like me?"

"A bad boy. A player. You know, the kind of man who is only interested sex."

"What makes you think I'm only interested in sex?"

"Well, aren't you?"

"Actually, I've been thinking about settling down myself." He wasn't sure why, but her perception of him bothered him and he had the sudden urge to prove her wrong.

She gave him a skeptical glance. "Is that so?"

"What? A bad boy can't settle down?"

"Bad boys never settle down."

"How do you know?"

"Eye-witness account. My mother was married four times before Fred and they were all bad boys."

"Maybe it wasn't the men. Maybe it was your mom."

"And maybe you should mind your own business."

Because he was right. Matt read that truth in her eyes. Shay had wondered the very same thing more than once, but then she'd quickly dismissed the notion. She was the spitting image of her mother. To consider that her mom might have commitment issues meant that she might have her own, as well.

She didn't. She believed in love. He didn't just see that truth, he felt it. In the hope bubbling inside her. The determination to steer clear of him. Because she didn't want another night of sex.

She wanted the perfect man.

Just as much as he wanted the perfect woman.

A woman who smelled like peach pie.

"How long am I supposed to wear this?" her voice slid into his ears and distracted him from the dangerous thought.

He glanced at his watch. "Time's just about up anyway. Let's get you rinsed off. Then I'll show you how to do a hanging sit-up."

She grinned. "Or maybe I'll show you." When he looked surprised, she added, "You're talking to a woman who owns an ab buster, a thigh master, a glute toner *and* a biceps builder. There isn't a work-out device I haven't tried."

"That explains it."

"Explains what?"

"Why you have such a great body." He didn't mean to say it, but he couldn't help himself.

"You obviously didn't see a thing last night."

"Says you."

She gave him a sharp look and he grinned.

"You're beautiful, Shay."

The words whispered through Shay's head, feeding her fragile ego, making her think that peeling away her clothes right here, right now, in the bright light of day, wouldn't be such a bad thing.

But she was through clinging to the here and now. She wanted a future. A nice guy.

Matt Keller with his wicked green eyes and his sinful smile looked anything but nice. Fierce? Yes. Dangerous? Amen. Sexy-as-hell? Straight up.

She stiffened and did her best to avoid contact as she scooted past him and pulled the towel off her head. She concentrated on adjusting the warm water and then leaned over the kitchen sink.

"I'll do it," she blurted the minute his hand touched the back of her neck. She shoved her head deeper beneath the spray and washed out the gunky egg.

Last night was over and done with. Ancient history.

Her head knew that, even if her body didn't seem to be getting the message. Her skin tingled to feel the rasp of his fingertips. Her nipples ached for his mouth. The slick folds between her legs throbbed to feel his body pushing harder and deeper and—

Water sloshed onto the cabinet and the floor, and she forced a deep breath.

Distance. That was the key. To keep her distance and learn as much as possible from him. Then she would say goodbye, do a thorough and knowledgeable write-up in the newspaper and add the specialty services to her menu back at the shop. She would stick to her vow—nice guys only—and he could go back to playing the field like every other bad boy she'd ever met.

In the meantime, all she had to do was steer clear of any physical contact. As long as he didn't touch her again, she would be fine.

"What's next?" she asked, grabbing the fresh towel from the counter and blotting at her drenched hair.

His grin was slow and tantalizing. "Full body massage."

Uh, oh.

7

"ARE YOU SURE YOU DON'T need a demonstration?" Matt followed Shay out onto his front porch and watched her haul ass down the steps toward her car.

"What's to demonstrate? Full body. Massage. Pretty self explanatory."

"But I've still got a few more tried and true tricks after that."

"I've already got plenty to keep me busy. Thanks for everything. I'll call you if I need you."

She wouldn't call. He knew it just as surely as he knew his hardon had returned full-force.

Forty-eight hours, he reminded himself. Until then, he was satisfied. Hunger completely and totally sated.

So why did he have the crazy urge to run down the steps, hoist her over his shoulder, tote her back into the cabin and plunge hard and deep into her voluptuous body?

Because Garret had been wrong. Dead wrong. Matt had barely lasted forty-eight minutes, let alone forty-eight hours.

He needed to feed again. No way was he this hard up because of Shay. Because he wanted *her*.

She could have been any woman and he would have reacted the same way. Any woman. Every woman.

He watched her pull out of the driveway, swing the car around and head back down the road. Once she disappeared, he walked back into the cabin and headed straight for the kitchen. He pulled out the bag of blood Viviana had given him.

And then he started to drink.

SHE WASN'T GOING TO CALL.

That's what Shay told herself for the rest of the week as she tried to forget Matt Keller and their one night of hot, wild sex. She did her damndest not to think about the desperate way he'd kissed her. Or the reverent way he'd stroked her body. Or the hunger in his gaze when she'd walked away from him.

As if their one night together hadn't been nearly enough for him. Right.

They'd spent a full hour together going over the different hair-growth techniques. Ample time for him to make another move if he'd still felt something for her. Something that went beyond lust.

She shook the notion away and finished spreading one of the oil mixtures Matt had told her about onto her long hair. It was late Friday afternoon. Usually one of her busiest at the salon. But other than a brief visit by Sue Ann who'd stopped by to pick up some of Shay's homemade cucumber cleanser, she'd had not one customer.

"Give it time," Sue Ann had told her. "You're just in a funk. Believe me, I know the feeling. I tried to interview the Whites yesterday—they've been married fifty-five years. Five minutes into the interview, they started arguing about denture cream. The next thing I know, they're spraying each other with Fixodent and I'm caught in the middle. Needless to say, they're now at the bottom of my happily-ever-after list and I'm back to searching for a front page feature for the Valentine's issue. I think I'll try the Humphreys next."

"Didn't they separate last year because she wanted to spend their retirement funds on Botox and he wanted a new tractor?"

"Christ, I think you're right. Still," she told Shay, "there has to be at least one successful love story in this town."

But the fact that she couldn't seem to find one was fast confirming Shay's worst fear—that true love didn't really exist. That the reason Shay herself hadn't found it wasn't because she constantly hooked up with non-committal, sex-only, bad boy types, but because there was no such emotion in the first place.

Love was a pipe dream. A fairy tale.

Which was why Matt Keller had made zero effort to stop her when she'd high-tailed it to her car. No running after her, hauling her into his arms, kissing her passionately and begging her to stay.

He'd wanted sex, he'd gotten sex, and now it was over as far as he was concerned.

As far as she was concerned, too, she reminded herself. She had no designs on him. No expectations. It was all about business.

Speaking of which… She finished smoothing on the oil mixture, wrapped her hair in a warm towel and walked back to the reception area. Pulling up her daily schedule on the computer screen, she stared at the empty spreadsheet. Nothing for today, or tomorrow. Her Saturday was empty. Void of even a footbath for old man Wexxler's cracked heels.

Despair rushed through her and she spent the next fifteen minutes nursing a pint of Chunky Monkey. But the sweet cream did little to ease the anxiety knotting her insides. It was a feeling that grew as she unwrapped her hair, combed and dried the long strands and measured her progress.

Not even a measly quarter inch.

Which meant the eucalyptus and lavender hadn't worked any better than the protein wrap. Or the upside down sit-ups. Or the pound of bacon she'd been scarfing every morning to feed the hair follicles. While she hadn't tried the full body massage recently, she'd had a few over the years and none had resulted in any notable hair growth.

Which meant that after four days and as many ideas, she was SOL. Unless…

Drawing a deep, steadying breath, she picked up the phone.

"It's Shay," she murmured when Matt's deep voice rumbled over the line. "I need you. Meet me at my place in two hours."

Plenty of time for her to close up shop and give herself a great big mental pep talk about priorities.

Her biggest? Hair growth techniques to boost her business.

That's the only reason she'd called him for help. Not because she wanted to see him again. Or talk to him.

No sirree. The last thing, the very last thing she wanted was to talk to Matt Keller again. Talking would lead to liking and liking would lead to a big, fat waste of time because he didn't like her back.

Even if he did show up at her place an hour early.

Faded Wranglers clung to his muscular thighs and a soft white cotton T-shirt hugged his broad shoulders. He smelled of fresh air and leather and a rugged sensuality that filled her nostrils and did dangerous things to her common sense. A straw Resistol sat tipped back on his head. Concern glittered in the green depths of his eyes. "You sounded desperate," he said by way of explanation.

"I was. I mean, I am." He stood there staring at her for a long moment and she shrugged. "Well, don't just stand there."

A strange expression lit his gaze. "Are you inviting me in?"

She had the sudden thought that she should shut the door and get as far as possible while she had the chance.

Before she gave in to the sudden urge to lean forward and press her lips to the pulse beat at the base of his throat. To feel the steady thump against her lips. To taste the salty sweetness of his skin.

"Are you?" His deep voice shattered the spell and the alarm clanging in her head faded as she stared deep into his eyes. "Inviting me in?"

"Of course," she murmured. "Come in."

Relief gleamed in his eyes as he followed her inside the living room.

"I didn't expect you so soon." She started snatching up the spa magazines littering her coffee table, suddenly desperate to ignore his presence and pretend that her heart wasn't pounding ninety miles an hour. "Or I would have cleaned up."

He watched her for a few seconds before turning his attention to the fireplace mantel and the assortment of trophies and pictures.

He eyed the row of pictures before shifting his attention to a small trophy shaped like a typewriter. "Did you win this?"

"A long, long time ago. I wrote a short story about a beauty pageant queen who stumbles onto the dead body of one of the judges."

"Based on an actual experience?"

"I'm afraid not. The closest I've ever gotten to a crime scene is watching CSI."

"That's too bad."

"Not really. Fiction is always a hundred times better than real life and I've got stacks of journals to prove it."

"These journals?" One minute he stood in front of the mantel and the next, he was reaching for one of her spirals.

"How did you do that—" she started, but then he flipped open one of the journals and she blurted, "Don't read that."

"Why not?"

"Because…" Because there was just something about seeing him holding the spiral and reading something she'd written that seemed so intimate. Too intimate considering she wasn't the least bit interested in him and he wasn't the least bit interested in her.

Her heart gave a double thump and she shook away the strange feeling. "Read it," she blurted. "What do I care?" She didn't. Not about him or her writing.

"So you like to write," he said after a few silent moments.

"I used to." Shay started straightening sofa cushions, determined to ignore the strange expectancy sitting in the pit of her stomach. "I don't really have time for it anymore."

"You're good," he stated after reading a few more pages. "What made you change career paths?"

"What do you mean?"

"Why did you ditch the writing for facials and mineral waxes?"

She wasn't sure why she answered him. There was just something about the intent way that he looked at her that made her think that he actually cared what she had to say. That he cared about her.

She shrugged. "Writing was a hobby. It's not like I could actually pay the bills with it."

"Why not?"

Yeah, why not? The question struck, niggling at her the way it had so many years ago when she'd been dividing her time between her writing and the pageant circuit.

"Play to your strengths," her mother had told her time and time again. *"You're too beautiful to waste yourself on something that may or may not pay off. Go for the sure thing, dear."*

She'd done just that. She'd entered pageant after pageant until she'd had enough money to open her own business.

A business that was now failing.

She ignored the last thought and fluffed a seat cushion. "How many working writers do you know?"

"None."

"My point exactly. I needed something practical."

"And writing for a living isn't nearly as practical as spreading peanut butter on someone's feet." At the mention of her latest menu offering, she couldn't help but grin.

"That's crunchy peanut butter. It sloughs off the dead cells and leaves the skin silky smooth. I know it seems unconventional, but it works."

"If you say so." His gaze zeroed in on the journal page and silence stretched around them for several long moments. "*This* is what works," he finally said. "It's good, Shay. Really good."

A tiny thrill went through her. A crazy reaction considering she didn't care about Matt or his opinion. She stiffened. "I really think we should pick up where we left off with the hair growth techniques?"

He closed the journal and slid it back onto the shelf. "Full body massage?"

She had a quick image of herself stretched out on the bed, his strong hands roaming her body. "After that," she blurted. "You just tell me what comes next and I'll write everything down."

Disappointment flashed in his gaze before he seemed to remember something. His mouth settled into a serious line and he nodded. "Sounds good." He settled himself on the sofa and Shay sank down next to him.

A bad move, she realized, over the next half hour as she wrote down several more recipes rumored to stimulate hair growth—everything from a castor oil hair mask to a milk and honey bath—and did her best to ignore the man who sat just inches away. So close she could cuddle up next to him if she scooted just a tad to the right.

Cuddle? She didn't want to *cuddle* with Matt. Even if he did like her writing.

Because he liked her writing.

It would be too easy to fall for him, to start hoping and dreaming and— *No*.

He wasn't her type. And she wasn't his. That much was obvious by the way he held his body so stiff. As if he wanted to be anywhere but sitting next to her.

That truth echoed home when they finished and he all but jumped up and ran out the door.

"Thanks," she called after him as she watched him head for his Jeep.

He gave her a husky "Don't mention it," climbed behind the wheel and then he was gone.

No, he didn't like her and she didn't like him.

And if you believe that, I've got some really nice beachfront property just a few miles outside of town...

Shay forced aside the notion, turned on her heel and headed for her kitchen. Time to stop thinking about Matt and start growing some hair.

The sooner, the better.

8

MATT HEADED BACK TO HIS CABIN and straight into an ice cold shower. The freezing spray pelted him but it did little to cool his burning skin or his throbbing cock.

He'd drunk himself into a blood stupor over the past few days, but it hadn't been enough to satisfy the hunger. He wanted sex. He needed it. It was all he'd been able to think about since that night with Shay. That, and the morning after.

He'd liked cooking bacon for her and talking to her. Being with her. He'd liked it way too much. That's why he'd raced over when she'd called.

He'd wanted to see her so badly. To smell her. To feel her. It had almost killed him not to press her down onto the sofa, settle himself between her luscious thighs and feel her wet heat close around him.

He'd wanted her desperately.

Correction, he'd wanted a woman desperately. Any woman.

It wasn't *Shay*. Sure, she was more determined than any woman he'd ever met—her coming after him like a bulldog for his hair growth secret was proof. And she was courageous. She'd been frightened on his doorstep that night, but she hadn't backed down. She'd faced off with him, propositioned him, and for that, he admired her.

But none of that made him want to kiss her senseless. Or sink into her sweet, delectable body. Or pull her close when it was over and never let go.

The hunger.

He sure as hell didn't want a future with Shay Briggs. His future mate was out there waiting for him, and he had every intention of finding her.

But first he had to satisfy the need clawing at his gut.

He killed the water, climbed from the shower and reached for a towel. He dressed in jeans, a T-shirt and a pair of worn boots. The Jeep squealed as he backed it up and swung around. In a matter of minutes, he cleared the trees and hit one of the farm roads that led to the interstate.

He drove several miles and ended up at a small honky tonk on the outskirts of the next town.

Cooter's Dance Hall had once been an ancient barn. The outside still sported a rusted red tin roof. Heavy wooden doors stood open and colored lights pushed out into the gravel parking lot. A rowdy Gretchen Wilson tune made the walls vibrate.

Matt killed the engine of his Jeep and climbed out. The steady crunch of his boots echoed in his head as he made his way toward the entrance. He paused in the doorway, his eyes adjusting to the bright glow of neon that sliced through the dim interior. Smoke fogged the air and the steady clack of pool balls echoed off the tin walls. Small round tables surrounded the perimeter of an old wooden dance floor sprinkled with sawdust and hay. A dozen couples slid this way and that, keeping time to the fast two-step.

He drank in the assortment of women, from the tall redhead in the far corner to a cluster of twenty-something blondes near the pool table, to a long-haired brunette standing by the bar. It was a smorgasbord—just what he needed to sate the damned hunger clawing at his gut.

Fixing his gaze on the brunette, he headed for the bar. Her name was Jeanine and she was a waitress in one of the nearby towns. She'd had a rough day, several asshole customers, not nearly enough tips and she was desperate to blow off some steam.

As the thoughts registered, he shook his head. He wasn't sure if he would ever get used to reading people's minds. At the same time, it definitely came in handy—he didn't have to talk to her to know that she wanted only sex.

She had enough complications in her life with her job, two kids and a deadbeat ex she fought with constantly.

She wanted a little fun, and Matt was just the man to give it to her.

The truth blazed in her eyes as he stepped up beside her and signaled the bartender for a beer.

"I don't think I've seen you around here before." Her soft words slid into his ears, but oddly enough it didn't stir the expected zing of excitement. "I'm from Carson Pass just a few miles up the road. My place isn't far." Her eyes twinkled. "I could give you a tour." *And a helluva lot more.*

She wanted to strip naked and ride him all night. The image was there in her head. The two of them naked and hot and sweaty. He'd clasp her hips and work her body while she writhed and moaned and exploded around him.

Her heartbeat kicked up a notch, echoing in his ears and drowning out the sound of an old Brooks & Dunn song that had just started up. She licked her lips and her chest heaved as she drew an extra breath.

Watching the luscious lift of her breasts beneath the ultra tight tank top, he braced himself for the sudden tightening in his gut as desire sliced through him so sharp and sweet and demanding. The way it had with Shay the moment she'd opened the door to him that evening.

Instead, he felt only the slightest twinge.

Because he didn't want this woman. Or the blonde standing near the juke box. Or the redhead who sashayed up to him and rubbed her breast against his arm as she leaned over the bar to order a drink. She leaned just so and he caught a glimpse of her nipple and...

Nothing.

His mouth didn't water for a taste and his hands didn't itch to touch and his damned cock... It was still hard, but it wasn't budging.

What the hell's wrong with you? They're all beautiful. Willing. Ready.

It didn't matter. He didn't want them.

The realization hit him and he downed his beer in several gulps. He dropped a twenty on the bar, turned and walked out. Outside, he climbed into his Jeep, gunned the engine and sped out of the parking lot.

The cool wind rushed through the open top and windows, but it did little to cool his raging body temperature. Only one thing could do that.

One woman.

Shay.

He knew that now. He hadn't wanted to face the truth before— that he was a helluva lot more attracted to Shay Briggs than he wanted to think. That he felt more for her than just lust. That he actually *liked* her.

She isn't The One. She's human.

He knew that. He also knew there was a female werewolf out there somewhere, waiting for him, wanting him. She would be his perfect match. His future.

But suddenly Matt wasn't half as concerned about settling down with another werewolf as he was with seeing Shay Briggs again.

And letting her see him.

She'll never accept you, buddy. Never.

Maybe. Maybe not. There was only one way to find out.

Matt floored the gas and headed for Skull Creek.

9

SHAY TURNED THE FLAME DOWN on the small stock pot. Her nose wrinkled and she waved a hand to dispel the fumes. *Ugh.* She knew castor oil didn't taste all that great, but she'd never realized that it smelled just as bad. At least, it did when warmed with cabbage and several other key ingredients per Matt Keller's recipe.

She stirred the mixture one final time before heading for the nearest window. Gripping the edge, she shoved the glass up and drank in a huge draft of fresh air.

Closing her eyes, she relished the faint breeze on her face. The slight wind slithered over her skin and tickled the edge of her T-shirt. Awareness rippled through her and she felt the purposeful sweep of Matt's hand up and down her back.

Her eyes snapped open to see him standing in front of her house. He leaned against his Jeep, his arms folded, his gaze fixed on her. A dozen explicit images rushed through her head, along with a fierce jolt of desire.

Get a grip. So what if he's here? It doesn't mean that he wants you as much as you want him.

She blinked, but he didn't disappear. Rather, he pushed away from the Jeep and started for her front door.

She watched his swift strides, his jeans pushing and pulling in all the right places until he disappeared onto her front porch. Her mouth went dry and excitement rippled through her.

She set the bubbling mixture aside, wiped her hands on a nearby dish towel and yanked off her apron. A quick glimpse at her reflection in the refrigerator and she stalled. She looked terrible. Her hair was wet—fresh from the shower and ready for another hair treatment—and she wore an old Miss Corn Queen 2000 T-shirt and raggedy sweats. No girdle. No body firming cream. No wrinkle-reducer foundation and blush. Nothing but eau de castor oil.

So? It's not like you're trying to impress him. Sure, he might be knocking on your front door. And maybe, just maybe, he might even want sex. But that doesn't mean you're going to give it to him. He's all wrong for you. You're keeping your head and your distance, remember?

Another whiff and her nose wrinkled.

With the way she smelled, he would surely turn right around and head for the Quick Pick and a can of Lysol.

Another knock sounded. She drew a deep breath, gathered her courage and hauled open the front door. "Yes?"

"I need to show you something."

"If it's another hair treatment, forget it. I've got enough to keep me busy for the time being. If they all fail, I'll let you know and we can start over."

"It's not a hair treatment…" His words faded as he sniffed. "You doing the castor oil?"

"I was about to, which means the smell is going to get much worse once I have it all over my head. You might want to bail while you've got the chance."

"Can I come in?" A wealth of meaning fueled his words and awareness zipped up and down her spine.

"I—I don't think that's a good idea." Particularly since she didn't trust herself. He was too close. Too handsome. Too wild.

She started to close the door, but his hand reached out, his fingers closing around the jamb. "I really don't have time—"

"Five minutes," he cut in. "Just give me five minutes."

The sudden desperation in his voice touched something inside of her. She stepped back and motioned him inside.

"So what is it that you need to show me?" she asked after a long, silent moment. "I can't imagine it could be any more impressive than the half dozen treatments I've already written down."

"I wouldn't be so sure about that," he murmured and his eyes seemed to grow hotter, brighter. Unearthly.

She blinked, but the color didn't fade. Instead, it intensified, glittering and shimmering and changing—

Wait a second. Wait just a motherfriggin' *second*.

She blinked. But the color intensified, shifting from green to a brilliant, blazing purple?

"What the—?" Her words died in her throat as he pulled his lips back and she saw the sharp ends of his incisors.

Fangs?

She clamped her eyes shut as her heart started to pound.

A dream. It had to be a dream. A weird twisted version of the fantasy she'd been having where Matt showed up at her front door and they had hot, wild sex in her entryway. And then her living room. And then the bedroom.

"And then the bathroom," his raw, guttural voice pushed past the pounding in her ears and finished her train of erotic thought.

Her eyes popped open to see him, his eyes glowing and his fangs still gleaming for several fast, furious heartbeats.

"I can hear your thoughts in my head," he murmured, as if the admission bothered him as much as it did her. "I didn't believe it myself when you showed up on my doorstep, but it was there. I could read you so clearly. I know all about you, Shay. I know your favorite color is red and your favorite ice cream flavor is Chunky Monkey. I know that you had the chicken pox when you were six and you still have a tiny little scar on your ear which is why you don't wear earrings. I know about your mother and her rotten taste in men."

"Because I told you," she managed to argue, more to convince herself than him.

"Her first husband left her on their wedding night," he added. "Just walked out and stuck her with a hefty hotel bill. She had to call your grandma to loan her the money."

"I didn't tell you that. I've never told anyone that."

"I know about marriage number two. She brought you a bunch of those little bottles of shampoo from the hotel in Austin. That one lasted about six months and then he ran off with a clerk from the feed store."

"Darlene," she whispered, the past rushing through her mind. She saw her mother standing on the corner at Main and Center, her face streaked with tears as she watched Dwayne's 4x4 motor toward the interstate, Darlene in the passenger seat.

"Darlene Monroe," Matt added. "Marriage number three was basically a repeat of number two. That's when you started to think that maybe it wasn't the men, but your mother. That there was something wrong with her that made her gravitate toward losers. That there's something wrong with you—"

"Stop. Just stop." Shay pressed her hands to her ears, not wanting to believe what was right in front of her. She shook her head. "This is just a hallucination." She latched on to the only excuse she could think of.

"There isn't anything wrong with you, Shay. You're just scared to put it all out there for someone because you don't want to be rejected again. But this isn't a hallucination caused by castor oil and cabbage fumes." He voiced the explanation echoing in her head. "Deep in your soul, you know that. You just don't want to admit it because then you'll have to accept this." His gaze locked with hers. "You'll have to accept me."

"W-what are you?"

"A werewolf. I think." When she gave him a puzzled look, he added, "I used to be a full-blooded werewolf, but now I'm something different." He gave her a brief explanation about Viv and the struggle and the vampire bite. "Now I'm something different. Half-werewolf, half-vampire."

"That's crazy." Even as she said the words, her mind rushed back through the past week and everything started to make sense. The furry picture of him in last week's newspaper. The unnatural glow of his eyes. The way he seemed to read her every thought, sense her every need. The wild, incredible, earth-shattering sex...

She saw him poised above her, his eyes gleaming, his fangs glittering... Her imagination, or so she'd thought.

"I always knew there was someone out there for me. I've been searching for my mate for three years now." His gaze locked with hers. "I've been searching for you, Shay. I love you."

"This can't be happening," she said again, denial rushing as fast and furious as her heart. "This can't be real. *You* can't be real."

He opened his mouth and a growl vibrated the air between them. His eyes glowed purple then the pupils shimmered to a bright, intense yellow. His fangs grew longer. His features shifted. His hair started to grow.

She heard the scream from far away at first. But it quickly grew louder until she realized that it was her own. The floor seemed to tilt. The smell of castor oil and cabbage burned her nostrils.

She had the brief thought that she was about to faint. A crazy thought because she didn't cry, much less crumple into an unconscious heap. That only happened in books and movies.

This only happened in books and movies.

She had one last glimpse of Matt, his body morphing and changing, and then everything went black.

10

No way was he a werewolf. Or a vampire. Or some weird cross between the two.

No *way*.

That's what Shay told herself when she opened her eyes a little while later to find herself tucked safely in her bed, with Matt nowhere in sight.

Things like that… They just didn't exist.

Even so, she kicked off the covers, pulled off her sweats and spent fifteen minutes doing a frantic search over her naked body for bites. She didn't find any. A discovery that sent her straight to the fridge for a pint of Chunky Monkey.

Not that she was disappointed.

Hardly.

The last thing she needed was to turn into some guy's chew toy. A crazy, disturbed, warped guy who actually thought he was a bonafide *werewolf*. Even worse, he was convinced he was a werewolf who'd been bitten by a *vampire*.

And she thought she'd reached her lowest moment whipping a bunch of meatballs at what's his name? Talk about a headline waiting to happen: *My Hot Night with a Werewolf*.

Forget losing her customers. They'd cart her off to the funny farm for damned sure.

Forget it. Forget him.

She tried. She really did. She gave up the ice cream and headed into the shop the next morning. She spent Saturday doing inventory and sending out post-cards to her client list. But no amount of work could make her forget the night before. It played over and over in her head like a broken record, taunting her, reminding her until she finally admitted the truth to herself—he was a werewolf, all right.

A werewolf hellbent on finding his one and only.

She'd seen the sincerity in his eyes and heard the conviction in his voice.

He *loved* her.

Even more, she loved him.

The realization hit her later that evening as she locked up the salon and headed home. She stood in her living room and stared at the stack of journals on her bookshelf and her heart lodged in her chest.

He'd taken one.

While that fact should have made her incredible uptight and insecure, it didn't bother her now. She wanted him to read her stories. She wanted him, period.

It didn't matter that they hadn't dated for months, taken long walks in the park or gone on romantic picnics. Deep in her heart, she *knew*. She'd known the moment their eyes had met outside of the Piggly Wiggly. It had been an attraction more intense than anything she'd ever felt before.

Because it was more than attraction.

It was the real thing. Deep down, 'til death do us part *love*.

She loved his strength and his passion and the fact that he knew her every thought, her every weakness, and loved her in spite of them.

And it was high time she showed him just how much.

MATT WAS STANDING ON THE FRONT porch when Shay pulled up in front of the cabin. She knew the moment she saw the expectant look in his eyes that he'd been waiting for her, his senses tuned to the surrounding forest.

Because he was more than a man.

Her hands tightened on the steering wheel for a brief moment as a wave of hesitation swept through her. She had to be crazy to be doing this. At the same time, she'd waited her entire life for just this moment. This man. And no way was she letting her inhibitions get the best of her.

Leaving the lights on, she killed the engine. She gathered her courage, took a deep breath and opened the door. A few seconds later, she stepped into the blaze of headlights. Her gaze locked with his and she reached for the hem of her T-shirt, pulling it up and over her head. Trembling fingers worked at the catch of her bra, freeing her straining breasts. The scrap of lace landed at her feet. Her jeans followed until she stood in nothing but her panties and a slick layer of perspiration. She hooked her thumbs at the waistband and pushed them down. The silk slithered down her legs and she stepped free.

The warm night air whispered over her bare shoulders and breasts and she fought the instinct to cover herself. She was determined to show Matt the real woman just as he'd shown her his true self.

"I love you, Matt," she murmured. "I still have a zillion questions about all of this, about you, and I'm scared to death, but I love you anyway."

She barely managed to blink before he reached her. Strong, muscled arms wrapped around her and drew her close as his mouth captured hers in a deep, thorough kiss that sucked the air from her lungs and made her legs tremble.

She clutched at his shoulders. Denim rasped her sensitive breasts and thighs in a delicious friction that made her tremble and clutch at the hard muscles of his arms.

Strong hands slid down her back, cupped her bottom and urged her legs up on either side of him. Then he lifted her. He cradled and kneaded her buttocks as she wrapped her legs around his waist and settled over the straining bulge in his jeans.

As anxious as Matt was to sate the beast that lived and breathed inside of him, he'd been waiting for this moment—for her—far too long to have it over at the flick of a zipper. He wouldn't scare her off and risk losing her.

He *wouldn't*.

He gathered his control and his body shook from the effort. "I want you so much," he murmured. "I don't know if I can hold back."

"I don't want you to hold back. I want all of you. Werewolf. Vampire. It doesn't matter. I love you both."

Her words whispered through his head and sent a rush of joy through him. An emotion that quickly faded into a wave of passion when she rubbed herself against him.

"Please."

He carried her inside to the bedroom, stretched her out on the bed and flipped on the bedside lamp. "I want to see you this time. I want you to see me."

And then he kissed her, hard and deep and urgently. His tongue tangled with hers, stroking and coaxing until she whimpered and tugged at the waistband of his jeans. He shed the denim, slid on a condom and settled between her legs. His weight pressed her back into the mattress. His erection slid along her damp cleft, making her shudder and moan and arch toward him. And then he plunged, fast and sure and deep, burying himself to the hilt in one luscious thrust that tore a cry from her lungs.

She wrapped her legs around him, the motion lifting her body so that he could slide more fully inside of her. He started to move, building the pressure, pushing them both higher, higher, until her climax hit her. Sweet, dizzying energy rushed through her and into him, feeding the hunger.

She milked him and he closed his eyes against the incredible sensation. But it wasn't enough. The more she gave, the more he wanted. Hunger gnawed at him, pushing and pulling inside of him until he felt her fingertips on his face.

He stared at her through a rich purple haze, seeing every feature so clearly. Her lush mouth. Her heavy-lidded gaze. Her flushed cheeks.

"All of you," she murmured and she arched her neck in silent invitation.

He dipped his head and sank his fangs deep. The red heat filled his mouth and desire speared him.

Her fingers plunged into his hair and she held him close as her lifeblood pulsed through his body. His own orgasm hit him hard and fast and he bucked, spilling himself inside the woman beneath him.

When he finally pulled away and collapsed next to her, she snuggled up against his body, happy and content and his.

His woman.

His mate.

"That was pretty incredible," she murmured into his shoulder. "Is it always that intense?"

"I don't know. You're my first bite."

She raised her head and stared down at him, into him, and if he hadn't known better, he would have sworn she could see his every thought just as he saw hers.

"Your last bite," she told him, love shining in her gaze.

He grinned. "Possessive, aren't we?"

"And demanding. I want my journal back."

"Is that so?" He touched her nipple, rasping the edge until she caught her bottom lip. "Maybe we can work out a little trade." And then he dipped his head and captured her lips in another deep, seductive kiss.

IT WAS STILL DARK WHEN SHAY opened her eyes to find Matt sleeping soundly next to her. She touched the prick points at her neck and a rush of desire bolted through her. When he'd drank from her, it had been the most erotic thing she'd ever felt. And the most intimate. She felt connected to him now. Really and truly connected, as if they were one. His heart beating in her chest. Her blood flowing through his veins. *One*.

She barely resisted the urge to snuggle up next to him. There would be plenty of time for that. An entire future, she realized. But she had something much more important nagging at her at that particular moment.

She pressed a kiss on his shoulder, climbed from the bed and walked into the living room. After rummaging in her purse, she found a pen and notepad and settled on Matt's couch. And then she started to write.

"WHAT'S THIS?" SUE ANN ASKED when Shay showed up on her doorstep later Sunday morning and handed her a small spiral notebook.

"Something sweet, sexy and romantic," she told the newspaper editor. "It's for tomorrow's Valentine's Day feature." And then she turned on her heel and headed back to Matt's place for the first day of the rest of her life.

Her future.

MY HOT NIGHT WITH A WEREWOLF by Shay Briggs.

Shay stood on Matt's front porch early Monday morning and stared at the front page headline.

"I thought you said you wrote a fictitious piece for the paper." Matt came up behind her and slid an arm around her waist. He wore nothing but a pair of jeans and a smile as he nuzzled her neck.

"What can I say? I was inspired by true-life events." Not that anyone in town realized that. They thought Shay had written a sexy piece of fiction. At least that had been Sue Ann's take when she'd called Sunday afternoon gushing about the story. She'd ran with it for the Valentine's issue and Shay had gone from columnist to feature writer just like that.

She thought of her empty schedule at the salon and the uncertainty of her future as the resident beauty expert. Particularly since she'd heard a rumor yesterday that half her clients were gravitating toward the hair salon which had started offering waxes and facials. The piece of FYI hadn't bothered her near as much as she'd expected it to.

Because she didn't love the citrus scrubs and the peanut butter wraps half as much as she loved writing. And while she hadn't managed to save her career, perhaps she'd found a new one. One that made her as happy as the man standing beside her.

"Nice pic," Matt murmured, drawing her attention to the photo at the far corner of the page that featured Shay in the parking lot of the Piggly Wiggly the day she'd spotted Matt for the first time. Her eyes sparkled and her face glowed. She looked happy.

"I don't remember anyone taking a picture." Her gaze zeroed in on the credit. *Photo by U.R. Luckyday.*

A smile tugged at her lips as she remembered Ulysses and his timely entrance into her salon the morning she'd been moaning to Sue Ann. He'd been the one to spark her interest in Matt's hair secret in the first place.

U.R. Luckyday.

The truth crystalized as she looked at the by-line. She knew then that Ulysses wasn't an ordinary photographer. There was something special about him. Not that she was speculating on what the something special was. She wasn't questioning fate. She was accepting it. Relishing it. Loving it.

She was loving Matt.

"It's the happiest Valentine's Day of my life, too," he murmured, reading the thoughts that whispered through her head. And then he gathered her close and kissed her.

And they lived sexily ever after…

Once upon a bite, in a small Texas town, there lived a beautiful maiden to whom beauty meant everything. Until the day she met the savage beast. He was ferocious and deadly and did his best to scare her away. She fell head over heels in love with him despite his fanged and furry status and they settled down together and lived happily ever after.

* * * * *

MY, WHAT A BIG...
YOU HAVE!
Leslie Kelly

To Kim and Rhonda, two fabulous authors
and two wonderful women—I've loved
working with you both.

And to Brenda Chin—thanks for giving me
the chance to!

1

CONSIDERING Scarlett Templeton wrote children's books for a living, she probably shouldn't have let herself get caught on camera telling someone to kiss her ass. Then again, since it was Cupid she'd told, and that half-naked little bastard with the arrows had screwed up her life more than once, she didn't feel too bad.

Her last breakup, which had been public and ugly, had occurred four months ago, as the smarmy reporter she'd run into at a recent media event *must* have known. So when he'd asked whether Cupid had set his sights on her for Valentine's Day, she'd told him what Cupid could do. The quip had ended up all over the Internet, eventually landing on some site called kissmyasscupid.com. She'd become a finalist for the "least romantic woman on the planet" award and a poster child for the anti-romance movement.

Ahh, well, it could be worse. She could be the poster child for the evil-authors-who-are-corrupting-our-children movement.

Oh, wait, she *was*. At least to *some* people, who didn't appreciate her seriously twisted humor and dark streak.

That would include her mother. The woman couldn't decide whether she was proud or horrified at Scarlett's success. She'd wanted Scarlett—named after her favorite literary heroine—to write romance novels or sweet, little-girls' books.

Yeah, right.

Having grown up hearing her too-romantic mother weave tales of gallant knights and damsels fair, Scarlett had hit the world with her head in a cloud and glass slippers on her feet.

Talk about a hard landing. It was a wonder she didn't still have shards of glass in her toes.

At thirty, after a dozen years of *realistic* life, love, sex and relationships, she was *over* the happily-ever-afters. So the kids' books she wrote weren't exactly Mother Goose rhymes or whimsical fairy tales. They were more like dark, twisted fables where Mother Goose could end up in a pot, and the princess would find out her Prince Charming was a two-timing scum-bucket. Most important of all, the princess wouldn't wait for anybody to save her, she'd get off her butt and do it herself. Or else get eaten by the wolf.

That was something Scarlett had learned long ago. Save yourself...or get eaten by the wolf.

"My children just love your books Ms. Templeton," said the customer in line at Scarlett's latest never-ending book signing. The tightness of her mouth indicated the woman wasn't finished. "Though I really don't understand *why*."

Being a *New York Times* bestselling writer...wow, what a great job. "Thank you," Scarlett said, not thrown by the reaction. She focused on the smiling faces of the girls at the woman's side. "Lady Bethany kicks some serious troll tail in this one!"

Both girls burst into a cacophony of excited chatter, all of which Scarlett genuinely appreciated. She didn't write for the parents, she did it for the kids. Her reader was the girl who didn't look like Rapunzel, the one who had enough brains to chop her damn hair off and climb down out of that tower herself.

"I saw you on YouTube," the older of the girls said in a whisper, trying to avoid being overheard by her mother. "And I voted for you in the contest on the kissmyyouknowwhatcupid site."

Oh, joy. She was well on her way to being crowned queen of stone-hearted bitches, helped along by adoring little girls.

"You know," she said, wondering if it was too late for damage control, "I was in a bad mood when I said that. You should probably take it as more of a warning of what happens when you don't watch what you say and when you say it. Especially in front of a camera."

The girl nodded. "Oh, sure." But the sparkle in her eye said she was still titillated. Then, when their mother harrumphed in impatience, the girl and her sister hurried away.

"You okay?" asked the owner of the quaint French Quarter shop where Scarlett always did signings for her new releases.

Scarlett shook her right hand and flexed her fingers. "If my hand can hold out, I guess the rest of me can."

The book-signing was only scheduled to last until four. It was now almost six. But Scarlett would never get up and leave when her young fans had waited patiently to speak to her.

"Well, it has to end soon. We're almost out of books," said the middle-aged woman who probably didn't understand Scarlett's stories, either. But she definitely understood the cha-*ching* of the cash register. "We have only two copies of your newest release left and we've sold out of all your backlist titles, too."

"Great, thanks again," Scarlett said as a customer handed her one of those last two books to sign. She did, then watched the man leave and waited for the next person. But there was no one else. Four hours and two hundred books later, she was done.

Rising, she stretched her back, which ached from sitting in the same position for so long. As she glanced at her watch, she realized she was running very late. Having decided to pay a surprise visit to her elderly grandmother for the weekend, she'd hoped to arrive before dark.

Granny lived in the middle of the bayou and swore she wouldn't leave until she was hauled out in her coffin. The route ran through miles of swamp, with roads only a few yards from 'gator-and-snake-filled water. Scarlett *really* didn't like driving out there at night. She needed to hustle if she was going to pick up the tabloids and junk food Granny always demanded and hit the road before it got too late.

Before she could hop to it, though, a voice interrupted. "I see I have procured the very last copy."

Startled, she glanced over and saw a stranger standing on the opposite side of the table.

It was all she could do not to stare because he was such an *odd-*looking man. She'd written a book once that turned the Rumpel-stiltskin story upside-down. In it, a clever milkmaid and her gnome-like friend conspire to trick an evil king out of his ill-gotten gains by pulling off a straw-into-gold scam. This guy could play *her* Rumpel in the movie.

Slight and diminutive, he probably stood as high as the base of Scarlett's throat, and she was five-six. His slumped shoulders further reduced his height and were emphasized by the long, thin gray hair that hung past them.

It got better. His protruding eyes were a murky grayish-green, and a hairy mole dominated one cheek. He boasted the most unusual nose she had ever seen. It curved down like a spotty, flesh-colored banana, the tip almost reaching his upper lip.

His clothes were old-fashioned—a navy worsted-wool three-piece suit, a walking stick, and a bowler hat. And he wore on his lapel a small pin—a beautiful, highly crafted set of wings that almost appeared to be made out of straw-spun gold.

He was, without doubt, the strangest-looking person she had ever seen. And she adored him at once. "Fantastic! I don't have any say in casting, but oh, wow, I will make a recommendation."

One brow went up over a rheumy eye. "I beg your pardon? I came simply to buy a book."

She hesitated, wondering if she'd really made a mistake. Leaning over to take the book from his hand, she got close enough to check for cosmetics, spirit gum on the prosthetic nose, or the line of a wig.

There was nothing. Either the man had a makeup artist to rival any in Hollywood, or he wasn't wearing a costume.

"I, uh…sorry, I thought you were someone else."

"I sometimes am," he replied, with a smile so enigmatic, Scarlett could only stare in confusion. "I do like your books. They're oddly shaped and eccentric…like me."

She couldn't help but chuckle along with him.

"There is, of course, a definite lack of romance in them."

"Yes, there is."

"You're not a romantic? You don't believe in true love?"

She bent over to the book, opening it to the flyleaf. "Romance and true love belong in fairy tales. I don't believe in any of it, which is why my books are dark and realistic."

He tsked and shook his head, as if she'd disappointed him. "Ah, well, I'm sure you have your reasons. Now, will you please inscribe the book to C? Just the letter will do."

Embarrassed to have mistaken him for an actor, Scarlett signed the man's copy. "You got here just in time. I was about to leave."

"Going out of town, are you?"

Surprised that he hadn't assumed she was going home, since she was a well-known author living right here in New Orleans, she mumbled, "I'm off to visit my grandmother, actually."

"Ah. A visit to Granny. Are you bringing her sweeties?"

Sweeties? Had this guy stepped out of a time machine or what? "She's a chocoholic," she admitted, "and a potato-chip junkie. If I show up empty-handed, I'll be in big trouble."

He laughed softly. "We old ones do like our treats." He reached for the book, and their fingers brushed. For such a frail-looking old man, his skin gave off a strong, almost electric vibe. As crazy as it seemed, the contact left her hand tingling. Her thoughts snapped and sizzled in her head.

"I suppose Granny told you not to stray from the path."

She blinked. "What?"

"I mean, to remain on the main road through the forest."

"It's a bayou," she said, wondering why she felt as though she'd just been injected with an overdose of caffeine.

"Sometimes *straying* from the path can lead to adventure."

Paths and adventure, forests and sweeties. The images jumbled. She suddenly wanted to get out of there, away from the odd man and into the refreshing air outside. "I have to go."

He smiled and extended his hand. "I so enjoyed our chat."

She really didn't want to touch him again, but courtesy demanded it. Slowly reaching out, she braced for more of that strange reaction—not revulsion, in any way, despite his appearance. On the contrary, she expected—and *got*—more of that strange, sizzling energy.

Then, with a tip of his hat and a tiny smile, he was gone.

The feeling, however, didn't go away. The intensity increased. Her back pain was gone, any fatigue forgotten. Even the rainy weather didn't bother her. She merely flipped up the hood of her trendy red raincoat and walked to a local shop for the latest rag sheets and junk food.

Armed and ready to meet even Granny's exacting standards, she got into her car for the drive out of New Orleans. Night had definitely fallen, and she had second thoughts about driving that route after dark. The trip was a surprise, so Granny wasn't expecting her, and she could easily have waited until morning.

But the darkness didn't intimidate her. Instead, she whistled as she drove, tapping her fingers on the padded leather steering wheel of her convertible.

Stray from the path…stray…

The strange words whispered into her subconscious for some reason, though she tried to focus on Granny's delight at seeing her, her next book, on not killing that reporter for asking her about Valentine's Day.

She almost missed the road sign. Dark green with sloping cursive lettering, unlike any sign she'd ever seen; it appeared a good five miles before the exit she normally took. She couldn't remember ever having noticed it before. It listed the name of the town closest to Granny's—Hastings.

Well, sort of. "Hastings *Towen*?" she mused.

Somebody needed to fire their sign painter.

She considered exiting. The sign claimed the distance to be much shorter than the route she usually took. Fewer miles through the swamp was a good thing. But it seemed so strange that she hadn't seen the marker before, and her senses went on alert, telling her not to.

The exit wasn't so much an off-ramp as a quick veering away from the highway. She *almost* drove past it. Almost listened to her sixth sense and continued on her way, not comfortable with trying out an unfamiliar road at night.

Stray.

At the last possible moment, though, she veered. The car's tires skidded on the gravelled surface but quickly regained traction as the highway became a pitted road. Ahead of her lay a winding, narrow thoroughfare overhung with sagging willows and skeletons of dead trees looped with tangled Spanish moss. It was dark and deep and unfamiliar.

In her stories, when the heroine was confronted with two paths, one bright and sunny and the other scary and full of mystery, she always went to the dark side.

Too bad Scarlett wasn't one of her heroines.

She decided to swerve right back out onto the highway, because, though lined with marsh on either side, the regular route was still a solid, well-maintained river of blacktop. Unlike this version of hell's Yellow Brick Road.

Stray.

She intended to go back. Really. But instead, she kept driving. And driving. Straight into the woods, almost into another world, a primeval one far from civilization. Soon the haunted trees seemed to close in behind her and she lost sight of the lights from the highway.

The curved canopy of trees nearly blocked out the sky, obscuring the bright, full moon overhead. The forest—it suddenly felt like a dense wilderness more than a typical marsh—crept closer to the road, until it seemed to hug her car in its green embrace. The throughway narrowed to the width of her single vehicle, meant for only *her* to drive.

A voice kept telling her to turn around. A louder one—*stray*—refused to allow it.

The electric tension that had driven her out of the store earlier didn't diminish. Instead, with each mile she drove, it built, making her heart beat faster and her breathing more ragged.

"What is happening to me?" she asked, wondering where the sensible, no-nonsense, no-romance Scarlett had gotten to. Why was she so excited? Why hadn't she turned around while she still had the chance? *Why didn't she care?*

There was no time to answer. Not even in her own head, because suddenly, in the trees a few yards ahead of her, she saw something. She had an impression of movement, then a shadow splitting the night.

The shadow took physical form as it sprang out of the woods, leaping directly into her path.

Jet-black hair. Feral, almost reddish eyes. Ripples of muscle across a powerful torso.

Impossible!

She screamed and swerved.

And crashed.

2

HUNTER THIBODAUX had been following his quarry for nearly a month. He'd picked up the trail soon after the suspect had arrived in New Orleans, followed him to Houston, then Arizona. Now he was back where he'd started, in the swampy marshlands of southeastern Louisiana.

He could have saved himself the effort and just waited here for four weeks, because Hunter had known the prey he sought would return to this place with the next full moon.

In that time, however, two policemen had lost their lives. Hunter had been too late to stop the murders. But suspecting who the third target would be, and staying close to his quarry, he'd managed to prevent that last murder from taking place. The heat he'd provided had stopped Lucas Wolf—the suspected killer Hunter was chasing—from carrying out his deadly mission of vengeance.

If, indeed, he was guilty. Something Hunter just didn't know yet, despite the circumstantial evidence.

That Hunter *hated* the man whose life he'd protected didn't change the fact that he'd done the right thing. Preventing a murder made the weeks of stalking, tracking and lying in wait worth it. Even if he had come up empty-handed.

Not anymore, though. This cat-and-mouse game was coming to an end. He'd catch Lucas—on this side or on the other. He was experienced in both. Licensed to carry a weapon in both. A successful bounty hunter in both. And since he was no longer a cop, he was even able to skirt the edges of the law occasionally to get his man.

He'd just never imagined that he'd ever need to hunt *this* particular man. And part of him wondered if he'd even been able to do it.

"Are you guilty, Lucas?" he whispered into the near silence, the words barely touching his lips. "Could you be *that* ruthless, even with good reason?"

It was possible. Even probable. Lucas had been in a bloody, vengeful mood after the murder of his younger half-sister Ciara. Just a kid in the wrong place at the wrong time, she'd seen something she shouldn't have and had paid for it with her life.

Hell, maybe Hunter would have done the same thing in Lucas's shoes. He didn't have a sister, but he knew the pain had to be almost unbearable. Especially for someone like Lucas Wolf: someone whose senses were especially…heightened.

Hunter needed the truth. For his own sake, for his mother's. Hell, even for Lucas's. Because Hunter being the one to take him in could mean the difference between Lucas Wolf's life and his death. No matter what, Hunter didn't want the man killed by an angry cop who'd rather take Lucas down than take him in.

He wanted to do it here. Tonight. Because if he missed Wolf here and was forced to go *traveling,* his schedule would get a whole lot tighter. He'd have tonight to get to his destination. One—two at most—to hunt. And one to get back. Or else he'd be stuck *there* for weeks until the moon completed its eternal cycle and began to swell again. The veil of mist between the lands became sheer enough to slip through only when the moon was either full, or nearly so.

He had been waiting near that mysterious border all week. Leaving his truck parked miles away to avoid detection, he had hiked in. He'd camped in the woods, living in silence, lighting no fire that might betray his presence in the dark night. Lucas might expect him to be here and would be wary. Strong and dangerous at any time, Lucas would be especially formidable now, so Hunter had done all he could to melt into the bayou, to disappear from sight, from scent, from sound.

He lived like a wraith. Waiting.

Then that patience paid off. He sensed movement in the trees, felt the air part as someone moved through it. Heard the cries of the night animals disappear as if extinguished—on alert because of the predator in their midst.

There. A shadow. Time to end this.

It's over, Lucas. Your vigilante days are done.

But suddenly, he was almost blinded by bright lights that seemed to come out of nowhere.

"No!" he snapped, catching only a glimpse of the dark-haired man as he leapt across the road. The shadowy form was silhouetted against the lights, then it disappeared, racing with animalistic speed toward the border.

Cursing, knowing the advantage would change over there, Hunter began to give chase. But he stopped abruptly at the jarring, horrific sound of brakes screaming and metal slamming. Glass shattered and the night air seemed ruptured with the violence of the unfamiliar noise.

The car that had so shockingly wandered into this *nowhere* that existed at the edge of two worlds had just crashed.

"You fool," he snapped, turning to glare at the car, which hung off the edge of the road. Its front end hugged a massive oak. Its back had swung around, nearly sliding off the gravel altogether. It clung to a narrow patch of soft earth just a few inches above a swampy mess of muck. "Damned fool."

Because only someone with no common sense would drive out here on this trail impersonating a street. It had no lights, no signs, no painted lines and no civilization within miles. That the driver had even found the path amazed him.

Unless the car was being driven by another traveler.

Leave him. Hunter's inner voice tempted him to simply abandon the stranger to his fate, and pursue the far greater danger.

Something inside him, however, couldn't do it.

Shoving his weapon into its holster, Hunter darted toward the car. The rear tires were losing their grip on the soft ground, sliding slowly toward a quick descent into the swamp. He had no idea how deep the water was, if the car would sink and the occupant drown. He only knew he didn't want to find out. Given the slithery sounds and the croaking, he had no doubt the water moccasins and 'gators were licking their chops in anticipation.

Still cursing the crazy occupant, he ran for the driver's-side door. He yanked at it, but it didn't budge. Looking inside, he saw only a sea of red, and at first, he thought the driver had to be dead given the amount of blood. But he soon realized he was looking at a billowing coat.

He noted one more thing. The lock stood upright. Meaning the crash had bent the frame and jammed the door shut.

"Hold on," he yelled. "And stay down."

The windshield was crackled and shattered into a thousand spiderwebs, but still held together in its frame. He considered smashing it in, and might *have* to if there was no other option. But showering the driver with glass wasn't his first choice.

He quickly assessed those options. Hunter couldn't get around to the other door, there wasn't enough ground to walk on. Even if there were, he couldn't risk the driver shifting his weight onto that side to get out.

It had to be the top.

Pulling his broad hunting knife from its sheath, he stabbed through the soft convertible top. The back tires slid another inch. "One minute, just give me one minute…"

He hated to add his own weight to the mangled wreckage, but there was no other way. Carefully, he climbed onto the hood, feeling the shift and sway of the metal beneath his knees. Hoping his added weight on the front end would help keep the vehicle up, he knelt over the windshield and finished cutting through the soft top.

Thrusting the thick fabric out of the way, he peered inside. The dim dashboard lights remained on, illuminating the driver, who was slumped over the wheel, against the already deflated airbag. The driver with the long blond hair.

"A woman," he muttered, wondering why he was so surprised. Maybe because he just couldn't imagine why any woman would be out there alone. And she *was* alone, a quick glance confirmed that.

"Can you hear me?"

Nothing. Damn. More careful than he'd ever been, Hunter stretched further, hearing the crackle and snap of the windshield glass. "I'm trying to get you out. Stay still, okay?"

Knowing he couldn't reach her seatbelt buckle, he slid his knife under the belt and sawed through the thing. The back of the car lurched, not just an inch this time, but several before it paused again. He was out of time, out of options. "No choice, *cher*," he murmured. "Keep your head down and your eyes closed."

Tugging the hood of the woman's raincoat over her head and face, he hoped it would be enough protection. Then, using the blunt end of his huge knife, he punched the broken windshield. The glass burst inward, showering the interior of the tiny car.

The blow had knocked the vehicle even further, but the slow slide didn't halt this time. He actually *felt* it when the back passenger tire left the earth and slid out into nothingness before the rear lurched downward.

Operating on pure adrenaline, Hunter knelt on the broken glass, reached down and grasped the woman beneath the arms. Hoping like hell that her legs weren't caught beneath the dashboard, he yanked with all his might.

She groaned. *Alive.* But she didn't come off the seat.

The car picked up speed. The second tire was heading over. He nearly fell off the hood. He had one more shot at it. "Come on, woman, I'm *not* going into that water for you."

Getting a moment of resistance from the seatbelt he'd cut, he feared they *were* both about to go for a swim. But with one more surge of strength, he heaved and watched the cut ends of the belt slid through the fasteners, freeing her at last.

She came out of the driver's seat like a rag doll, almost weightless, sending both of them flying. They hit the ground hard mere seconds before the convertible slide down the embankment into the swamp.

It was completely submerged in the water in under a minute.

The still-working headlights sent twin beams of weak, muddy illumination from beneath the surface. Through them, he spotted the heads of two alligators. Then the lights flickered out and it was gone. The car had disappeared as if it had never existed.

Disappearing. Huh. That wasn't such a rarity around here.

Hunter lay panting on the ground for a full minute, willing his heart to stop racing. Beside him, the woman softly groaned, and he rolled toward her. The moon reflected brilliant sparkles on her coat…glass. "Sorry, darlin'," he murmured, reaching to push the long strands of blond hair off her bloodied face.

He plucked a few errant bits of glass from her cheeks, then spread her unbuttoned coat to look her over, from top to bottom. Her brow was bloodied and a lump had already started forming; she'd obviously banged her head in the crash.

Carefully running his hands over her shoulders, limbs and midriff, he checked for broken bones. And because he was a half-decent guy and she was unconscious, he managed not to notice how attractive she was, or that her body was enough to make a man howl at the moon—if one was into that sort of thing.

"You're gonna be okay," he told her. Because other than the lump and the cuts from the glass, she appeared intact. She'd been wearing her seatbelt, and the airbag had deployed, so her shoulder, chest and collarbones would probably be sore as hell when she woke up. But, nothing appeared broken.

If he hadn't been here, though, he imagined her situation would have been very dire indeed. She would have gone into that water unconscious. The only question was whether she'd have drowned before the alligators paid a visit. Or after.

"What am I going to do with you now?" he whispered.

The reality of his situation was just starting to sink in. He was on the ground with an injured, unconscious woman, deep in the bayou, far from any help.

His truck was parked five miles away. He could carry her, but it would take a while. And even then, they would still face a long drive to anything resembling civilization.

One thing was certain. He would never make it back here before dawn. Not with the way time operated in these parts.

There was only one alternative. He could take her somewhere close. Very close. Somewhere safe and warm where swamp became stream and the bayou a welcoming green forest. He knew of a place just like that, less than a mile through the veil. In it were bandages, medicine, clean water and comfort. Safety.

If she'd been badly injured, he wouldn't risk it. But she didn't appear to be. He'd had enough accidents and mishaps of his own to recognize a simple concussion and a cut that might require a stitch or two at most.

So…take her to a hospital? Or take her over *there*?

One way would send him far off course and put him a full day behind his quarry. The other risked exposure of something this woman could never possibly understand.

She doesn't have to know.

Right. She never had to know. A hunter's cottage looked much the same on either side. He'd take care of her, leave her to recover, and go finish his job tomorrow night. Then he'd bring her back here after it was all over, being very careful to limit where she went and the things she saw in the meantime.

And if she did see anything she shouldn't?

"It'll be a dream, darlin'," he whispered. "Just a dream."

3

SCARLETT was having the nicest dream.

She dreamt, oddly enough, about being in bed. She was tucked into the most comfortable one she'd ever felt, covered by a blanket of pure softness. It gently caressed every inch of her, rubbing against her naked skin, silky and smooth.

And she wasn't alone. A man with big, strong hands and a deep voice was with her. He touched her, stroked her, each movement tender, as if she might break if he was too rough. There was no sexual element in the contact, yet with every brush of his fingertips on her brow or his palm on her shoulder, the drugging, sensual awareness increased.

She'd had erotic dreams before, but they'd always included actual erotic content. She'd never felt her sex moisten and her nipples harden in anticipation of a longed-for caress unless some seriously hot activities were happening in her dreams.

They weren't. Not yet.

She wasn't deeply asleep, but in that place where consciousness almost seemed able to control the unconscious. A voice deep in her head ordered the dream to change, demanded that it shift into something erotic and wild.

Then came another voice, this one more distant. "Can you hear me?"

She frowned, not wanting to hear more than sultry whispers.

"I know you're at least partially aware of what's going on," the voice said, sounding much too harsh to be a lover. "So listen, lady, you'd better wake up and stop me. I'm a total stranger and my hands have been all over you tonight."

Was he kidding? Why on earth would she want to stop him? Or to wake up at all? She sighed and burrowed deeper into the delightful bed. "Touch me," she whispered to her dream lover.

"It's the herbal tea," he snapped. "I spooned a little into your mouth while you were unconscious. It'll make you feel better, but it can also hype you up and make you horny as hell if you're not used to it."

The angry tone, and the sudden lightness of the bed—as if the person sitting on the edge had gotten up—began to penetrate the mist in her mind. The dream faded and reality gained a stronger hold.

Not yet. Please.

She focused on the last thing he'd said—horny as hell. God, yes, she was. She ached, deep down, feeling hollow and empty. She needed an orgasm, but she needed penetration even more. Her hips thrust up in silent demand.

She shifted on the bed, kicking at the covers, wanting nothing touching her, nothing on her skin, unless it was a man's hands. That man's, the one with the deep, accented voice and the strong but tender stroke.

Her own touch would be a poor substitute, and she knew it. But the need was tremendous. She slid one palm across her stomach, the other to the bottom of one breast. Both slowly began to move farther, one up, one down, but were suddenly stopped by the clamp of strong fingers around her wrists.

"Huh-uh, lady. I might be one of the good guys but I'm no damned saint." His tone was a mix of frustration and anger and just a hint of throbbing sexual desire.

And that was when she realized she was no longer dreaming.

Her eyes flew open as she realized the truth. Strong hands *were* wrapped around her wrists. A big, powerful-looking man *was* at the other end of those hands, leaning over her, though her vision was blurry and she couldn't make him out clearly. She did, indeed, lie in an incredibly comfortable bed, against silky-smooth sheets that felt so good she wanted to roll all over them. Most shocking of all, she *was* nearly naked—wearing only her skimpy panties and a sheer, lacy bra.

Oh, yeah, and she was definitely hornier than she'd ever been in her life.

"What's going on?" Despite the sensual awareness that had her legs shaking and her breath coming in short gasps, Scarlett tugged her hands free and struggled to sit up. Grabbing for the sheets, she pulled them up to cover herself, because, physically aroused or not, she had no idea where she was or who the hell she was talking to. "Where am I?"

"You had an accident."

"Oh, and all my clothes were ripped right off my body?"

The man stepped back from the bed, his hands up in a nonthreatening pose. "You were covered with glass. So were your clothes. I took them off so I could shake them out and clean them, as well as tend to your cuts. I needed to make sure you didn't have any other injuries or broken bones."

Scarlett blinked rapidly, her flash of anger at being nearly naked in a strange bed dissipating with the realization that she *had* been hurt. Her body ached, her head throbbed. Her collarbones felt as if they'd been pulverized and her left shoulder felt as if it had been used as a punching bag.

"You're sure nothing's broken?"

He nodded. "I'm sure. But you're gonna have some bruises, especially where you flew against the seatbelt and got a face full of airbag."

"Seatbelt...airbag?" she murmured, trying to remember.

"You don't remember crashing your car?"

The car. Oh, God, yes, the car! She'd been driving on that crazy, tunnel-like road, plowing on even though her every instinct had been screaming to turn around. And then she'd...what? The recollection got fuzzy and dim. She remembered something moving in the trees—a shadow. Then nothing.

"I saw it happen. You were almost 'gator bait," he said. "A minute or two later and you would have gone into the swamp with your car. You were unconscious. I had to break the windshield in order to get you out." He gestured toward her face and shoulders, where she could feel the sting of tiny nicks. "That's why you got a little cut up. Sorry 'bout that."

"Don't be, you saved my life. Thank you."

And he had. He'd saved her life. She could have died.

Next time, don't stray from the damn path.

"Road," she mumbled. "Don't veer off the main *road.*"

"What?"

"Nothing." She lay back on the bed. "Who are you, anyway?"

He remained a few feet away, in the shadows. Though her vision was clearing as she pulled herself farther and farther from her fuzzy sleep, she still couldn't see him well. And she wanted to. Remembering the dreams she'd been having, she wanted to put a face to the voice, a body to the touch. Right now, all she could tell was that he was very tall and very broad. And had a great voice.

"Hunter."

"You're a hunter?"

He chuckled softly, for some reason. She modified her assessment: he had a great voice *and* great laugh.

"I'm Hunter Thibodaux."

"Cajun."

"N'awlins born and bred, *cher*."

God, she loved Cajuns. She'd moved to New Orleans ten years ago because she'd been so enraptured by the city. And, she had to admit, also by the sexy, mysterious quality of the men it produced. Men like this one.

"Who are you?" he asked.

"My name's Scarlett Templeton."

"Scarlett?" he asked, sounding disbelieving. Her name sounded especially Southern when spoken with his lyrical accent, which seemed to lengthen and soften each syllable at the same time. *So hot.*

One other thing she noted—he hadn't reacted to her name because he'd recognized it. That was good. He'd merely sounded as though he thought she might be lying. "You've got a lot of room to talk. I guess Hunter's the next Bob, right?"

"Sorry. That was rude. It's not a name you often hear."

"My mother was a book-inhaling romantic."

That was putting it mildly. Her father had walked out on them both before Scarlett was even born. And her mother had retreated into a complete fantasy world, believing he would someday come riding back on a white steed, after fulfilling whatever glorious quest must have drawn him away.

Personally, if she were her mother and the man ever did come back, Scarlett would greet him with a closed fist, not open arms.

"Ah. I half wondered if you were on the run or somethin'."

"On the run?"

"Well, you were out in the middle of nowhere."

"So were you."

"I was camping."

"In a swamp?" she asked.

"Forget it," he said. "Just be glad I was there."

She nodded, conceding the point. "This doesn't seem like a hospital, Hunter." She liked the way his name tasted on her lips. It was sexy. A little dangerous.

Which pretty well described her current situation, didn't it? Nearly naked, vulnerable, with a complete stranger. And still overwhelmingly aroused.

Dangerous. Sexy. Oh, yeah, it fit.

"No. Like I said, I was camping and my truck was miles away. It would have taken too long to get you out."

"You sure know how to pick your camping sites," she said, unable to resist. That need to get the last word in had always driven her mother nuts. And her exes.

He ignored her. "You were unconscious. It was easier to bring you here and take care of you than try to carry you through the bayou in the middle of the night."

Here. Where was here? She glanced around, moving slowly since her head hurt. Though, honestly, it didn't hurt nearly as much as she would expect after being knocked unconscious in a car crash. And her confusion merely grew.

The low lighting didn't allow for a thorough inspection, but she did realize at once that she was in a spacious, one-room cabin. The rough-hewn log walls and unfinished pine floor made that clear. It was obviously a very rustic one judging by the hanging lantern providing the only illumination. *No electricity.*

But as she'd already noted, the bed was incredibly comfortable, the coverings on it as soft as any 500-thread count sheets she'd ever owned. Interesting accommodations: luxurious sheets, no power.

Then she noticed the single door that must lead out, meaning there was probably no indoor plumbing. *An outhouse? Oh, wonderful.*

"What is this place?"

"Just a hunting cabin in the woods," he said. "I knew there were first aid supplies here…"

"Not to mention aphrodisiac tea." Which still had her in its grip, given the way the muscles of her legs kept clenching and releasing, and her body still thrummed beneath the sheets.

He said nothing, watching her from the shadows a few feet

away. Her eyes had adjusted, so she could now roughly make out the shape of his face and the gleam of his eyes.

Not enough, though.

"That's an occasional side effect," he admitted. "But it's also a very good pain reliever. I only gave you a few spoonfuls. Are you feelin' better?"

She did a little shoulder roll and carefully turned her head from side to side. To her surprise, the pain was diminishing and her arm didn't fall entirely out of its socket as it had felt on the verge of doing only minutes ago. And the fuzziness in her brain was completely gone. In fact, she felt more wide awake now than she usually did after a full night's sleep.

"Yes, I am." She glanced toward the wall again, wondering what time it was, but a heavy cloth covered what appeared to be the only window. "How long have I been unconscious?"

"About an hour. It's around midnight."

Midnight. She had finished buying Granny's guilty pleasures and left town at seven. The drive to her grandmother's place usually took no more than two hours. The math didn't work. "That can't be."

"It's the truth."

"Are you sure? I mean, I'm missing a good couple of hours."

He said something under his breath.

"What?"

"Driving through the woods can make time seem…flexible."

She grunted in disbelief.

"I'm not lying. See?" He stepped closer and extended his arm, showing her the face of the plain watch on his left wrist. She noted the time, but was more interested in the visible strength of his hand and forearm.

Then she looked up at the rest of him. And was way more interested in that.

She'd sensed he was sexy and dangerous. She just hadn't expected that he'd be so damned handsome he'd nearly make her heart stop beating in her chest.

His shaggy, shoulder-length hair was light brown, maybe dark blond, shot with streaks of gold that glittered in the soft light thrown from the lantern. His deep-set eyes were green, a vivid, deep jungle green. His hollowed cheeks were lightly whiskered, as was his strong, jutting chin. The mouth was the only soft-looking thing about the man, and she suddenly wondered how much more devastating he'd be when he smiled.

Right now, there was no smile on hint of a those lips. Nor did any humor linger in his eyes. He was intense, on alert, his whole body held stiff, as if he was ready to leap into action at the slightest provocation.

She could definitely think of some action she'd like this man to leap into. And if she hadn't been beaten up so badly by a vicious beast disguised as an airbag, she'd consider provoking him.

"See? Midnight."

He must not have noticed the dumb, glazed way she'd been staring at his gorgeous face. That was good. She hoped he hadn't noticed the drool, either.

Even though her mind grew more sharp and clear by the second, physically she felt pretty banged up. Yet it didn't matter. She didn't know if it was that tea or his big, hard body, or the fact that she hadn't been touched intimately by a man in months, or that she was a woman who really liked sex—*or all of the above*…she was ready to pull him down on top of her.

Thinking about it, she realized her chest and collarbones probably wouldn't appreciate his weight. So maybe she'd pull him down and roll on top of *him*.

You're crazy. She was lusting over a complete stranger, who'd taken her to a remote cabin in the middle of nowhere, stripped her and admitted he'd had his hands all over her.

Mmm. Those big hands all over her.

As if finally noticing that she was staring at him as if he was an ice cream sundae and she a diet-deprived housewife, he stepped back. The shadows wrapped around him once more, though now that she'd laid eyes on him her mind filled in all the spaces she couldn't see. And all the ones she hadn't yet seen. Especially because, from here, his body looked just as delicious as the rest of him.

"It's the tea," he said flatly.

Damn. The man was a mind reader.

"It'll keep you awake and pretty much pain-free all night. And that, uh, side effect will wear off soon."

"I don't know what you're talking about."

"For a writer, you're not a good liar, Ms. Templeton."

Double damn. He had recognized her. "You know who I am?"

He nodded. "It took me a few minutes. The name sounded familiar. I saw your picture on a poster at a bookstore once. You write books for kids, right?"

Probably not the kind he imagined. "For the most part."

"Are people going to be looking for you?"

In a normal situation, if she felt in any way threatened, she would have snapped, "Hell, yes, the National Guard will be out searching for me by now, buster."

But she didn't.

"No."

"Okay." He stepped across the room, lifted the heavy curtain and peered out into the night. "Look, I have to go out for a little while."

Her jaw dropped. "At midnight?"

"You'll be fine," he insisted. "There's more tea on the table beside you if you start hurting again, but try not to drink too much."

"I'll pass, thanks. I've had quite enough of the side effects. Don't you have a bottle of aspirin lying around?" She always did. Of course, hers was in her purse, which was in her car, which was now resting at the bottom of a swamp.

Wow. Her insurance agent was not going to be happy.

"No, I don't." He dropped the curtain and walked over to the bed, staring down at her. Frowning, he murmured, "I know you could have a concussion, and I'd stay if it wasn't so important. The tea will keep you awake, so just lie here and try to relax, okay?"

She did feel incredibly jazzed up, nowhere near ready to fall asleep. Almost the way she had felt when that strange, Rumpelstiltskin-like man had touched her earlier.

"That man," she mumbled, suddenly realizing he was the one she'd been hearing as she drove blindly through the woods. *Stray from the path.* His words. And his voice.

"What man?" Hunter asked, his tone sharp. "Did you see someone in the woods?"

"Someone crazier than you?"

His eyes narrowed. "The tea can make you a little jumpy, but that mouth, it's all you, isn't it?"

Scarlett couldn't contain a cocky grin. "'Fraid so."

His lips might have quirked the tiniest bit. But whether he was going to smile or sneer, she honestly didn't know.

She wasn't going to find out, either.

Because without another word, Hunter swung around and crossed the room, grabbing a long duster coat off a hook. He tugged it on, then put a tattered fedora on top of his head.

The Indiana Jones look *so* worked on this guy.

He reached for the doorknob. "I've gotta go." Before he slipped out into the night, however, he added a warning. "Stay inside until I get back. You don't want to be wandering around in the dark. There are...things out there. And do *not* open the door to anyone."

He mumbled something else under his breath.

"What?"

He grudgingly explained. "Strange people live around here. If a grumpy-looking dwarf shows up, just stay quiet and pretend you're not here."

Scarlett couldn't contain a snort and she rolled her eyes. "Yeah, and, uh, I have to beware of old crones bearing apples, right?"

"That's ancient history," he muttered.

Then he was gone, leaving her to wonder just what the hell she'd gotten herself into.

And why she didn't seem to care.

4

HUNTER HEADED BACK to the cottage at dawn. The night had proved fruitless, as he had thought it would. Morning came earlier here—the days were shorter all around—and he'd had just a few hours to track. The only good thing was the daylight hours would pass quickly, too. He'd be back out to start all over again the moment the sun went down.

Lucas wouldn't be able to stay in after dark. It didn't matter where he was holed up, he'd be drawn outside into the moonlight as surely as a salmon was drawn upriver to spawn every year.

Hunter glanced at his watch. It was 3:00 a.m. But streaks of pink and orange sliced the sky, preparing it for the arrival of the sun. The woman in his cabin would almost certainly notice.

"Of course she will," he mumbled, shaking his head. Half frustrated, half ruefully amused, he changed his watch to a time she'd find more realistic.

The sharp-tongued blonde he'd rescued seemed to notice a lot. While the tea he'd spooned between her lips had probably worn off, he didn't think the ten-cups-of-coffee high it had given her had been the reason for her sharpness. Huh-uh. He suspected that was all Scarlett Templeton.

"Scarlett," he said, rolling his eyes. She was about as far from a Southern belle as he was from Rhett Butler. No, she was fast-talking, quick-witted, aggressive and strong.

Not to mention beautiful enough to fry every brain cell in his head and leave him breathless.

He hadn't been prepared for that, for her to clean up like something straight out of every man's fantasy.

His fantasy, truth be told.

Not that he allowed himself such luxuries anymore. His last re-

lationship had ended two years ago. That had been just before his
mother had died. After she'd told him the truth about the world he
thought he knew. And the life his mother had lived in another place
entirely—with Lucas Wolf's father. He'd sort of soured on relationships after that.

He'd since had offers of just about anything, just about any way
it could be had—after all, he lived in the Big Easy. But he hadn't been
interested. Not while his life was focused on one thing: tracking down
the criminals who slipped back and forth between the worlds, using
each realm to hide from their crimes in the other. He'd worked as a
cop for ten years back then, seeing people evade prosecution for their
crimes. Finding out how some of them had disappeared so completely had been a personal gauntlet thrown at his feet.

But, in times gone by, when he had enjoyed normal pleasures
like an active sex life—*ancient history*—Scarlett had been exactly
the kind of female who'd driven him crazy with lust.

He'd seen the blond hair when he'd rescued her, of course. But
out in the bayou, he hadn't realized how silky it was, or how the
soft waves would feel in his hands. Since her eyes had been closed,
he hadn't known they were a deep blue the color of the sky on a
starry night. He'd been too concerned about picking bits of glass
off her cheeks to realize how creamy and smooth her skin was. Or
to judge the beautiful shape of her face, the softness of her full lips
or the gracefulness of her slim neck.

It wasn't until he'd gotten her to the cabin, laid her on his bed
and carefully started removing her clothes that he'd realized any of
those things. Cleaning her up, gently washing off her tiny cuts, had
been like revealing a masterpiece beneath a painted-over canvas.

He'd begun the task with resolve and impersonal concern.

By the time he was done, he'd been shaking with desire and
unable to think straight.

Thank God she'd awakened when she did. Because he'd done
as much as he could while still retaining his sanity. Moments before
she'd come to, he'd noticed a drop of blood on the snow-white lace
barely covering her full breasts. But it would have taken a much
stronger man to go that far. No way could he remove the last bits
of her clothing. Not without being instantly overwhelmed with the
need to touch her for reasons other than to tend to her wounds.

Seeing her reach to touch herself in her sleep had almost put him over the edge. He'd known what she was dreaming. The gentle thrust of her hips, the restless quiver of her legs, the visible tautness of her dusky nipples beneath the lace had made it clear.

"Damned tea."

That was it. She was under the influence. The tea might have dulled her pain, but it also heightened all her other senses. No decent man would ever take advantage of that.

Some perps might argue it, given the brutal tactics Hunter had occasionally needed to use on the job—both his former one, with the NOPD, and his current one—but he was still a decent man. Even if he'd been entertaining a lot of indecent thoughts in the hours since he'd left Scarlett.

Not gonna go there, he reminded himself. She was a woman, just like any other woman. He was a professional and had a job to do. From this moment on, his sex drive was going to pretend Scarlett Templeton was a ninety-year-old nun.

He knocked before opening the heavy oak door. Ninety-year-old nun or not, God help him if he walked in on the woman naked.

Getting no response, he knocked again. "Scarlett?"

Nothing.

Hoping she was just asleep, he pushed the door in, his gaze shifting toward the bed where he'd left her.

It was empty. A quick glance confirmed that the rest of the shadowy cabin was as well.

"Damn it, woman, I'm not rescuing you again!"

Then a scream split the dawn air, piercing and terrified.

And he realized he might have spoken too soon.

SHE HADN'T seen that.

She had *not* seen that.

It was the same thing she had *not* seen right before she'd crashed.

"A man," she whispered as she raced through the woods, in the direction she hoped would lead back to the cabin. "It was a man," she repeated, the words becoming a mantra.

Not an animal. Not a beast. A dark, swarthy man. One who had scared the bejesus out of her. She didn't have one bit of bejesus left. Whatever bejesus was.

Damn it, where was the cabin? She should never have left it. *Why didn't you listen to him?*

Because she'd been bored and jittery and stubborn. And because there hadn't been a damned bathroom.

She would have sworn she hadn't gone more than a few dozen steps from the door. She'd picked her way carefully, using the lantern he'd left to light her way so she wouldn't accidentally tumble into the mouth of a hungry alligator. Or worse…a big-ass snake. God, she hated snakes.

But even with the lantern and the sun on the verge of rising, the woods seemed to close in around her, growing darker rather than lighter. Nothing appeared familiar. She couldn't even see the outline of the cabin's roof through the thick forest.

Running was still better than stopping, though. Better than once again seeing what she *so* hadn't seen before the crash, or just now, in the woods.

Damn that tea. It had made her a little crazy. And a little wild. Crazy and wild and horny. Not a good combination.

Only she hadn't had any tea before the crash.

Screw that. You imagined it. Now run!

She kept going, her legs pumping even though her feet hurt like hell as she ran across jagged earth, dead brush and rocks. Her soles would be a bloody mangled mess if—*when*—she got back to safety. She'd found her clothes without any problem, but had only been able to locate one of her shoes when she'd gotten up a little while ago. So she had ventured out barefoot.

It wasn't the smartest thing she'd ever done. But all she could think about was answering nature's call and getting back before *he* could return. Because having to ask him to take her to "use the facilities" seemed infinitely worse than risking stepping on a sharp stick.

But perhaps not worse than seeing a…*a man. Just a man who ran supersonically fast!*

"Scarlett?" a voice called.

Hunter. Oh, thank God. She almost cried in relief.

True, he was still a stranger. But she'd take her chances with the one who'd stripped her and yet managed to remain a gentleman—which hadn't exactly thrilled her at the time, to be perfectly honest—over the guy she'd just glimpsed through the trees.

"Here! I'm over here." She darted toward the sound of Hunter's voice, so glad he'd come back, she couldn't even worry about his anger that she'd disobeyed his order to stay put.

Bursting from the shadows, she spied him running toward her, the cabin silhouetted beneath the rising sun directly behind him. She stumbled a little over her own injured feet, pain giving way to just a bit of awed lust at the way the golden morning framed his big, tough body.

She hadn't imagined it. He really was that handsome.

And furious.

"What happened? Why did you leave the cabin? Why did you scream?" She almost flew into his arms. He wasn't exactly in the mood to catch her. Instead, he grabbed her, and shook her lightly, the way a parent would after a kid ran out in front of a car. "Jesus, you almost gave me a heart attack."

"I almost gave myself one, too," she said, gulping in deep breaths of refreshing morning air. It was almost too refreshing—she wasn't used to it. Give her the pungent scents of beignets and booze and the Mississippi over the great outdoors any day. All this pine, flora and fauna was making her dizzy.

Pine. Flora. Fauna.

No swamp.

She tugged away, her eyes narrowing. Slowly turning in a circle, she ignored his questions, focusing only on where she was. She'd barely even noticed her surroundings in the darkness when she'd wandered away from the cabin, but there was no creepy road, no bayou, no Spanish moss or skeletal oaks.

That road. It had been so strange. She hadn't been able to decide, when driving through it, whether she was traveling through a forest or a bayou. It had seemed to be both. Now, there was no bayou at all.

"Where did you bring me?" she whispered.

"What?"

She cleared her throat. "This doesn't look familiar. Just how far are we from where I crashed?"

She turned around in time to see the way his eyes shifted as he answered. "Not far."

Scarlett crossed her arms, knowing he wasn't being completely honest with her. "So take me back."

"Back to your car? You bet, darlin'. Have fun digging it out of the muck."

Narrowing her eyes, she ordered, "Take me to civilization."

He shrugged. "Can't do it."

"Why not?"

"I've got work to do. I lost enough time taking care of you. You're going to have to wait here with me until I finish what I came here to do."

Her jaw dropped. "You're *kidnapping* me?"

His unconcerned shrug told her just how worried he was about that. "So much for the 'thanks for saving my life.'"

"You saved my life. That doesn't mean you get to run it." Unable to help herself, Scarlett cast a quick, worried glance over her shoulder. Those damn woods looked Hansel-and-Gretel innocent now, unlike the trap they'd become when she'd been racing through them. Remembering what had happened to that mischievous twosome, and how close they'd come to being dinner, she snapped, "I want to go home."

He frowned, pushing a weary hand through his hair. "I'd like to accommodate you. But I can't. Give me one more day, all right? Then I promise I'll get you back where you belong."

One more day. She didn't want to be here for one more hour. But she couldn't deny the idea of spending another whole day with Hunter didn't exactly break her heart.

Swallowing and forcing the thought of the shadowy figure from the woods out of her mind, she nodded. "Okay. But you…you'll be nearby, won't you?"

She should have kept her mouth closed. Because the quiver in her voice and her quick glance at the woods reminded him of what she'd kind of been hoping he'd forget.

"Why did you leave when I told you not to?"

"Like I said. You don't run my life."

His jaw tightened, fire snapping in those green eyes. "I warned you it was dangerous."

"No," she replied, "you didn't. You told me there were temperamental dwarves, and 'tings' out there. Not *dangerous* things."

His voice low, intense, he asked, "What did you see?"

She shook her head, wanting nothing more than to go inside and crawl into that soft bed. She didn't hurt—the magical tea still had a good grip on her pain—but some of the energy had waned and she almost felt as if she could drop where she stood.

The other side effect had, thankfully, disappeared, too. Right now, what she most wanted to do with the man in front of her was punch him and make him take her home.

Okay, okay. He was still incredibly hot. And maybe, once she got him home, she'd want to keep him for a while. But the sexual urge wasn't quite as intense as it had been during the night when sensuality and lust had filled every cell of her body.

"Damn it, woman, tell me what you saw."

Woman? *Woman?* "Don't call me woman."

"You sure ain't a man from where I'm standin'," he said, raking a hot gaze from the top of her raggedy hair to the bottom of her.... "Aww, hell, *cher,* what'd you go and do to your feet?"

Before she could answer, he swept her up. But not at all like Rhett Butler had swept *that* Scarlett up the stairs. Instead Hunter hoisted her over his shoulder and dumped her there, hanging like a big sack of dog food. With one hand wrapped around her thighs, the other on her bottom, he kept her where he wanted her. *Humiliating.* But oh, lordy, did the position give her a great view of his strong, muscular back, lean waist and a tight butt she wanted to grab with both dangling hands.

He'd probably drop her.

He kicked the door open with the toe of one boot, carried her across the room and dumped her onto her back on the bed. She bounced twice, then collapsed back into the pillows.

"No sense," he mumbled. "I shoulda hidden your clothes."

"Like you hid one of my shoes? Were you planning to play Prince Charming and present it to me when you got back?"

"Musta come off when I carried you here, Cinderella."

She rolled her eyes, not entirely believing him.

"I didn't know I had to play tricks to make you stay put."

"I had to use the freakin' john, okay?" she snapped, unable to stand it anymore.

He stared down at her, the anger fading from his eyes. A twinkle appeared there, a twinkle of laughter. Damn. She should have let him stay mad. This was so embarrassing. Far beyond run-in-your-hose embarrassing and into fall-on-your-ass-in-public territory. Embarrassment to the nth degree.

"Sorry," he said softly. "I shouldn't have left you."

"I didn't need an escort."

"Yeah, seems like you did." He turned his back on her, crossing to the wood stove, on which sat an old-fashioned, wrought-iron kettle. Picking it up with a thick pad, he poured water into a large ceramic basin, then carried it over.

She had no idea what he was going to do until he sat on the end of the bed and pushed her calf-length, flowing skirt up and out of the way. Then he lifted one of her feet into his warm, solid lap. Surprised, she could only gasp as he took a rag and soap from the bowl and began to wash her dirty, torn-up foot.

Oh, my God. She loved having her feet pampered. She had a standing weekly pedicure appointment and she considered it one of her few true indulgences. But nobody—not the pricy salon she usually went to, or the massage therapist she occasionally visited, or any spa employee—had ever handled her with such tenderness and care as this man did.

She closed her eyes and settled into the pillows, a smile on her lips. His strong hands provided intense pleasure as he slowly and deliberately cleaned her wounds, just as he must have done the night before when she had been unconscious.

Oh, what she wouldn't have given to be awake for those ministrations! Especially since she'd noticed the flecks on her chest where the glass had gone down the neckline of her blouse.

Maybe the tea's effects hadn't worn off after all. She was once again falling into that strange place where sanity gave way to impulse and desire overpowered common sense.

Stray. Go someplace even wilder this time.

Though she barely knew the man, at this moment, she'd gladly pull him down to join her on the bed. Well, after he'd finished the lovely foot massage.

Almost cooing with the pleasure of it, Scarlett closed her eyes and relaxed, feeling the press of his strong fingers in the arch of her other foot and around her ankle. His hands were magnificent and every inch of skin covering her bones wanted to be touched by them.

"Better?" he asked, his tone husky.

"Mmm-hmm." She opened her eyes to smile her thanks, but he was still focused only on the task at hand.

Setting the bowl down, he reached for a jar. "This'll help, too," he said before slathering some kind of thick salve from her toes to her heels. It smelled unfamiliar. Nice, but not an obvious scent like peppermint or jasmine. It was earthy, spicy, but not anything she could put her finger on.

And it felt divine. Cooling and soothing, it removed any lingering sting from the scratches and blisters until she couldn't even remember they'd existed. "How amazing," she murmured as she stretched in physical contentment.

"It's good stuff."

That, too. But she hadn't been referring to the salve. "I bet it would really help my legs." Had that sounded hopeful or merely pathetic? "They got pretty scratched up in the accident."

She was such a liar. Whatever the shattered glass had done to the top half of her body, her lower half had been spared by the spread of her billowing coat across her lap, and her skirt below that. She did, however, have one scrape up the side of her left thigh. Probably from where he'd hauled her out of the car.

He might have cleared his throat. Or that might have been a low rumble of laughter. Whichever it was, he scooped another dollop of the white, pasty salve into his hands and moved them to her ankle. Sliding them around her calf, he began to gently massage her, kneading the muscles there, running the tips of his fingers all the way up until he reached her knee.

That was when sensual awareness and lazy desire turned into heat. The tender skin on the backs of her knees had always been an erogenous zone, though only one of her lovers had ever been around long enough to figure that out.

This guy seemed to realize it right away. She must have gasped or something, because he shifted his gaze, watching her through half-lowered lashes as he caressed her.

She bit her lips, trying to remain still and silent, as if simply appreciating the care and not getting off on the feel of his hands on her body. Fat chance of her managing that for long, but it was the best she could do.

So tell him. Or better yet, show *him.*

She could. But he'd proven last night that he was noble and a gentleman. He'd probably think she was still suffering the effects of the tea, or that she'd consumed more of it while he was gone.

She wasn't. And she hadn't. Frankly, this wasn't even just about pure desire. It was about the edgy need she'd been feeling ever since she'd left the bookshop the evening before. The need to do something different, to veer from the path. To stray from the familiar into something dark and dangerous and terribly exciting.

Like sex with him.

He shifted, as if about to stop, and Scarlett sat up in the bed, resisting the urge to clamp her thighs together and keep his hand right where it was. Instead, she offered him a smile.

"Thank you so much," she murmured. Then, as if simply wanting to reiterate the thanks, she leaned close, until their faces were inches apart. She let herself study the depths in those dark-green eyes—not to mention the surprise there—before pressing her lips against his for a soft, gentle kiss.

It was just a kiss of thanks. If it happened to turn into something else, well….

His form remained stiff for an instant, then, with a deep groan torn from somewhere within him, he thrust his hands into her hair.

And it turned into something else.

Cupping her head, he turned her so that their lips could part and mate more fully. It was Scarlett's turn to groan. With pure, deep pleasure.

He tasted hot and spicy, and kissed the way a man should kiss. Forcefully. Deliberately. Their tongues met and entwined, and their breaths joined as well. Her thighs trembled and she longed to shift them apart, inviting him between them.

Before she could do it, he ended the kiss. Yanking his hands from her hair, he muttered a curse and jerked to his feet.

"Hunter…"

"What'd you see in the woods?"

He busied himself putting the salve away, not looking at her face, so he probably didn't see her start of surprise. Though she'd lay money he knew there was one.

"Trees," she snapped, almost choking on disappointment. He'd changed the subject, caught her by surprise intentionally. That kiss night even have been his way of setting her up. And here she'd been priding herself on initiating it. Now she had to wonder if he'd been playing her all along.

Damn, he was good.

"Trees made you scream like that?"

She flushed, deliberately looking at her own hands. No way was she going to tell Hunter she thought she'd seen a man with amazing speed, reddish eyes and more thick, dark hair than any guy she'd ever seen.

"Scarlett," he said, staring at her face, "I need to know what you saw."

She waved an airy hand. "It was dark."

He frowned, but slowly nodded. "Yes, it was."

"I'm sure it was nothing. Just an overactive imagination."

He stared into her eyes for a moment longer, then nodded. "You're probably right. You had quite a knock. I'm sure whatever you saw out there was just your imagination, almost like a dream."

A dream? Maybe a nightmare. But she didn't say that. It sounded stupid enough in her own mind. She wasn't about to voice the words. Especially not when the dreams she could fulfill here—inside this cabin, with this incredibly sexy man—were so much nicer to contemplate.

She only had to figure out a way to make those dreams come true.

5

HUNTER NEEDED sleep. Badly. It had been a rough week, and last night he hadn't even tried to close his eyes. The bone-deep weariness was going to catch up to him, probably at the worst possible time—like when he finally came face-to-face with Lucas—if he didn't do something about it.

But he didn't know that he could trust *her.* Scarlett. His unwelcome, unwanted, unbelievably sexy guest. Despite her scare, he wasn't sure she wouldn't up and leave the minute he nodded off, if only to prove to herself that she wasn't afraid to.

She could get into real trouble here. Or, at the very least, see things that would make her question her own sanity. He hadn't been joking about that damn dwarf from up the road, whose No Trespassing signs were backed up by his ax.

God knew, the first time Hunter had crossed the border—not even sure he believed there was one, despite what his dying mother had told him—he hadn't believed his own senses. And he'd been prepared. Scarlett wasn't.

He should never have brought her here.

She'd been bad enough when woozy and hyped up on tea. Now, with all her faculties firmly in place, and that mouth giving back as good as she got, he found her even more distracting. More frustrating.

More damned attractive.

In silence, she was completely sexy. Conscious and aware, she delighted him.

Still, kissing her? Dumbest thing he'd ever done.

"Is my shoe really lost?" she asked, still lying on the bed, relaxed, oozing physical satisfaction as though she'd just had great sex rather than just getting her feet tended and sharing one little—all right, big—kiss.

He should have handed her the water and ointment and let her take care of herself. Then there would have been no soft whispered, "Thank you," followed by a kiss of gratitude that had turned into one of pure carnal pleasure.

If she hadn't set out to make it that way, he'd give up his truck. And damn, he loved that truck.

"Yeah," he said, remembering her question. "I guess it fell off your foot when I carried you here."

"How far did you have to carry me again?"

The softness of her query didn't disguise the sharpness of her interest. The woman was thinking about leaving, trying to find her way out all on her own. He was never going to be able to get any sleep.

"A long way," he told her, hoping to discourage her. And it wasn't a lie. Maybe they hadn't gone far in conventional distance, but metaphorically, they'd gone over the freaking rainbow. There was a dusty, gold-tinged paved road not five leagues from here that proved it.

"We went over some pretty rough terrain," he added, "so don't get any ideas, *shoeless*."

Her lip curled in derision. "And somehow we left the Louisiana bayou and ended up in something resembling Carolina woods."

She wasn't too far off, really. Everything was smaller over here, not just time. If he walked to the next border crossing over, maybe half a day away on this side, he'd come out several states away from where they'd entered in Louisiana.

Choosing to ignore her skepticism, he said, "I'll rig up something for you to wear on your feet when we leave."

"You're a cobbler too, huh?"

He shook his head, unable to resist smiling a little. The woman was just too damned cute when she was being snarky. "Actually, I think there might be something in that trunk you could use." He crossed the small cabin, opening the big wooden chest where he, and other travelers who used this place, left the basic supplies and stuff they no longer needed.

He first found a pair of small wooden clogs. They'd probably been left here by the hunter who'd saved those two bratty kids from that crazy old child molester, whose house most definitely had not been made of gingerbread. The story had sounded scary enough from his childhood story books… The truth, though, was a whole hell of a lot worse.

Finding a pair of rough, flat leather shoes, he figured they could be cut down to do the job. "These'll work."

"As *snowshoes?*"

"You're not exactly diminutive, darlin'," he replied, baiting her deliberately, hoping to glimpse the fire in those blue eyes.

He got it. "Are you saying I have big feet?"

"Calm down," he said with a soft laugh, unable to help it. "I was kidding." Because, in truth, the woman was just right. From the top of her blonde head to her pink-tinted toenails. Perfect all the way down.

He shifted a little, thrusting the image of all that naked perfection out of his head. He'd somehow managed to smooth ointment into her long legs without getting much more than a minor hard-on. The kiss had made it major. The last thing he needed was to think himself into a zipper-busting one now at the memory of how she tasted, and all that soft creamy skin covering soft creamy woman.

Determined to ignore the attraction, he turned his back on her and retrieved his knapsack. "Are you hungry?" He was. He needed food almost as much as he needed sleep.

Neither of which he needed as much as sex. But that wasn't gonna happen. Not here. Not now. Not when he had to be alert for danger at every moment, not to mention keeping her from finding out just where on earth he'd brought her.

If this *was* earth. He *thought* it was. Sort of. Just maybe another layer…a few degrees to the right of everything he'd once considered reality.

"Depends."

"Oh?" He glanced over his shoulder just in time to notice the way she pulled her skirt up even higher to study the sharp scratch marring the side of her thigh. Her long, silky thigh. Her smooth thigh that he wanted to feel wrapped around his hips.

Lord have mercy. So much for his plans to stay away from her. Heaven help him if she asked him to rub ointment on that thigh. Last night, when she'd been unconscious, had been one thing. Putting his hands that close to heaven when she was awake and urging him on with every heavy-lidded look?

No man alive would be strong enough to resist.

"Depends on what?" he managed to mutter.

"On whether you have a box of Pop Tarts, or you're going to offer me some freshly slaughtered Bambi."

He rolled his eyes.

"Well, this is a hunter's cabin, isn't it?"

"I'm not that kind of hunter."

Reaching into the pack, he pulled out the rations he'd brought with him. Enough for the two of them for another day, at least. Without having to go…local. He didn't trust anything growing wild in this place. Too many witches in the vicinity.

Though he liked having her all the way across the room, where she couldn't mess with his head with a word or a look, or see the effect she had on him, she didn't cooperate. She hopped out of the bed, bouncing a little on her freshly tended feet, as if wanting to test them out. He could have told her they'd be fine. The analgesic properties of the salve would have her feeling like new.

She ought to be glad she hadn't tempted him into sliding more of that stuff higher on her legs. Some of that cool, energizing stuff on her most intimate parts would have her needing sex for ten hours straight just to gain some relief. He'd probably kill himself trying to give it to her.

But what a way to go.

She smiled. "You should open a business in foot repair."

"I've got a job, thanks." Though, honestly, having his hands on her beautiful, slender feet and luscious legs had been a whole lot more pleasant than anything he'd done at work for a very long time.

"Well, if you ever need a career change, I'll give you a dazzling recommendation, or hire you full-time myself."

Huh. Hired to do nothing but touch this woman?

It had its advantages.

Still smiling, she began to clear off the small, rickety wooden table, which stood in the middle of the room, setting the table for their so-called breakfast. He wondered what she was going to say when he handed her the beef jerky and trail mix.

"Thank you." That's what she said. Then she sat on one of the two stools, grabbed a fistful of the nuts and dried fruit and popped them into her mouth.

Hunter had to hand it to her. The woman wasn't a complainer. And she knew how to hold her own. "Coffee?"

"I'd kill for my regular café au lait from Café du Monde, but I'll settle for anything that comes from a bean."

"Don't say that." Those were dangerous words in this part of the world. Not that she'd ever realize that. At least, God, he hoped not. "It's growing season," he murmured, more to himself than her, and he did a quick mental calculation as to exactly when the more daring farmers around here put in their crops.

"You got something against coffee beans?"

He shook his head, mumbling, "No. Just, some of the stuff farmers grow around here can, uh, lead to trouble."

She coughed a little, choking on a nut. "Are you talking Children of the Corn stuff?"

"Wrong genre," he muttered, shoving a mug of water at her before turning to make the coffee. Grabbing the small bag of grounds, he prepared them each a cup, black, no sugar, and carried them to the table.

She took one, sipped, made a face, then sipped again.

Something evil made him say, "There's always more tea."

Her smirk should have warned him he was playing with fire. "You sure you can handle me drinking more of that tea?"

Dangerous. But he couldn't help responding. "You might be surprised at how much I can handle."

She shivered lightly, though the cabin was comfortably warm. Through the thin fabric of her blouse he noted the way her skin puckered. He could tell she wasn't wearing her bra—she must have seen the small cut on her breast and cared for it herself. Her dark nipples tightened, jutting in silent invitation as they had last night.

He suddenly wanted to drop to his knees in front of her and cover the tip of one breast with his mouth, suckling her right through the sheer material.

"So how much can you handle?" she asked.

Hunter swallowed hard, cursing himself for starting a round of verbal foreplay that couldn't lead anywhere. Not here. Not now. Maybe in the real world?

Hell, his life was too crazy even to remember what the real world was like. Living in-between had left him sometimes unable to see clearly the difference between reality and fantasy,

Her being here…maybe that was a fantasy.

His fantasy.

And maybe he ought to do something about it.

Forget it. You have a job to do.

"Drink your coffee."

She leaned across the small table. So close he could feel the warmth of her soft breath against his throat. The invitation to kiss her again couldn't have been more plain. "I might be up for tea, if you drink some, too."

He slid back in his seat with a gruff laugh. "I'm immune."

She stared at him for a moment, as if reading his underlying meaning—whether he was claiming to be immune to *her,* or to the aphrodisiac qualities of the tea. One was the truth. The other total fabrication.

She chose to misunderstand completely. One delicate brow rose and her tone was purely wicked. "You mean you're immune to women? I didn't take you for…"

"To the tea," he snapped, knowing what she was about to say. "I've worked up a resistance to its side effects."

She half lowered her lashes, disguising her amusement at getting a rise out of him, and lifted her steaming mug to her mouth. "So what kind of hunter are you?"

The subject change startled him. And relieved him. Sort of.

"What?"

"You said you're not that kind of hunter. What is it you're after?"

Wishing he hadn't said anything, he admitted, "Criminals."

She dropped her jerky. And her mouth. "Are you a cop?"

"Not anymore."

"But you were?"

He nodded.

"In New Orleans?"

Another nod.

"Do I have to pry the words out of you with a crowbar?"

"What words?"

"You can't just tell me you're an ex-cop who hunts *people* and not elaborate."

He elaborated, just a little, knowing she wouldn't shut up until he did. "I was a detective in New Orleans until a year ago." One year ago—when he'd seen firsthand that the cops weren't always the good guys, and, in fact, could be more corrupt and vile than any perp he'd ever gone after.

Finding out his own partner and two other detectives in the squad had discovered the other world along their border—and had been plundering it for their own gain—had been a shock. They'd been running drugs from one side to the other, corrupting people over here who had never heard of the kinds of pills or rocks they were pushing. And had brought back massive quantities of that crazy tea and other unusual items to sell on the streets of New Orleans.

They'd gotten away with it. At least until one innocent young girl—Ciara Wolf—had walked in on a deal, seen too much, and had been permanently silenced.

"What happened? Why'd you stop being a cop?"

"It's a long story," he said. "One I really don't want to get into."

He could make it succinct. Could tell her how Lucas Wolf had come to him with irrefutable proof. Could explain that there had never been any doubt Hunter would cross the blue line to stop his former partner and fellow cops. But how to voice the frustration he'd felt when, before he could do it, all three of the suspects had disappeared? They'd melted somewhere between New Orleans and never-never land, anonymous and free to continue their reign of terror.

That was when Hunter had quit his job to go after them, doing everything within the boundaries of the law to bring them to justice.

Unlike Lucas Wolf, his dark shadow, who'd gone after them in his own fashion. Vigilante-style.

"So what do you do now?"

He thrust the dark thoughts away. "I left the force and went into business for myself."

"Are you a bounty hunter like that blond guy on TV?"

"I'm *nothing* like that blond guy on TV," he insisted. "But yes, I'm a skip-tracer. I track down criminals who skip out on their bail." *As well as some who have never been caught.*

Scarlett's hand clenched around her mug, though she didn't seem to notice the heat on her fingertips. "You said you were out here working. Are you chasing someone now?"

He nodded. "A very dangerous man."

"Oh, my God."

Hearing that she'd gone past curiosity right into dismay, Hunter lowered his own cup. "What is it?"

"What does he look like? This criminal you're hunting? Is he intense-looking, about your height, with very dark hair and a swarthy complexion?"

Almost holding his breath, Hunter bit out, "You saw him."

She nodded.

Rising so quickly the stool fell over, he put both hands on the table and leaned over her. "When? Where?"

"Last night, before the accident. I swerved to miss him. That's why I crashed."

Last night. Thank God. For a moment he'd feared she had seen him over *here*. Lucas's distinctive qualities were more noticeable on this side. Especially since the moon had been at its fullest a few hours ago.

There was no such thing as an outright *change* for those like Lucas. But things became more clear in the full moonlight. Perceptions were heightened. Just as the gossamer-light, veil-like border between the worlds thinned to near incandescence once a month, many other things unseen in the light of day became sharply obvious.

Such freedom was irresistible to Lucas and his kind.

He straightened, then turned the stool upright. "It's okay. He's long gone by now. But I can track him."

Maybe the fact that Scarlett had seen Lucas—had seen how dangerous he sometimes seemed to be—wasn't a bad thing. It would make it easier to explain why he was moving the man bound and gagged. Trying to cross the border during the full moon with Lucas unbound would be impossible. The only way would be to incapacitate him and truss him up like…like an animal.

Damn it. I'm sorry, Mama. It has to be that way. If anybody else finds him first, it could cost him his life.

"Why are you so sure he's long gone?"

Sitting down once more, he noted the trepidation in her voice. He didn't like the way she tilted her head forward so her blond hair shielded her eyes and grazed her cheeks. "What?"

She sighed deeply. "I might have seen him again."

Hunter shot up again. And again the stool flew. "When?"

"This morning, when I screamed."

"Impossible." Why would Lucas stay here, knowing Hunter was

on his trail? He'd had hours to get away, to hide in some deep burrow in an effort to evade his true nature and not relent to his driving need to see the moonlight. "You can't have."

"I really think…"

"You said you didn't see anything," he snapped. "You were just scared of the trees."

She stood, too, crossing her arms. "Well, what kind of nitwit is scared of trees?" ·

Around here? With these *trees? A smart nitwit.*

"I'm nearly certain it was him."

He muttered the kind of four-letter word his mama would have washed his mouth out with soap for saying.

"Sorry. I should have told you."

Yes. She should have. But it wasn't entirely her fault.

He'd known better. He'd known she'd seen something, but he hadn't *wanted* to admit it. He had deliberately chosen to convince her she'd imagined it because of her head injury, figuring she wouldn't take much convincing. Because the sights to be seen over here could make anyone doubt their sanity. He, himself had seen any number of things that would drive a rational, sane person to madness.

And a person with a huge imagination, like a kids' writer? He didn't even want to think of the places her mind could take her if she ever realized where she was.

She wouldn't be the first. A visit to any library in the States provided evidence that other authors had been…travelers. Hell, there was even a statue to those German brothers in a village not far from here that confirmed it.

They did deserve some credit though. At least they managed to convey some of the darkness of this place in their so-called fairy tales. Unlike others who merely glossed over the bad to capitalize on the magical.

With Scarlett's background writing children's books, he wondered how'd she react. Would the truth behind happily-ever-after change the nice kids' tales she probably wrote? For all he knew, she might end up writing Stephen King-type stories.

As they returned to their seats and resumed their simple breakfast, Scarlett asked, "How bad is this guy?"

He answered instinctively. "Bad as they come." But even as the words left his mouth, a part of him wondered.

"Is he a murderer?"

Good question, though he couldn't answer it. He wasn't certain. And he wouldn't be, not until he found Lucas.

One thing was sure: Lucas Wolf could be deadly. Considering what had been done to his sister, the man probably felt justified in seeking vengeance.

But had he done it? Could he really have turned into judge, jury and executioner? Had Lucas killed two people—and gone after a third—in revenge for his sister's murder?

He wanted to know. He *needed* to know.

That Hunter partially blamed himself for that murder was an understatement. It had been three men he knew—cops he'd considered good men, one of them his own partner—who had been responsible for it. He had no idea how they'd found the crossover to this place. God help him if they'd followed him. The guilt would be too much to bear.

Not that he'd live long to bear it. Because if it was his fault, Lucas might hold Hunter every bit as responsible for his sister's death. And might be out for his blood, too.

The hunter might actually be the hunted. Which could explain why Lucas was still in the area.

God, I'm sorry, Mama, he thought again, knowing this would break her heart. Because this was going to end ugly.

Either Hunter would haul Lucas to jail.

Or Lucas—his own brother—would kill him.

6

Hunter didn't have to tell her he was exhausted, Scarlett could see the physical weariness washing over him with every moment that passed. He'd been out all night—chasing a criminal, pausing only to carry an unconscious woman for a few miles and then take care of her. Who wouldn't be bone-weary?

Maybe that was why he hadn't answered her question about the man he was after. He looked ready to fall asleep in his seat. Or maybe he just didn't want to admit that she had nearly come face-to-face with a killer. Twice.

Scarlett thrust the thought away, feeling so safe in this man's presence, she couldn't muster up any concern. Though, if he was going to keep her safe from some psycho ax-murderer, he really ought to take a nap, at the very least.

Funny that she felt so safe with him, considering the sense of danger wrapping around the man like some extra layer of skin. He sounded gruff when he talked about his job—and those he hunted— yet he'd shown her nothing but thoughtful concern, even if his bark had, occasionally, been worse than his bite.

Mmm. Bite. Wouldn't she love to take just a little nibble and offer him one in return.

Unlike Hunter, she was still wide awake, though she imagined she must have dozed off during the night without realizing it. Because it was now morning and he'd left at midnight. No way had six or seven *conscious* hours passed.

Whatever the case, she'd had more rest than he had. So, even though she knew he didn't entirely trust her, after they'd finished eating, she urged, "Why don't you lie down and sleep for a while?" Swallowing, since making girly promises was not in her character, she added, "I promise I won't go anywhere. I'll stay here and keep watch until you wake up."

He tilted his head to the side, eyeing her from across the small table. "Keep watch?"

She clarified. "Well, I'll listen. How's that? I'll sit here and if I hear anything at all outside, I'll wake you up."

His eyes narrowed as he thought about it. Rubbing a weary hand against his stubbled jaw, he admitted, "I don't trust you."

She could have taken offense, since she'd sworn she wouldn't go anywhere. But in Hunter's line of business, she suspected he couldn't put much faith in people's promises.

"You can hide my other shoe," she said with a soft smile. Then, having an even better idea, she rose to stand beside him.

He watched in silence. Only the parting of his lips and a quick, audible inhalation betrayed his reaction as she unbuttoned, then unzipped her skirt. She caught it as it fell with a soft swish, and then dropped it onto his lap.

Hunter's eyes widened, all evidence of fatigue disappearing like mist in the sunlight. "What do you think you're doing? Because if this is supposed to get me into bed, it's working. But I'm not exactly gonna get any sleep."

Oh, she loved that idea. But he needed that sleep. "I'm not trying to seduce you, just putting your fears to rest. I might have risked bare feet," she said with a saucy smile, "but I won't risk a bare bottom."

Her fingertips went for the skimpy elastic at the top of her panties. As she expected, however, he immediately reached out, grabbing her hands. "Don't even think about it."

The words sounded ripped out of him, deep and hungry. For a moment, she considered saying to hell with it. He'd already admitted it wouldn't take much to get him into her bed. And oh, did her body quiver and her thighs quake at the thought of it.

She could push him over the edge. She'd like to see the man refuse her if she dropped her panties then sat on the table in front of him and spread her legs in pure, raw invitation.

It wasn't exactly ladylike, but it would be expedient and effective. And incredibly wicked.

Two things stopped her: the fatigue causing his shoulders to slump a bit. And the thought of splinters in her butt.

"Go to bed." Noting his slight hesitation, she sighed heavily and grumbled, "Alone."

"You sure?"

Sadist. "I'm sure."

He let go of her wrists and rose to his feet. Because she stood so close, the motion became a slow, torturous slide about two inches from her body. Heat rose as his warmth traveled the lazy distance from her belly to her cheek.

Finally they were nose to nose, breath to breath. And as if he could no more stop himself than stop the setting of the sun, he groaned deeply and cupped her face in both his big, rough hands. "I might have to keep you," he muttered, then he lowered his mouth to hers.

This kiss was slower, more sultry. He tasted her thoroughly, his tongue lazily thrusting against hers. He held her tightly, their bodies pressed together, from neck to knee. And Scarlett just sagged there against him, too weak and hungry to do anything more than enjoy it.

I might have to keep you.

Considering she was at his mercy, she probably ought to be a little worried about that ragged declaration. Right now, though, she could only manage deep, bone-rattling pleasure.

He finally pulled away with a dark frown. "Wake me if you hear anything at all."

Scarlett hoped her voice didn't shake. "I will."

He said nothing else, merely collapsing onto his back on top of the bed. Still completely dressed, he appeared ready to leap up and into whatever action might come his way. And within moments, judging by his deep, even breaths, the beautiful-but-deadly man was sound asleep.

Scarlett watched him for a long time, alert for any sounds outside, but also trying to make none within that might disturb him. And though her legs eventually stopped shaking from that kiss, her mind continued to churn with possibility.

The possibility of what might happen when he woke up.

THOUGH Hunter didn't sleep more than a few hours, it felt like mid-afternoon by the time he awoke. The light oozing in from around the heavy quilt over the window was bright and intense. Outside, the sky had probably become its typical brilliant blue with puffy white clouds, the kind only ever seen in storybooks. Or here.

Give him smog and humidity any day. Things here were a little too perfect on the outside, while darkness lay just beneath the surface. He'd rather know what he was getting into at first sight.

For a moment, he remained still, unmoving on the bed, trying to clear his head from its post-sleep fuzziness. It took only a second to remember everything.

He jerked upright, wondering if Scarlett had been true to her word and had stayed put. God, what if she'd gone out, what if Lucas had been watching and had taken her to get to Hunter?

What if she'd stumbled into someone even worse?

He realized at once that he needn't have worried. She hadn't gone, she was still right here in the cabin with him. The sight of her, however, almost made him lie back down, and retreat into the relative safety of his dreams. Because there was nothing safe about staying awake and confronting his deepest, darkest sexual fantasies.

Scarlett had obviously found the large washtub that had been tucked beside the woodstove. He'd forgotten it was there, since it was usually stacked full of firewood.

She had emptied it. And had then put it to use.

Right now, she knelt in the thing, her long blond hair pulled up onto her head in a loose bun, a few curls falling to brush her shoulders. Her bare shoulders.

Her bare shoulders above the equally-as-bare rest of her.

The woman, a stranger to him a day ago, had stripped naked to bathe, trusting him to remain a gentleman or stay asleep.

Hell. Nobody had ever called him a gentleman. And Rip Van Winkle himself couldn't have slept through a sensual exhibition like this one.

As he watched in dry-mouthed silence, she ran a thick, soapy sponge over one long, slender arm. She was half-turned away from him, intent on her task. The position afforded him a delectable view of the back of her body, from her creamy shoulders, down the vulnerable curve of her spine, the indentation at small of her back, the swell of her hips. The edge of the tub and the soapy water within it prevented him from glimpsing what he suspected was a magnificent ass.

But it didn't hide her other magnificent assets when she turned a little to rinse the sponge. Her full breasts shimmered and gleamed, slick with soap and topped with taut, puckered nipples. Hunter's heart pounded hard in his chest with the need to have, to take, to taste. His blood surged downward, settling in his cock, which swelled hard against his jeans. The waves of sexual need threatened to drown him. And when she began to stroke her breasts with her own soapy palm, he couldn't contain a low groan of pure, primal hunger.

She heard. But she wasn't startled and she didn't immediately grab for a cloth to cover herself. Instead, she merely glanced over, lashes half-lowered over sultry eyes. A slow smile widened her lush lips. "Awake at last, I see?"

Hunter realized the truth. "This was intentional."

She laughed softly, and rose to stand in the tub, the water dripping off her in rivulets. Lifting a pitcher, she dribbled clean, fresh water over herself to wash away the soap.

"You set me up."

"Well, of course I did."

Pivoting his legs off the bed, he sat on its edge. Half of him wanted to stalk out, not give in to her obvious seduction attempt. The other ninety-nine percent demanded that he take her and be done with it. "Why?"

Bending gracefully at the waist, she reached for a rough towel, which lay across the back of a chair. She patted herself dry, not rubbing the coarse fabric against that incredibly soft-looking skin. "Today *is* Valentine's Day. Don't you want a present?"

"I don't like chocolate," he snapped.

"Shameful." She tsked and shook her head, as if she'd never heard anything more sacrilegious. Then she smiled, her blue eyes gleaming. "But don't worry, your mouth is safe. I didn't bathe in chocolate."

Meaning she wanted him to dine on *her?* His mouth went moist with hunger at the very thought of it. He'd nibble there, suck there. Move his mouth over every last inch of her. Make her come right against his lips and satiate his hunger with her body's hot and steamy response.

She stepped out of the washtub, slowly crossing the room, her breasts swaying with each step. Her long legs were still damp and slick, and she left moist footprints in her wake. He stared at the pale thighs, not allowing himself to dwell on the juncture between them, or on the small tuft of curls she made absolutely no effort to hide.

He gave it one more shot, growling, "Why?"

"Can't it just be because we want each other? So why not take what we want? Why not...*stray?* We're here, we're two adults, we're single." Her eyes widening, she added, "We are both unattached, right?"

He nodded once.

Her audible sigh of relief almost brought a smile to his mouth. "Okay, back to the point. We're incredibly attracted to each other. So why shouldn't we do something about it?"

She made it sound so simple.

Maybe it is. And maybe it should be.

She stepped again, until she was within a few inches of the bed, all that soft, creamy skin inviting him to touch her in a thousand places. His eyes zoned in on a few of the closest ones and another low groan emerged from his throat.

"You can't know whether you want to keep me until after you've had me," she said, her voice thick with hunger.

Remembering what he'd said to her before—the dumb admission he shouldn't have voiced—he gave up all resistance.

She'd get her way. They'd both get what they needed.

But if she thought her seduction had given her the upper hand between them sexually, she needed to think again. She'd thrown the match on the tinder. Now he intended to make her burn like she'd never burned before.

He slowly rose from the bed. The slide upward was more intimate than it had been earlier, for this time, only an inch of air separated her beautiful naked body from his mouth. His lips scraped a path up her belly, her midriff and her chest. The woman's skin was supple and smooth and smelled of the wildflowers that grew around this cottage, and were used in making that local soap.

A heady smell. Intoxicating and a little dangerous. Like many other things in this place.

Brushing his cheeks against the inside of her soft breasts, he heard her hiss and felt her jerk against him. Her dark nipples tightened in visible need, and he knew she wanted his intimate attention there.

He didn't give it to her. Instead, he kissed and licked his way farther up, pressing his mouth to the hollow of her throat, then over the pulse point in her neck.

"Hunter…"

"You've talked enough."

She sucked in an indignant breath. "Are you telling me to shut up?" Her sigh of pleasure took any bite from her words.

He nibbled the lobe of her ear. "Yeah."

She didn't obey, opening her mouth to say something, but he cut her off, plunging his tongue between her lips. She shuddered, sagging hard against him. Turning her head, she wrapped her arms around his neck, tugging him closer, beckoning him deeper. Her warm mouth both offered and delivered intense pleasure, and the feel of her naked body pressed against his sent him almost over the edge.

Her hands were tugging his shirt free of his pants as his explored that fragile back and the generous curve of her hips. Needing more, he cupped the round cheeks of her ass, lifting her a little, making himself at home between her thighs. She welcomed him, rising on her toes, thrusting helplessly against his rock-hard erection. Whimpering, she jerked again, and again taking the kind of contact she most needed.

He watched her closely, letting her use him, certain he'd never seen a more erotic sight. Seeing the flush rise in her face, and her lips part on a soft, helpless sigh of pleasure, he smiled in self-satisfaction.

She'd come. Just like that.

Any other long-deprived man might have joined her at the glorious sight of this beautiful blonde gaining her release. But the realization of just how responsive the woman was only threw down another gauntlet, made him want to do wild, intense things to her for hours. To make her reach that shattering peak and explode into a thousand pieces again. And again. And again.

"Would you…"

He kissed the words away again, not ending the deep mating of their mouths until he had to back away to finish yanking his shirt off. Her cool hands immediately began to stroke his chest, to toy with his nipples, and she leaned forward to lightly bite the skin above his collarbone.

When she reached for his belt, he pushed her hands away and unfastened it himself, then unsnapped his jeans. It had been a long time since he'd had sex. A very long time. And even though he told himself he would hold back and make love to her until she begged him to join her in another climax, he knew he was no damned sex robot. Holding himself together long enough to do a decent job of it wouldn't be easy if she wrapped those soft, greedy hands of hers around his rigid cock.

Or if she used her…

"Hell, *cher*," he muttered, the words exploding from his vocal cords as she suddenly dropped to her knees in front of him. Stunned, he could only watch as she tugged his jeans down, the tips of her fingers traipsing over the erection straining against his shorts.

When she replaced those fingers with her warm mouth, he had to grab the wooden bedpost. The earth seemed to sway beneath his feet. As far as he knew, there was no giant out there making it happen. Just sweet, sultry Scarlett Templeton whose hot breaths sifted through the cotton to increase his insanity.

"Let me," she begged, as if they were long-time lovers used to such intimacies. As if right now, nothing was off-limits, nothing too much to ask or too much to take.

He'd never known a woman to be so bold, so ravenous about taking what she wanted. And he had no strength to resist her.

When she eased the cotton down and out of the way, then pressed her lips against the head of his shaft, he could only reach down and twine his hands in her soft, blond hair. His breaths tripped over themselves to leave his body as she spread her warm tongue around the tip of his cock, then opened her mouth wider to suck an inch or two of him inside.

Blissful.

"Mmm," she groaned. Wrapping her hand around him, she squeezed and caressed him, driving him to insanity when that soft hand slid further to cup him.

Another caress, a deep suck, and he felt on the verge of coming right into her mouth. Which might be incredibly satisfying, but wasn't going to fulfill his need to drive her out of her everloving mind.

With gentle force, he tugged her away, his hands still wrapped in her hair. She glanced up at him, a pout on those shiny lips, but he shook his head and grabbed her shoulders to help her up. No sooner had she reached her feet before he pushed her back onto the bed.

"Hunter," she whispered hoarsely, "I totally forgot—we didn't talk about protection."

Damn.

"I get contraceptive shots every three months," she said, and quickly added, "and, uh, I have no other health problems."

"Ditto."

So relieved he wanted to kiss the ground, he settled for kneeling beside the bed…and kissing *her*. This time, he didn't deny himself the pleasure of her lush breasts. Cupping them in his hands, he lifted one nipple to his mouth while toying with the other, rolling it between his fingers, squeezing and plucking her into near frenzy. She gasped as he thoroughly laved her, her head rolling back and forth on the pillow.

"You are like a fantasy come to life," he admitted gruffly as he pulled away to watch her.

She didn't reply, but merely reached for his hand, pushing it down her front in one long, smooth stroke—until their joined fingers reached that soft nest of hair and slid into it.

"Oh, yes," she groaned, thrusting upward, showing him what she liked, where she wanted it.

As if he'd needed the instruction.

Gently pushing her hand out of the way, Hunter slid his index finger against her taut clit, playing it like a pretty little bell until she was positively ringing. She thrust up for more, panting and almost cooing as he took her higher.

Needing to feel even more—and wanting to drive her even wilder before allowing her another climax—he moved his hand, slipping his fingers into the drenched lips of her sex. She was steamy-hot, silky-smooth and beautifully tight. He didn't know who groaned louder at the realization that she was literally dripping with want.

"Take me, Hunter."

He could have dragged things out, built her to another climax, but he suddenly needed to be inside her so badly, he just couldn't wait. Ripping off the rest of his clothes, he climbed onto her, settling between her silky thighs. They wrapped tightly around him, clenching his hips, and she thrust upward in silent demand.

He hesitated in pure anticipation. Knowing bliss was only an inch away, he savored the delay, bending to kiss her deeply. Their tongues mated as he began a slow slide into her warm body.

"Oh, yes," she mumbled against his lips. She lifted up, welcoming him, enveloping him in all her wet heat.

He meant to take it slowly, but when she clenched her legs tighter and arched harder, he had to thrust deep, making a place for himself inside her.

Scarlett cried out. He instantly paused. "You okay?"

"Don't stop." She thrust her hands into his hair, twining it around her fingers. "Don't you dare stop."

He grinned down at her, loving the sparkle in her eyes and the flush of pleasure on her face. "Wouldn't dream of it, *cher.*"

The endearment brought another smile, then whispers and smiles gave way to deep, hungry kisses that mimicked the deep, hungry movements of their bodies. Scarlett matched him thrust for thrust, taking everything he had to give her, until, finally, when he knew he wouldn't be able to hang on more than a few seconds, he reached down between their bodies, stroking her clit. "Let's go together this time," he said, feeling her clench even tighter as he caressed her inside and out.

"You got it," she said on a long, deep groan. Then she gasped, buried her face in his throat and together they rode out their deep, shattering orgasms.

7

ONCE AGAIN, Scarlett was having the loveliest dream.

This time, though, she was conscious enough to acknowledge it wasn't a dream. She really was lying naked in an incredibly comfortable bed, rubbing her bare skin against the silky sheets.

The only thing she had to think about for a moment was whether she'd imagined the incredible lovemaking that had taken up a good bit of the afternoon or not.

The warm, hard body in the bed beside her said *not*.

"Mmm," she groaned, without opening her eyes. Reality had been so much better than anything she'd ever dreamed about. Hunter had given her more physical pleasure than she had known it was possible to experience. Twice.

She tucked in closer to him, wanting more of the intimacy that seemed so natural between them, and which she'd never felt before. He might have been a stranger to her a short time ago, but physically, she already somehow felt connected to him.

It wasn't just the amazing sex. The draw went deeper than chemistry. The soft whispers and quiet conversation they'd shared between bouts of lovemaking still warmed her. Maybe it was because of how safe she felt with him, how much she enjoyed teasing him into one of those rare smiles. Maybe because he wouldn't let her get away with too much and she wouldn't let him glower his way out of anything.

They had something. Something nice. Something she wanted more of.

More sex would be good, too. God, she was a glutton. Dying of orgasm, wouldn't that read well in her obit? Yet as far as deaths went, it would have to be pretty high up on the list of best ways to go.

Lifting a bare thigh, she slid it over his legs. But instead of warm male skin, she felt rough fabric. He'd apparently gotten up and got dressed at some point, then came back to bed. She'd been so exhausted, she'd fallen into a deep sleep and hadn't even noticed. "Why did you bother?" She ran a hand lazily down his chest. "I'm just going to rip your clothes off again."

Repeating that as boldly as possible, she moved her hand down to cover the crotch of his jeans, cupping the massive bulge there. *Oh, yeah.* Their sex drives were definitely compatible.

"You might have to carry me out of here the way you carried me in," she said as she caressed and toyed with him. "I don't think I'll ever be able to bring my legs together after today."

He chuckled, the sound making his chest rumble a little.

Yawning, she murmured, "What time is it?" She no longer felt warmth from the streaks of sunlight that had been pouring around the edges of that heavy window blanket earlier. And even without opening her eyes, she could tell the room was dark.

Or maybe that was because her face was buried in the neck of her sexy Cajun lover.

Mmm. Wanting to taste him again, she pressed her mouth to the hollow of his strong throat, feeling the rhythmic beat of his pulse against her lips. The scrape of his grizzled jaw against her skin made her shiver, just as it had when it had so deliciously brushed against her inner thighs a little while ago.

Now, though, it felt particularly rough, as if his five-o'clock-shadow had just struck midnight. She might go home reddened and sore. Well, actually, she already knew she was going home won-derfully sore, for different—delightful—reasons.

"You need a shave."

Rubbing her cheek against his jaw, she realized something. He wasn't grizzled. He was almost bearded. And unless he was some kind of Chia Pet who sprouted when water was poured on him, she had no idea how that could have happened in a few hours.

Her heart skipped a beat and her breath turned to a solid lump in the middle of her throat. She tried to swallow it down, willing her rising panic away, without any luck.

What if this isn't Hunter?
You're crazy.
But what if she wasn't crazy?

Finding some deep well of courage, she slowly lifted her eyelids. She first noticed the swarthiness of his skin, the roughness of the thick shirt covering his enormous shoulders. Hunter was a big guy, but she didn't remember his shoulders being twice as wide as her own.

Tilting her head back a little more, she spied that beard. Not golden, as she'd expect Hunter's to be. Instead, it was dark, almost black.

Oh, God. She was in serious trouble.

Inch by inch, her gaze moved up, taking in the strong nose, the slashing cheekbones, the thick, almost jet-black hair hanging in disarray around his shoulders.

And the blazing brownish-black eyes staring down at her.

"You," she whispered.

It was the man she'd seen in the woods. The killer. Though now, up close, he looked just like a dark, swarthy man. Not…anything else. But that was still frightening enough to stop her heart.

Scarlett was wrapped around a psycho murderer. Not only that, she had a handful of his most male part, which was hard enough to tell her exactly how he'd reacted to their encounter.

She jerked and threw herself backward. "Don't touch me."

"You were doing all the touching," he said, his voice husky. Not melodic like Hunter's, more gruff. "Not that I minded."

Scarlett felt her face redden, wondering why the guy hadn't pulled out his ax or something. Or just killed her in her sleep.

Inching back, she reached the edge of the bed and slid off it, falling onto the floor. Scrabbling for the blanket, she tugged it down to cover herself. "He'll kill you."

"No he won't."

The man's calm confidence confused her. He didn't sound the least bit concerned. And suddenly, her fear for Hunter was even greater than her fear for herself. Where was he? How could this stranger be so sure he wasn't in danger.

Oh, God. What if he'd already done something to Hunter?

Staying low, she began to scoot along the floor toward the door. But she hadn't gone far when his big, booted feet came off the bed and landed on the blanket, trapping her.

Earlier, she'd told Hunter she wouldn't run bare-assed through the woods. Now, faced with the alternative, the idea wasn't without merit.

"You're not going anywhere."

"What do you want?" she whispered, edging a little further—as far as she could go without losing the blanket completely.

"I just want to talk."

Her eyes widened. "You want to talk to me?"

"Hell, no, if I had the time, talking would be the *last* thing I'd want to do with you." His eyes narrowed as he raked a thorough stare over her, from the top of her tousled head down to her bare thighs, no longer covered by the blanket. The heat in those eyes left no doubt about what he meant.

Part of her wondered why he hadn't just done it—taken advantage of her while she was asleep and naked beside him in the bed. She wouldn't have even realized it, not at first anyway.

The thought that she could so easily have been raped made a long shudder roll through her body.

"I want to talk to *him*."

The shudder passed as she sighed in relief. Wanting to talk to Hunter meant this crazy guy hadn't killed him already. "He's not going to be much in the mood for talking if he comes back here and finds you attacking me."

He put his hands up, palms out. "I haven't laid a finger on you. Your hands and mouth were doing all the traveling."

Her jaw stiffened in angry embarrassment.

"Don't worry, Red," he whispered, his eyes glittering in the semi-darkness. "I won't tell him."

"My hair's not red."

Those dark, knowing eyes dropped to her bare shoulders. "Your skin is. You two have been having quite a time today."

"Pig."

"Wrong species."

She glared. "You better get out of here. He drove to town to get the cops. They'll be here any minute."

To her surprise, he began to laugh. Softly at first, then louder, as if she'd genuinely amused him. Bastard.

Sick of sitting at his feet staring up at the man like some helpless harem girl, she tugged at the blanket. He stepped off it, allowing her to rise to her feet. She tucked the blanket around herself, then lifted her chin in defiance. "I mean it. Go. I think I hear a siren."

"You have no idea where you are, do you?"

"Of course I do. I'm in a cabin in Louisiana, and we're only a few miles from the closest police station." She wasn't sure there was a police presence in the small town where Granny lived, but hopefully he didn't know that.

A smile appeared on that mouth again. "You really don't know. He brought you over and didn't tell you."

"Over where?" she snapped, feeling left out of a big joke.

He rubbed a hand on his lean jaw. He had big hands. Dark and strong-looking, with more hair at the knuckle than she was used to seeing. "I don't quite know how to say it."

"*Now* would be good."

"You're not in Louisiana. You're far, *far* away from there."

She glared. "Forget it. I don't want to hear your lies."

"Not lies, Red. You're in a place that doesn't exist on any map. I guess the only way to say it is, uh, my brother brought you over the rainbow."

She didn't know which shocked her more. The idea that this man was crazy enough to think they'd flown here over some rainbow. Or his claim that he was Hunter's brother.

Then she remembered the smile, and wondered. Could the killer Hunter Thibodeaux was chasing be his own sibling? There was a hint of a resemblance…it could it be possible.

But as for the rest? Well, it only confirmed one thing. She was trapped with a complete madman.

HUNTER HEARD voices as he returned, carrying the bucket of spring water to resupply the cabin. He'd pictured coming back and warming it up so Scarlett could have another bath while he went out hunting tonight.

He'd never imagined coming back to find Lucas with the innocent woman Hunter had dragged into their private struggle.

Moving quietly, he put the pail down, tugging his weapon from its holster on his hip, thankful he wasn't stupid enough to have left without it. He did not want bullets flying. Not just because Scarlett could get hurt, but because, deep down, he didn't know if he had it in him to kill his half-brother.

You didn't come here to kill him. You came to arrest him.

Only Lucas wouldn't let himself be arrested easily.

He considered his options, finally realizing the pair inside stood close to the door, meaning they were not close to the window. He crept toward it silently, knowing Lucas would sense him if he made the slightest sound. Reaching the square opening, he pushed the lower corner of the blanket in.

And found himself face-to-face with his brother.

"You should have just come in the front door," Lucas said. "I smelled you five minutes ago."

"Hunter!" Scarlett rushed toward the window, stumbling a little on the long blanket wrapped around her naked body.

"If you touched her, I'll kill you," he growled as he climbed inside. He reached for Scarlett and pulled her behind him, blocking her with his body.

"I didn't touch her. We were just having a conversation."

His fingers still wrapped around the grip of his 9 mm, Hunter peered through the near-darkness, trying to see what kind of weapon Lucas was holding. He wouldn't come in here unarmed. The man was far too good for that.

"I have something for you."

Hunter waited. When Lucas reached into a knapsack on the table, he snapped, "Keep your hands where I can see them."

"If I wanted to kill you, I would have done it as you climbed into the window, little brother."

"You know I have to take you back."

"I don't think so."

"You might have felt justified, but you killed two men."

"Again. I don't think so." Lucas pulled a thick sheaf of papers from the knapsack and stepped closer, appearing unconcerned about the gun in Hunter's hand. Nor did he seem angry. "I didn't kill them. They deserved it, but I didn't do it. See for yourself."

Hunter reached out and took the pages. Not certain what he was looking at right away, he soon realized they were black-and-white snapshots, like those taken from a surveillance camera. And visible in the frame was Colin Frakes, his former partner.

"It was taken by a liquor-store camera an hour before Frakes was killed," Lucas said. "Look in the upper left corner."

He did. And stiffened in shock at the sight of another familiar face. "Harry Stafford?" Stafford was one of the other detectives…the one Lucas had not caught up with during his deadly spree last month. The one who was still alive out there somewhere.

Not understanding, he looked up at his half-brother. "But he was living in Arizona, nowhere near Frakes. They split up once they knew you were after them. I figured he went deep into hiding when he realized you'd tracked down the others."

"Wrong. *Stafford* killed Frakes."

Hunter waited for the rest.

"Look at the next shots—red-light cams a block from the second victim's apartment, taken within twenty minutes of his murder. See who was there?"

Hunter flipped the pages and saw exactly what Lucas had told him he would, including a time-stamp from the police camera. Harry Stafford had *indeed* been close to each man just before their deaths. "Why?"

"I don't know. Nobody to testify against him? He had to have known one of us would catch up with him sooner or later."

One of us. "You didn't kill them," he muttered.

Lucas shook his head once, his eyes never shifting, visibly resolute and certain. "Can't say I wouldn't have, if I'd gotten there first," he said, sounding cavalier. "But I didn't set out to. I wanted to bring them back here. I know what kind of easy justice system you've got over there. No way was I going to let them sit in jail for a few decades getting fat." His voice shook and his body tensed as he added, "Not after what they did."

Then, as if they'd said everything that needed saying, Lucas reached for the knapsack and hoisted it over his shoulder.

But Hunter wasn't quite finished. There was one more thing to say. "I don't know how they found their way here," he said, hoping his brother heard the genuine sorrow he made no effort to hide. "But if it was my fault—if I was somehow responsible for putting them in the path of your sister—I'll regret it for the rest of my life."

Lucas stared at him for a moment, then replied, "It wasn't. Frakes has been dealing on this side for years. Long before you paid your first visit."

Relief washed over Hunter. He closed his eyes for a moment, nodding and sending up a prayer of thanks. "I'm glad." Then, his voice still quiet, he added, "I'm sorry about Ciara."

Lucas nodded once, slowly, then walked to the door. Opening it, he peered outside, up at the sky. The full moonlight washed over him, and from a few feet away, Hunter saw the way he swayed forward, welcoming it. His brother's features looked longer, coarser and when he turned to look at Hunter one more time, Lucas's teeth glittered in the darkness. There was absolutely no denying his genetics, not now, not in this place when he was bathed in the moonlight that revealed all.

Beside him, Hunter heard Scarlett gasp. He put a hand on her shoulder and squeezed.

"I'm going after Stafford," Lucas said.

Hunter expected nothing less. "Try to take him alive. Because you're right. Shooting him won't be good enough. He does deserve the kind of justice he'll get over here."

Old-fashioned justice. An eye-for-an-eye justice. His half-brother's entire family would settle for nothing less.

Lucas cast a quick glance at Scarlett, who still watched, her stunned eyes wide. "You should probably get her out of here. It's growing season. You don't want to be stuck here for this next month." A small smile that looked more predatory than amused widened his mouth, and in the low light, his eyes gleamed. "Nice to meet you, Red. You make him tell you the truth, you hear? Because you sure aren't in Kansas anymore."

And then, without another word, Hunter's brother turned his face back toward the moon and slipped out into the night.

8

SHE WAS DREAMING again. She had to be. Because no way had the man she sensed she could truly fall for just told her the crazy story still ringing in her ears. No way. No how.

"It's the tea," Scarlett snapped, "you drugged me. This has all been a hallucination." Chewing on her lip, she eyed him from behind half-lowered lashes. "But the sex was real, wasn't it?"

He smiled as he finished cutting down the oversized, flat leather sandals he'd found for her. After he'd dumped that load of BS on her, he'd gone to work on the shoes, telling her she needed time to "absorb" it all.

She could have paper towels in place of skin and never absorb that nonsense.

"Everything I've said is true."

"Bullshit. I don't believe in fairy tales."

"They're not fairy tales here. They're history. I'd prove it to you if we weren't short on time."

More bullshit. This story about there being another world existing alongside theirs…pure fabrication. She didn't believe in fantasies. Or in crazy stories about alternative universes where fiction had actually happened and mystical creatures actually lived. She wasn't buying one single bit of it.

"I didn't believe it at first either. My mother told me on her deathbed about stumbling over here, and I thought she'd lost her mind. Until I came and saw the truth for myself."

She smirked and rolled her eyes.

He continued, undeterred, his voice never wavering despite the crazy words coming out of his mouth. "I don't think she'd have told me at all if she hadn't been calling out Lucas's name. I asked who he was and she told me the whole story." He looked down to work on the second shoe. "She was in love with Lucas's father, but she was never happy here. She wanted to go back to her other life, wanted him to come with her. But he hated it there as much as she hated it here and refused."

Drawn into the story, as any true storyteller would be, she couldn't help asking, "And Lucas?"

"Their son. She left him behind."

She huffed audibly. "I saw this plotline on *General Hospital.*"

Ignoring her, he added, "She knew she couldn't possibly take him away from his own kind."

His own kind. Riiiight.

Except…she'd seen. God, she'd *seen.* With her own eyes she'd seen the way Lucas had looked in the moonlight. He'd been a man…yet, not entirely human.

He was not an animal, by any means, and was nothing like some stupid old black-and-white werewolf movie. But in that flash of moonlight, his body had seemed too broad, his back too curved, his dark hair too thick.

And his teeth too long.

She'd *seen* it.

Swallowing, not even believing she was about to ask, she tried to sound nonchalant. "Is he a…a werewolf?"

Hunter walked over and dropped the shoes onto her lap. "There's no such thing. That was a story made up by superstitious villagers on our side of the divide. He's just part wolf."

Just part wolf. Sure. Uh huh.

You saw.

He bent in front of her, taking one shoe and sliding it onto her foot, fastening it with a leather strap. Then he did the same with the other.

Putting shoes on her feet. Just like Cinderella. *Gag.*

"So your mother, what, dumped her kid, and left?"

He didn't reply. Noting the tormented expression on his handsome face, she wished she could curb her sometimes wicked tongue.

"She couldn't take him. And she couldn't stay. So she went home, eventually met my father, had me. She kept her secret until her dying day, wracked with guilt and broken-hearted over the choice she'd made."

Was it possible? Could he really be telling the truth? The anguish on his face appeared too deep, too wrenching, to be faked. "And afterward? What did you do?"

"I came here and saw the truth for myself, including meeting my half-brother."

"Are you two…friends?"

He barked a humorless laugh. "I wouldn't say that. But we do have common interests. He's a lawman."

Lawman. Interesting word. Not cop, not detective, not police officer. Yet she sensed the description was still an actual title.

"Ciara?" she asked. "Who was she?"

"Lucas's younger sister." His jaw as hard as granite, he rose to his feet, quickly telling her what had happened. How men he worked with had been dealing and thieving over here, and how the teenage girl had been in the wrong place at the wrong time. Just a random victim of an act of horrible violence.

"And you thought he had killed the men who did it?"

"Yes."

She shook her head and ran a hand over her brow. "You know I can't believe any of this."

"I know. But it's true. I hadn't intended to tell you at all, only…"

"Only?"

"Only I'm not going to be able to take you across the border and never see you again," he admitted. He took her hand and pulled her to her feet. Brushing his fingers across her cheekbone, he added, "Like I said, I might have to keep you."

"It'll never work. You're an insane person," she said matter-of-factly.

He laughed, loud and long. "How can someone who writes kids' books have no imagination?"

"I write the dark, realistic side of the kiddie stories, where Prince Charming is a cheating schmuck…"

"He is."

She ignored him. "And where the helpless princesses get out of their own messes."

"They don't. Sorry. The ones I've met are brainless twits."

She groaned, poking her index finger into his chest. "Stop it. You're nuts. Either that or I'm in a coma in the hospital after my accident, and I'm going to hate waking up because I think I could fall in love with you, if only you were real and not a figment of my imagination. And, if only you weren't abso-frigging-lutely insane."

"I'm not insane and you're not in a coma. But just in case, here's a little something else for you to dream about there in that hospital bed." He thrust his hands into her hair and tugged her close, covering her mouth with his. His lips molded against hers, his tongue diving inside to taste her more fully.

Scarlett whimpered, turned her head and welcomed him deeper. They shared hot breaths and heartbeats and he kissed her so long he claimed a permanent place for himself inside her. No other man could ever kiss her—ever make her feel like this—again.

Then it ended. He drew his hands from her hair. "Believe me. Or don't. But I'm not lying to you."

She stared into his eyes, seeing nothing there but honesty, integrity and an emotion she couldn't quite define.

Thoughts swirled in her brain, the memories of everything that had happened to her over the past twenty-four hours, starting with the appearance of that strange little man in the bookstore.

The man…the electric feeling…the odd sign out on the highway. The road that narrowed into a swamp before disappearing into forest. The oddly colored sky, the flavor of the water, the damned tea. And Lucas.

They jumbled and twisted until her head pounded.

But in the end, it was just impossible. She couldn't bring herself to believe it. She'd learned from a young age that fairy tales weren't true and that believing in them only ever led to grief and heartbreak. Her mother had been waiting her entire life for her fantasy world to become a reality, waiting for Scarlett's father to come back, to make everything right, to give her the happily-ever-after. And Scarlett had spent her childhood waiting, too.

But she was no longer a child.

"I'm sorry," she whispered. "If this is a dream, I hope I get to keep seeing you every night for the rest of my life." Deep down, she knew it wasn't a dream, that she was here, with him. That he had made beautiful love to her and had begun making her wonder if she really could find happiness with a wonderful man.

If it wasn't a dream, there was only one other thing it could be.

"Honestly," she said, swallowing hard, "I think you should get help. And I want you to stay away from me."

Without another word, she hurried to the door, opening it and rushing out into the night. She'd find her own way back to the road, or to the town, or to Granny's. Her *own* way. She'd prove to herself, and to him, that the crazy story he'd spun back there had been just that: a story.

Except...bad idea. It was confusing as hell in those woods in the daytime. By moonlight? She was sure to get lost.

Great exit, genius. Now crawl back inside.

She turned around, about to swallow her humiliation and get Hunter to lead her out of here. But before she could do it, a loud sound rent the night air. Like an earthquake, only richer, deeper, as if the ground itself was stretching wide open.

Shocked, she looked again toward the woods. And saw something that simply couldn't be happening.

HUNTER HEARD the sound and recognized it immediately. He'd been grabbing his pack to go after Scarlett anyway. Now... "Screw the pack."

He almost ran into her. She stood right outside, her back to the cottage, staring up toward the sky. Her eyes were wide, her mouth open in complete shock.

He grabbed her hand. "Come on, we've gotta get out of here!"

She didn't budge, merely lifting her arm and pointing up.

"I mean it, Scarlett, move your ass. It's growing season." He yanked her harder this time, dragging her into the woods. Her shock wore off, her adrenaline finally kicked in. Within seconds, she was matching him step for step as they ran through the woods, racing toward the border.

"What *was* that?" she yelled without slowing her stride.

"A way up...and a way *down*," he snapped, not wanting to take the time to explain. Not until they were through.

He glanced up at the sky. The moon was still high, but it was later than he'd thought. They'd wasted a lot of time. Damn, he should have just brought her back then sat her down and told her the truth.

Finally spying a familiar copse of skeletal trees—trees that were out of place in this thriving forest—he squeezed her hand. "There," he said, nodding toward the spot. "That's the opening."

She didn't hesitate, just charged forward, trusting him com-pletely. When they reached the trees, they found themselves in a low-lying mist, which should have been unusual on such a clear night. But which confirmed their location. "A few more steps…"

Then they were *there*. They pushed through, the misty air giving one instant of firm resistance before the two of them burst past it and out the other side.

Into a bayou.

Scarlett skidded to a stop, bending at the waist, dropping her hands onto her knees to suck in deep breaths. When she looked up at him, long tendrils of blond hair hung in her face. "What the hell was that?"

"The border." He heaved in a few breaths of his own. "You okay? It can sometimes be a little constricting."

She glanced back toward the group of trees they'd just come through. Over here, the mist became moss, long, gray, looping and thick. He preferred coming back to going in. Walking into that Spanish moss was like stepping inside a witch's scraggly hair. Having met one or two of the old hags, he couldn't say he liked the visualization.

Scarlett slowly sank to the ground, ignoring the muck and mud, not that her skirt was in very good shape now, anyway. On her knees, she looked up at him, fear, surprise, excitement warring in her eyes. "I meant," she said, her breaths slowly returning to normal, "what was *that*? Over there?"

He thought about it, knowing what she was asking. He also knew she'd probably think he was crazy again, even though she'd seen it with her own eyes. Jesus, another few minutes and she might have seen a lot worse.

"It's growing season," he explained. "And some moron thinking he could get rich planted a bean."

She thought about it, her brow scrunching in confusion. Then, as though a light bulb had lit up over her head, she got it.

"Oh, my God."

He nodded.

"Are there really…"

"Yeah. Believe me, we would not have wanted to be stuck over there for a month if one of them comes down. Their feet are the size of Mack trucks and their breath smells like a sewage plant."

Scarlett was silent for a moment, unmoving, unblinking. Thinking it over. He was prepared for derision, for her to ignore her own senses and cling to the reality she'd always known.

Instead, she shocked him. "Giants," she said with a snort. She began to laugh…and laugh…and then howl until she had to curl up and clutch her stomach. And when her laughter was finally over, she wiped moisture from her eyes and said, "My agent's never going to forgive me."

Hunter squatted down beside her. "Why?"

She grinned up at him, looking so beautiful his heart twisted in his chest. "Because I think I just started to believe in fairy tales."

And They Lived Happily Ever After…

WALKING hand-in-hand through the night, Scarlett and the huntsman traveled out of the woods, eventually finding their way back to the city by the great river. Their bodies were weary but their souls were light. They had entered the dark forest, had battled monsters created by their own fears and had emerged safe and sound.

But forever changed.

While little Scarlett had learned a few lessons about faith and believing, what she'd learned most of all was that nothing was impossible. Nothing.

With that hopeful mantra as her guide, she allowed herself to open her eyes, her mind and her heart. With every day that passed, she fell deeper in love with her handsome huntsman. Together they explored other worlds, worlds of danger and excitement and fantasy. He sought out the wicked and she shared stories of dark magic and deep dreams.

Then one day he fell to one knee and asked her to be his wife. Having long since given him her whole heart, she agreed.

They wed on a summer day in a small village on the edge of a great sea, promising to love one another for the rest of their days.

Oh, and that happily-ever-after? It included a lot of fabulous, mind-blowing sex.

* * * * *

SEXILY EVER AFTER
Rhonda Nelson

To my novella mates, Kimberly Raye
and Leslie Kelly.

Poor Cupid will never be the same!

1

_____

THIS HAD BEEN a *bad* idea, Juliet Swan thought as she stared across the table at her most recent pre-Valentine's Day, rush-to-get-a-boyfriend blind date. The mall food court was packed, but the noise had receded to a dull buzz. Juliet blinked, certain she had to have misunderstood her companion. "I'm sorry?"

"I said that with a little bit of effort you could be sort of attractive," he said.

So she hadn't misunderstood him. She felt her expression blacken and her so-called date leaned back, seemingly startled. "'Sort of attractive?'" she repeated, her voice throbbing with irritation. "'With a little bit of effort?'"

He chuckled uneasily, then appeared to take offense. "Hey, look. I'm just keeping it real, all right? We're both getting up there in years and there's no point in beating around the bush with social niceties. I like a woman to want to look good for me." His gaze drifted over her hair and his lips pulled down into a frown. "And I get the impression that you aren't into that."

She'd had enough, Juliet decided. She snatched her purse from the back of her chair and stood. "You're right. I'm not." Seething, she managed to paste a smile on her face. "But while we're ditching the *social niceties,* why don't I give you a critique, too? A little bit of effort might make me more attractive, but no power on earth is going to make you anything but a crass, simple-minded bore." She gestured to his head. "And those hair plugs? Not working for me."

With that last comment, she turned on her heel and stalked away from the table. Why, why, why did she put herself through this? she wondered furiously. Every February it was the same old song and dance. She'd have a momentary freak-out over being single on

Valentine's Day—again—and she'd accept any invitation in order to find a little romance for the holiday.

And she was invariably disappointed.

She hurried around a mother pushing a baby in a stroller and a couple of perky teenage girls, then quickened her step toward the exit. Never again, Juliet decided. She was done. *Sort of attractive. With a little bit of effort*, she thought again, disgusted, and, damn him, stung by his less-than-tactful assessment. Men were bastards. Cocksure, boob-obsessed ingrates.

Juliet drew up short as a microphone was suddenly thrust in front of her face and a cameraman aimed a lens in her direction.

"Excuse me, miss, but would you mind if we asked you a couple of questions?"

As a matter of fact, she did. "Actually—"

"With the countdown to Cupid's holiday officially on, the scent of roses and chocolate in the air, what's *your* take on Valentine's Day?" The reporter smiled expectantly.

A cynical laugh bubbled up in Juliet's throat and something inside her just snapped. "You want to know what I think about Valentine's Day? Great. I'll happily tell you what I think about it."

A minute later, she left the bemused reporter standing in the same spot, shell-shocked.

Juliet Swan was officially finished with Valentine's Day.

One week later...

"HONESTLY, Juliet, it was crass. And you look so bitter." A formidable Southern belle, Juliet's mother, Cecilia Swan, clucked her tongue in disapproval and shook her head, passing the fried okra to her husband with a perfectly manicured hand. "What on earth were you thinking?"

Seated at her mother's dining-room table—just as her family and their guests did *every* Saturday at noon sharp—Juliet resisted the urge to make a snarky remark and instead, tucked deeper into her plate. Frankly, she'd actually thought her mother would never see it.

It being the newest viral video sensation via the World Wide Web and more specifically kissmyasscupid.com.

How was she to know when they'd stuck that camera in her face at the mall last week that her interview would be one of only three the Web site would choose to make fun of this latest Valentine's Day season? The damned thing had been featured on the front page of several Internet sites and had even been picked up by a couple of late-night talk shows. As a result, her inbox had been flooded with e-mail and her answering machine had been packed with messages, some from people she hadn't heard from in years.

And her mother was right—she *did* look bitter. Shockingly so, if she were honest.

Her gaze slid to her two younger, beautiful, perky blond sisters and their current dates. She suppressed a sardonic smile. Was it any wonder?

She'd *never* brought a date to Saturday lunch.

"Your mother forwarded the link to me, Juliet," her father chimed in. He squeezed a wedge of orange into his sweet tea, then, chuckling, shot her a smile. "If you weren't my daughter, I'd think it was funny. *'Valentine's Day is an overhyped commercialized crock of crap, focused on the most fickle of emotions, and celebrated by those rare, happy—usually beautiful—people who are fortunate enough to be in a relationship,'*" he quoted, much to her embarrassment. "But the best part was when you told Cupid he could kiss your—"

"That'll do, Warren," her mother said, darting him a frown of disapproval. "We've all seen it, unfortunately. We know which part of Juliet's anatomy she told Cupid he could kiss."

A muffled laugh emerged from Bianca's latest boyfriend—Victor, if memory served—and Portia's newest conquest wore a barely suppressed smile.

Bianca leaned over and gave Victor a little one-armed squeeze. "I happen to love Valentine's Day," she said, beaming. "It's only two weeks away. Victor and I are taking a dinner cruise."

"Really?" Portia asked, her bright-blue eyes sparkling with interest. "Joe and I haven't made any plans yet, but that sounds lovely."

Juliet grimaced, carved off a piece of ham and popped it into her mouth to keep from gagging. This was precisely why she loathed the holiday. Most of the time she was quite happy being by herself. She enjoyed her own company, didn't have to consider another person's feelings when making day-to-day plans and loved having sole power of the remote control. She slept in the middle of her bed—Romeo, her pug, at her feet—selfishly hogged every pillow, and never had to worry about sharing her closet space with anybody else.

There were perks.

Occasionally she would succumb to a little loneliness—laughing with someone was always preferable to laughing alone. But in those increasingly frequent instances when she wished she had someone to share a movie with—or her bed—Juliet would just channel-surf until she found a good Brit com or go into her studio and pick up a paint brush. The pungent scent of gesso and the sight of a swirl of color on a fresh canvas never failed to make her forget whatever else might be lacking in her life.

Or at least they always could…until Valentine's Day.

Then everything went to hell in a handbasket.

Thanksgiving and Christmas were always a whirlwind of activity—it was all about the food and the shopping and the last-minute gift for Great-Aunt Ida, spiced cider and her mother's squash casserole recipe. While having a significant other would be nice, the lack of one wasn't quite as pathetic because there was so much else going on. During those holidays, she was much to busy too focus on being lonely.

But Valentine's Day? Juliet blew out a resigned breath. Being unattached on February fourteenth was a.) significantly noticeable and b.) even more pitiful.

Juliet had spent much of her life feeling pitied. Despite her last name, she was definitely the ugly duckling in the family. Her sisters were petite and fair, with curling blond hair and vivid violet-blue eyes. Cherubic, everyone always said. She caught a glimpse of her own reflection in the mirror over the antique buffet and inwardly winced.

And if they looked heavenly, then she definitely represented hell.

Her hair was stick-straight—it absolutely would not hold curl, much to her mother's chagrin—black as a raven's wing and her eyes were even darker. And petite? Er…no. At five foot ten—eleven in shoes with any sort of sole—she towered over many men and was at eye level with most. To her perverse satisfaction, she found a lot of men—generally shallow, self-serving, oversexed, one-dimensional assholes—found her intimidating.

She'd heard her looks described by various family members as "striking" and "unique," as well as getting the occasional well-meaning pat accompanied by a "you're lovely, too, dear," but Juliet accepted them for what they were—patronizing compliments delivered with an awkward smile, usually after a gushing session over her younger sisters.

She was an afterthought.

It would be easy to be bitter about it if her parents had ever once made her feel that she was less attractive than Portia or Bianca. But they hadn't. To their credit—despite their love of all things Shakespearean, which accounted for each of the Swan girls' names—they had never played favorites. And while Juliet was occasionally jealous of her sisters' beauty and social ease—she couldn't quite forget the galling crush she'd developed on one of Portia's brief boyfriends a few years ago—she couldn't harbor any resentment toward them either. They were smart, accomplished young women. Both of them taught at the local elementary school, and Portia had just completed her master's degree.

No, the only person who had ever made her feel less than beautiful was Juliet herself. And that was because…she owned a mirror.

And, from an artist's standpoint, she could appreciate that she wasn't as aesthetically pleasing to look at. Her eyes were a little too dark, her jaw a little too sharp and her mouth a little too wide. She didn't care for makeup—her face always felt like it was smothering—and she'd long ago given up trying to style her hair. Every effort resulted in burns from a curling iron—*not* attractive—and clumps of scorched hair. Her so-called style of choice was the ponytail. Quick, efficient and timeless, Juliet thought, her lips twitching.

"Did you know you were going to end up on the Internet, Juliet?" Portia asked.

Juliet chewed the inside of her cheek and shook her head. "No. But I guess the camera should have tipped me off that it could turn up somewhere."

Her dad chuckled. "Yes, that should have been a clue."

"It's not funny, Warren," her mother chided. "Didn't you hear what she said? She hates Valentine's Day. *Our daughter*. Named after one of the most romantic characters in all of classic literature and the only thing she likes about the holiday are those chalky conversation hearts." Her mother gave a delicate shudder.

"She's named after one of the most tragic heroines in classic literature, Mom," Portia contended. Her lips twitched. "Given how her namesake's love life turned out, you should be glad that Juliet isn't interested in romance."

That wasn't precisely true—she'd been interested once. A vision of dark auburn hair, humorous mossy-green eyes and a crooked smile interrupted her thoughts, making an unexpected longing rise up her throat where it almost choked her. Her thighs gave a little quake and she felt her sex quicken, remembering. It had been more than a crush—utter infatuation, more like.

"Juliet's interested," her mother insisted. "She just hasn't found that special guy yet."

"It takes a special guy for a special girl," her dad said, offering one of his favorite platitudes. He glanced at each of the gentleman seated at his table and lowered his brow into a fierce line. "All my girls are special and should be treated accordingly. Keep that in mind, boys."

Smiling, Bianca rolled her eyes. "Why don't you just drag out the shotgun and start cleaning it, Dad?"

Her father grinned. "Don't think I won't."

They all knew he would. Warren Swan might be a mild-mannered podiatrist with a penchant for drama—both her parents were players at the local theater—but he took his fathering duties quite seriously.

Every guy Portia or Bianca had ever brought home had been given the third degree and found her father on the front porch polishing a rifle, awaiting their timely return. Extreme, yes, but effective. Dating one of the Swan girls had never been for the faint of heart.

As a teenager Juliet had both anticipated and dreaded her first date, seeing her own guy through her father's version of the Spanish Inquisition. Unfortunately, she'd never dated in high school—that miserable milestone had occurred in college—and she had completely skipped her prom. She regretted that now. At the very least, she wished she would have gone stag.

She had several friends who'd gone as a group, but Juliet simply hadn't been able to bring herself to do that. The prom was meant to be a couples' event. The idea of going by herself had simply been more than she could emotionally stomach. She'd spent the evening painting a gazebo scene on her bedroom wall instead. She still considered it among her best works.

Speaking of work...

Juliet set her fork aside and wiped her mouth. "I'm afraid I've got to be off," she said, carefully placing her lace napkin next to her plate.

"Off?" her mother parroted, startled. "But you haven't had dessert. I made pie."

She knew she was committing a cardinal breach of etiquette by abandoning the table before dessert, but she had no choice. She was meeting a new client today, one whose fancy address and interest indicated a hefty commission. Business was good, of course. She was a fine artist, if she did say so herself. She was prompt, efficient, had a good eye for scale and composition and completed projects on time. But each new job was only as good as her last and she depended heavily on word of mouth to keep her calendar full. A wealthy client meant equally wealthy friends, and her potential for income would increase exponentially.

Juliet winced. "Sorry, Mom. I've got to meet a client."

"It's chocolate," she said temptingly. "Your favorite."

Juliet wavered. "Can you cut me a slice to go?"

Her mother smiled, the balance in her genteel world restored. "Of course, dear."

"A new client, eh?" her father said. "Sounds promising."

"He lives in Whitetail," Juliet said, referencing Jackson, Mississippi's answer to New York's Hamptons. She took a final sip of tea and accepted the plastic container which held her pie from her mother, then stood.

"Whitetail, you say? Who is he?"

"Jamison Highgrove. He's an older gentleman who's interested in commissioning a set of fairy-tale murals for his wife."

Cecilia smiled and her blue eyes lit with maternal delight. "Oh, she must be expecting."

Juliet frowned uncertainly. Funny. He'd seemed quite odd about it. Purposely vague, even. "He didn't mention a nursery."

"Well, good luck, dear," her mother said. "Business in Whitetail is a coup."

It was, Juliet thought. And as long as she didn't have to paint Cupid, she'd be thrilled. At this point, all she wanted to do was get

through the next couple of weeks—and V-Day itself, of course—
as painlessly and quickly as possible.

Since she couldn't throw herself in front of a bus, throwing
herself into her work seemed like a good alternative.

2

"…AND IT makes us merely average girls even more painfully aware that we are eternal ugly ducklings without the hope or the faintest prayer of ever getting that handsome guy. It's a cruel holiday whose only redeemable benefit is the brief but memorable appearance of the large Hershey Kiss and conversation hearts. Quite frankly, Cupid can kiss my ass."

Gareth Harper stared at his PDA screen—at Juliet Swan, in particular—and laughed until tears gathered in his eyes. His sister had forwarded him the link to kissmyasscupid.com, along with the note "Another V-day hater. This is the girl for you."

He didn't know about that, but he couldn't deny that her assessment left him howling with laughter. "Conversation hearts and the large Hershey Kiss," he muttered under his breath. She was right. He loved those damned Kisses.

As for Juliet, Gareth had actually met her many years ago when he'd briefly dated her younger sister, Portia. To say that he'd been blown away by those dark eyes, that direct stare, in particular, would be a huge understatement. She'd been so different from everyone else in her family. All the other Swans, parents included, had been fair and blond.

Juliet wasn't.

Black hair, dark-brown eyes, tall. Compelling, Gareth thought, remembering the unmistakable current of attraction that had zapped his loins the minute he'd looked at her. He inwardly snorted, remembering. Hardly good form to be attracted to one sister when he was dating another, but…

He and Portia had parted ways—she'd been a little too perky for his tastes—and while he'd entertained the idea of calling Juliet, ultimately Gareth had decided against it. He had dated her little sister—which would be awkward to ignore at best—and there had been something about Juliet that had made him a little…uneasy.

She had a way of looking at him as though she could see right through him. There'd been several times during that fateful lunch— a family tradition, if memory served—when he'd caught a little sardonic smile cross her lips and he'd been left with the strange sensation that she'd been able to read his mind.

Gareth preferred being an enigma to being an open book.

And right now, he'd temporarily closed the book on romance.

In fact, Cupid could kiss his ass, too. The winged bastard certainly hadn't done him any favors of late. His last serious relationship had ended right before Christmas when he'd found an unexpected present under his tree—his business partner and girlfriend going at it like a couple of drunken elves on a three-day pass from Santa's workshop. It hadn't been a surprise, really. For some reason, he had a history of getting ditched on statutory holidays. Hell, the only one he had left was Halloween, and, considering it was more of a pagan ritual than an actual holiday, Gareth wasn't even sure it counted.

Understandably, he, his business partner and his girlfriend had parted ways.

Frankly, losing his business partner had been harder to take than losing the girlfriend. His landscaping and pool business was gearing up for prime season and he still hadn't found a suitable replacement. Besides, he and Keith had been friends much longer than he and Courtney had dated. Losing Keith had been more of a blow.

Then again, one could argue that if Keith had been any sort of friend, he would have bypassed screwing Gareth's girlfriend, but Gareth preferred not to get too hung up on that little detail. Keith had been drunk and Courtney had been an opportunistic, unfaithful bitch. He wanted Keith back. Courtney, on the other hand, could go to hell.

A few minutes later, Jamison Highgrove—who looked alarmingly like Sean Connery's younger brother—rounded the corner next to the house and whistled low at Gareth's handiwork. "It's coming along nicely, isn't it?" the older man enthused.

Considering this was the first time Gareth had ever been asked to build a grotto à la Hugh Hefner and his Playboy mansion fame—he'd researched it on Google to make sure he had the right idea—and he was working without a partner, Gareth did indeed think the work was coming along quite well. Highgrove was a well-connected client and it was in Gareth's best interests to knock this one out of the park, so to speak.

He'd incorporated some beautiful pottery inside the rather large cave, used cut stone for the steps leading in and out of the pool and had placed several little seating areas throughout the structure.

"I'm still working on the waterfalls and fountains within the cave," Gareth told him. "But everything else is coming together remarkably well."

Jamison rocked back on his heels and smiled. "Excellent. And are we still on schedule? You'll be finished before Valentine's Day?"

Gareth rubbed the back of his neck. "It'll be tight, Mr. Highgrove, I won't lie to you. But it will get done." Even if he had to work all night to complete the installation. Highgrove was a high-profile client. He couldn't afford to screw it up.

"It's a Valentine's present for my wife, you know," Highgrove reminded him for at least the tenth time. "I want everything to be perfect when she gets home."

"I understand."

Truthfully, he didn't understand. But then again, he didn't have to. If the elderly Highgrove wanted a sex grotto for his hot young wife—one who was currently at a resort island in the Caribbean undergoing a few "procedures"—then who was he to judge? His girlfriend had slept with his friend, for heaven's sake. Clearly his penis hadn't been enough to keep her satisfied.

Faithless bitch or not, that had stung.

Frankly, the fact that Highgrove was willing to go to these lengths to make his wife happy impressed the hell out of Gareth. Eccentricities aside, he liked the old man. He admired his grit. He hadn't let a little thing like age keep him down.

Literally, Gareth thought, remembering the penile implant demonstration Highgrove had offered to show him last week. "Best damn thing I've ever done for myself," Jamison had told him, going into explicit detail about how the device worked. "Getting it up and keeping it up is no longer a problem—powering that sucker down, on the other hand, was a bit tricky on the front end, but we've got it all worked out now."

That, of course, had left him with a mental image he could have done without. But what could he say? He hoped he'd never need a penile implant, but it was nice to know there were options available should the unthinkable ever occur. Hell, by then, they'd probably have invented a remote-control variety, complete with an internal vibrator option. The idea made his lips twitch and he passed a hand over his face to hide his smile.

Highgrove's ever-present walkie-talkie chirped at his waist. "Mr. Highgrove, there's a woman at the gate to see you. She says she has an appointment."

Highgrove's tanned face split into a broad grin. "Another surprise for Patricia," he explained.

Whatever cranked her tractor, Gareth thought. Like any other man, he'd cop to enjoying a little girl-on-girl action.

"Juliet Swan?" Highgrove asked the security guard.

Gareth blinked, stunned.

"Yes, sir," came the reply.

"Excellent," Highgrove said. "Send her in." He clipped the walkie talkie back to his waist. "My one o'clock is here, Gareth, so you'll have to excuse me."

Gareth frowned and gave his head a little shake. "Did you say Juliet Swan, sir?"

Highgrove paused. "I did. She's a local artist I'm commissioning to paint a few naughty fairy tales in our *special* boudoir. Patricia had seen a bit of her work at a friend's house and was quite impressed. She's an excellent muralist from what I understand." The older man paused, his dark browns knitting thoughtfully. "Do you know her?"

Naughty fairy tales? Juliet? In their special boudoir complete with the sex swing? Gareth couldn't stop a grin. He could just imagine Juliet's reaction to her new assignment. "I met her once several years ago." As for her art, she was more than talented—she was brilliant. He'd actually bought a painting of hers from a local gallery a few months ago. It was of a single canoe on a moonlit lake, with just the hint of a shadowed person manning the boat. It was dark and lonely and hauntingly beautiful. The damned thing had cost more than his high-definition television, but he hadn't been able to resist. He'd wanted it.

"Good, because if she takes this job, I'm going to get her to paint a few things out here for us as well. Vines and flowers and such."

Gareth nodded and thoughtfully stroked his jaw. "Er…does she know you want her to paint naughty fairy tales?"

Highgrove grinned, showing a full mouth of ceramic implants. The man's mouth was worth more than his own car, Gareth thought. "I might have left out that little detail. Thought it would be better if I pleaded my case in person."

"Right."

Highgrove's manicured brows formed a questioning line. "She's not a prude, is she?"

"I only met her the one time, sir, so I really couldn't say." He'd gotten the impression that she was inexperienced, Gareth thought, but not necessarily a prude.

"Perhaps you should come and meet her with me," Highgrove suggested. "Help put her at ease."

"Oh, I don't know—"

"I insist," he said. "I don't want her to think I'm some old pervert. Patricia and I, we just like to keep things fresh. There's nothing wrong with that, is there? It's not like we're going to host an orgy or anything. We aren't *deviants*. We're sexual pioneers."

Sexual pioneers. Right. Honestly, it was quite depressing for Gareth to realize this old man was getting laid more frequently than he was.

As a consolation prize, he supposed seeing the look on Juliet's face when Highgrove explained exactly what sort of art he wanted would have to do.

Gareth nodded and followed Jamison into the house, making sure to wipe his muddy boots before going inside. "So, when you say naughty fairy tales, just exactly what is it that you're looking for?"

"I've been thinking about that," Highgrove said. "I'm thinking 'Beauty and the Beast.' Beauty's got a little cleavage showing— possibly even a whole breast. 'Little Red Riding Hood' on another wall. She's wearing nothing but the cape and the Big Bad Wolf is trying to help her out of it, if you get my drift. Then 'The Ugly Duckling'—I'm having a harder time coming up with a concept for that one, but it's Patricia's favorite story, so it's got to be included. Hopefully Juliet can figure something out."

"Is this a Valentine's Day present, too?" Gareth asked, just as the front doorbell rang. His spine prickled and his heart rate kicked up a notch.

"It is."

"I'd keep that to myself if I were you."

"What? Why?"

"Trust me on this, Mr. H. Not all women are as keen about this holiday as you are," he said, remembering Juliet's recent video tirade.

Seeming baffled, Highgrove nodded.

Fran, one of Highgrove's staff, ushered Juliet into the foyer just as Gareth and his employer were making their entrance as well. Her surprised gaze connected with Gareth's, making a sizzle of unexpected electricity fire in his crotch and the back of his neck prickle with excitement. So he hadn't imagined it before. Damn.

He honestly didn't understand it.

Dressed in a shapeless black top easily two sizes too big, a pair of paint-speckled jeans, her hair in a sloppy bun on top of her head and secured with what looked suspiciously like chopsticks, she was hardly what one would call sexy. In fact, she was a walking fashion wreck—she even had on a pair of those godawful plastic shoes all the kids were wearing. Her only nod at any sort of current style was a pair of colorful, boxy glasses. They were funky, and definitely suited her, Gareth decided.

"Good afternoon, Ms. Swan," Highgrove welcomed her. "I'm so glad you could see me on such short notice."

"Certainly," she said, shooting him a curious look. She inclined her head. "Mr. Harper."

So she remembered him. His ego knew a fleeting moment of masculine joy. "It's nice to see you again, Juliet."

Highgrove frowned. "How is it again that you know each other?" he asked Gareth. "You never said."

Gareth smiled awkwardly. "I, uh—"

"Gareth came around for lunch with my sister a couple of times," Juliet said, letting him off the hook.

"How is Portia?" he felt compelled to ask.

"She's fine. I just saw her a little while ago as a matter of fact."

"Lunch?"

She smiled and something flickered in her gaze. "Right. Every Saturday, noon sharp. Be there or else."

"Sounds like a lovely family tradition," Highgrove said. "Those are becoming increasingly rare. I only see my kids and their families a couple of times a year. Brant's in Denver, Lucinda's in Maine." He grimaced. "We're scattered, much as I hate it."

Juliet made a commiserating face, then briskly changed the subject. "So, what sort of project did you have in mind for me, Mr. Highgrove?" she asked.

Highgrove shot Gareth an uncomfortable look. "It's of a different nature," he said. "I doubt you've done anything like it before."

"Oh, I've painted many fairy-tale murals." She reached into a big bag attached to her shoulder and withdrew a large leather album. "Actually, I brought my portfolio with me—"

"Er…that won't be necessary," Highgrove interrupted. "Why don't I show you the room, then you can get an idea of what sort of *tone* we're looking for."

To give her credit, Juliet didn't miss a beat. He knew she had to be thoroughly confused, but was professional enough not to show the slightest hesitation. She nodded briskly, then followed Highgrove to the back part of his Georgian-style mansion. The "boudoir" actually opened into the pool area, which would come in handy when they decided to move the festivities to the sex grotto, Gareth thought. After all, it was attached to the pool.

Gareth followed Juliet into the bedroom and had the privilege of watching her step falter at the sight of the heart-shaped bed, the champagne-glass hot tub and the sex swing. Recessed lighting and a disco ball rounded out the tacky porno-film decor.

"Oh," she said. "I see."

From the corner of his eye, Gareth noticed a rush of color bathe her cheeks and a single bright spot of red appear on her throat.

"As I explained to Gareth here, who's working on the grotto and pool area, the wife and I like to keep things…fresh."

Juliet nodded again, seemed to be inspecting the walls. In fact, she was looking everywhere but at him or Highgrove. "So, the fairy tales… What exactly did you have in mind?" Was it his imagination or had her voice become a bit strangled?

Highgrove mopped his face with a handkerchief. "Naughty fairy tales. Nothing too racy, of course. Just a slightly d-different take."

Gareth smothered a snort. There was nothing "slight" about this request. Highgrove wanted to take beloved children's fairy tales and turn them into a sexual stimulant. Granted, Beauty falling in love with the Beast appealed to him, and Little Red Riding Hood older, more mature, and decked out in nothing but the coat was an excellent idea. Still…

He didn't have any idea what was going on in Juliet's head, but he certainly hoped she'd sign on for the job. Watching her paint these scenes would sure as hell make his job more interesting over the next couple of weeks. His gaze slid down her back, over her rear, which was surprisingly full in the seat and another bolt of attraction knifed through him.

And if she'd paint them in nothing but her smock for inspiration, then all the better.

NAUGHTY fairy tales?

Juliet could feel Gareth's amused gaze boring a hole in the back of her skull as well as the twin flags of color, which had no doubt appeared on her cheeks, blaze their way into her hairline and down her throat. She'd never blushed prettily, dammit. She'd always blushed in giant blotches. More like a rash.

Honestly, when Jamison Highgrove had called her about doing the murals, she'd gotten a bit of a weird vibe. But this—her gaze strayed to the champagne-glass hot tub and what she could only assume was some sort of sex harness—*this* took the cake.

But if she hadn't keeled over in shock, or melted into a puddle upon seeing Gareth Harper again, she could certainly pull it together for this interview.

Gareth Harper. Here. *Wow.*

"I realize it's an odd request, but I assure you—"

"No, no," she said, swallowing her initial surprise. "Provided you give me creative license to make the scenes more evocative than sexual in nature, I think the concept could be quite nice."

It would be even more nice if Gareth would stop staring at her, Juliet thought, stomach churning. She could hardly think. She hadn't seen him in years, but he'd certainly featured prominently in many of her fantasies. He was the only one of her sisters' boyfriends she'd ever wished was hers. That dark-auburn hair—irreverent curls—and those mossy green eyes were especially sexy. Factor in his significant height—he easily towered over her and actually made her feel small—not to mention he tripped internal triggers that made her squirm inwardly, made her breasts go all heavy and wanting.

"Evocative," Hightower repeated thoughtfully. "Yes, that's it exactly. I don't expect you to paint 'Beauty and the Beast' in flagrante delicto," he explained, blushing sheepishly. He strode over to the bedside table and pulled a couple of books from the drawer, then returned. "More like these," he said.

Juliet inspected the covers. "Like romance novels?"

"Exactly. They're evocative, right? Without giving away too much?"

She could do this, Juliet realized, letting the thrill she always got with a new project tingle in her imagination. Visions of various fairy-tale heroines and their respective heroes flashed through her mind. She glanced at each wall, mentally measuring the scope, the amount of canvas she'd have to play with. Two long walls—one with a set of French doors which led out to the pool—then the one behind the bed. So three actual scenes, she decided, then the wall with the doorway could be a more of a mystical garden scene, with a gate painted directly onto the door. Hence, the doorway to their sexual sanctuary.

She smiled, shot Mr. Highgrove a smile and outlined her thoughts.

Gratifyingly, he beamed at her. "This is why you were so highly recommended. You've nailed it. You'll need to be finished by the fourteenth. When can you start?"

She blinked. "The fourteenth?"

"It's a gift for my wife," he explained.

She had other clients in queue. She couldn't possibly put them off to accommodate Mr. Highgrove, regardless how much she might want to.

Deflated, but resigned, Juliet shook her head. "Mr. Highgrove, I'm sorry, but—"

He scribbled a figure onto a business card and handed it to her. Juliet closed her mouth to keep her jaw from dropping. The amount was three times what she would have charged—and her services didn't come cheaply.

He merely smiled. "I want this, Ms. Swan, and more importantly, my wife wants it. I understand that your time and services are valuable and changing your schedule to accommodate mine is an inconvenience for you and your other clients. I hope my offer will rectify any problem."

Juliet wavered. On the one hand, she hated to be so greedy and self-serving, but on the other hand the next couple of projects she had slated weren't particularly pressing. Furthermore, Highgrove's bonus would go a long way toward that house on the lake she'd been saving for. She loved the water. It was the only place she didn't feel awkward and gangly.

Smiling, Juliet reached out and shook his hand. "Your offer is more than generous, Mr. Highgrove. I accept."

His grin made an encore appearance. "Wonderful," he said. "Other than 'Beauty and the Beast,' were there any particular fairy tales you were interested in?"

"'Little Red Riding Hood,'" he said. He winked at her. "That one ought to have some potential. And 'The Ugly Duckling.' It's Patricia's favorite."

'The Ugly Duckling,' Juliet thought, inwardly wincing. She'd been the ugly duckling her entire life and had completely given up on that whole turning-into-a-swan nonsense. Of course, with enough money and plastic surgery, anybody could be beautiful nowadays. Highgrove had mentioned something about his wife being out of town for surgery—no doubt that was the sort she was getting. In which case, for her, the story might actually fit. She'd get her happy ending.

Juliet nodded. "Certainly, sir. I'll see what I can come up with."

"I know you won't disappoint me." A walkie-talkie clipped to his waist chirped, announcing the arrival of another guest. He expressed his regrets, told her to take as much time as she needed today, and he'd see her tomorrow. Then he happily excused himself.

Interestingly, Gareth stayed behind. She was hammeringly aware of the heart-shaped bed and the naughty nature of what she'd been commissioned to paint as he continued to stare at her with a slightly bemused expression.

"So," she said, for lack of anything better. "What exactly is it that *you're* doing for Mr. Highgrove?" She scowled. "Or do I want to know?"

Gareth grinned and wandered over to the harness suspended from the ceiling, inspecting it thoroughly. "I'm building his sex grotto."

A startled chuckle erupted from her throat. "A sex grotto?"

Gareth shrugged. "Hey, if it's good enough for the Hef, then it's good enough for the Highgrove."

She wished he'd get the hell away from that contraption. She didn't have any idea how the damned thing worked, but just imagining him trying to figure it out—preferably with her—was making her blood pressure rise. "So you're still in the landscaping and pool business then?"

He nodded. "I am. But this is the first time I've built a sex grotto."

"Seriously?" she quipped, feigning surprise. "You mean people in the greater Jackson area aren't beating down your door asking you to build them?"

He chuckled, the sound every bit as sexy as she remembered. "I know it's hard to believe, but no. And I guess you get requests to paint naughty fairy tales every day, too, right?"

"Naughty fairy tales?" She shrugged. "It's old hat."

Gareth grinned again. "I could tell," he said. "By the strangled tone of your voice and that blush that hasn't quite gone away yet."

Damned cheeks. She gave her head a sad but resigned shake. "Gives me away every time."

The sound of Highgrove's booming voice drifted into the bedroom, jarring Gareth into action. He jerked his thumb toward the pool area. "I've got to be finished in two weeks as well, so I'd better get back to it." He paused and his gaze drifted over her face, lingered over her lips, making them tingle. "It's good seeing you again, Juliet."

Probably so he could hook back up with her sister, she thought. But she basked in the comment all the same. "I'll tell Portia you said hello."

A slight frown flashed over his face, but he covered it quickly with a smile. "Sure," he said. He started to walk off, then stopped short. "Want to share lunch Monday?" he asked. "You know, since we're both going to be here?"

"Sure," she said, startled. More than likely, he wanted to pump her about what was happening with her sister, but for the moment she'd pretend he was actually interested in sharing a meal with her.

His smile was quick and curiously relieved, then turned a bit wicked. "Excellent. I'll bring dessert." He chuckled under his breath "I, um…I recently found out that you were fond of Hershey Kisses and conversation hearts." And with that parting shot, he strode off, leaving her to blush in mortification.

This time, all over.

Excellent, Juliet thought. *Just excellent.* He'd seen that damned video, too.

Cupid really could kiss her ass.

4

"COME ON, sis," Gareth moaned. "Surely there's someone else who can do it."

"Gareth, you are my only hope," Jill needled, in that older-sister tone that had managed to extract all sorts of favors over the years. "These kids don't want their parents chaperoning their prom. Would you have wanted Mom and Dad at yours?"

"Of course not," he admitted. He accepted the lunch he'd ordered for him and Juliet from the delivery guy, nodding an apology over the handset. It was rude, but getting off the phone with Jill was impossible at the moment. "But I still don't want to do it."

A heavy sigh carried over the line. "Fine. I'll tell Jeremy that his favorite uncle doesn't care about his prom and the poor kid will simply have to make do with his meddling old mother there. I'm sure he'll love it."

Gareth checked the bag, making certain their order was correct. Asian chicken salad for her, steak sandwich and potato skins for him. Excellent. He frowned. "Tell me again why you're in charge of the chaperones?"

"It's part of my job description."

"You're a teacher, not a babysitter. Couldn't someone else have volunteered?"

"You think I volunteered for this?" she asked, her voice climbing. "I was assigned this job. I would never have volunteered for it." She snorted. "Hell, no one does. And it's my night in the barrel. Come on, Gareth. It's one night and it's in February instead of the summer, for a change. You can't have anything planned. It's not like you're seeing someone," she said significantly, fishing for information.

He glanced through the French doors into the kitchen where he and Juliet were meeting for lunch—Highgrove had stocked the fridge with drinks for them—and watched her stroll into the room.

Once again that unusual blast of heat erupted in his groin and an odd sensation winged through his suddenly tight chest. She looked up and her gaze caught his, making his breath catch in his lungs.

"Unless something has changed," his sister added, evidently sensing his hesitation.

"Er…no," he said, cursing his distraction. "Fine. I'll do it," he relented, more to get off the phone than anything else. "But I'm not wearing a tux."

Jill whooped in his ear. "Thank you, little brother. Jeremy will be pleased."

He didn't know about that. He imagined his nephew wasn't going to like having any family member at his prom, but given the circumstances Jeremy would probably agree that Gareth was the lesser of two evils.

"We'll see," Gareth said cryptically. "Look, sis, I've got to go."

"But—"

"Talk to you later," he interrupted, then quickly snapped the cell phone closed to end any further protest.

For reasons he couldn't begin to fathom, he'd been looking forward to this lunch with Juliet since the instant he'd suggested it. He'd been surprised he'd had the nerve to ask and, because Cupid evidently had it in for him, lunch would probably end in disaster. But…Juliet fascinated him.

He'd been intrigued by her the minute he'd laid eyes on her all those years ago and that interest seemed to have grown considerably overnight.

And now it was sexual.

He'd never been so preoccupied over a woman before and frankly, his reaction puzzled him.

After all, while compelling, Juliet wasn't exactly what one would call—and he winced even thinking this—but, well…pretty.

Unique, yes. Her face was an interesting composition of planes and angles, her brows a bit heavy. Her eyes were strikingly dark, the deepest shade of brown he'd ever seen and ringed in what could only be called black. It was an intense illusion, one that made him feel his thoughts were being stripped bare and exposed. Her nose was slim, feminine even, and her mouth was a bit wide, but full, rosy and surprising lush.

He'd spent a lot of time over the past twenty-four hours thinking about her mouth.

And what she could do to him with it—in the sex grotto, specifically.

It was sheer madness, Gareth thought, as he opened the door and stepped into the kitchen. "Hey," he said. "I've got lunch."

Juliet smiled. "Wonderful. I'm starving." She moved to the fridge and opened the door. "What would you like to drink?"

"A soda's fine," he said, setting everything down onto the table. He'd just finished unloading the bag when she placed his drink next to the takeout container.

Juliet sat down and inspected her meal, then picked up a condiment package and removed a napkin and utensil. "Ah," she said, grinning. "Nothing says haute cuisine like a spork."

Gareth nodded, smiling. "Part spoon, part fork. It's ingenious, really."

"I know. I can't believe that Oneida hasn't tried to capitalize on it yet."

"I'm sure that Highgrove wouldn't mind us borrowing the real thing if it bothers you."

Juliet shook her head. "No, no, not at all." She stabbed a mandarin orange wedge. "See how well this works? It's amazing." She took a bite, then washed it down with a sip of bottled water. "So how long have you worked for him?"

Gareth slathered a bit of sour cream onto a potato wedge. "I've been here around a month. He wanted the pool area completely revamped. I put in a new liner and built the waterfall at the deep end—I'm still working on the opposite one in the shallow end that hides the grotto. Then I tore out all of the original concrete and replaced it with the stone you see out there now. My crew has been taking care of some of the lighting and landscaping, while I've been primarily working in the grotto area myself." He nodded, pleased with how well it was turning out. "It's been a bit of a challenge. Highgrove wanted several water features inside the grotto, all flowing into a secluded pool, and several seating areas both inside the pool and outside of the water, tucked against the cave walls."

She smiled, seemingly impressed. "Sounds like a tall order. But a very nice one."

"It is," he admitted, feeling that smile of approval warm in his chest. "You should come out and look at it before you go home. And what about you? Think you can get those murals done before Valentine's Day?"

She grimaced at the mention of the holiday, forcing him to squelch a laugh.

"Er…yes," she said. "It's going to take a lot of long days and a few long nights, but I'll get it done. I'm sketching it out now. That's the hardest part for me. Once I'm finished with that and can actually pick up a brush, it'll go much faster."

He took a bite of his sandwich. "You're sketching out all of them in advance?"

"Yes. I want to know exactly what I'm doing and, of course, I'll need Highgrove's seal of approval before I apply the first bit of color."

"Good idea," Gareth told her, remembering some of the man's explicit instructions for him. He chuckled. "He has a very clear vision of what he wants, I can tell you that."

A droll smile rolled around her lips. "I sort of got that impression."

Finished eating, Gareth leaned back and shot her a grin. "You've got to admire him, though. He's not letting a little thing like age slow him down."

Her dark eyes twinkled. "I imagine that younger wife of his has something to do that that."

"How do you know she's younger?" He'd met Patricia, so he knew that she was at least half Highgrove's age. But how did Juliet know, or was she just making an assumption?

Juliet jerked her head toward the hall. "Pictures."

"Ah," he said, inclining his head. He decided to toss the line of conversation into a more personal pond. "So, other than startling unsuspecting reporters with your anti-Valentine's Day propaganda, what else have you been up to lately?" He had to admit he was very curious as to why she was so personally opposed to the holiday. Personal experience, he wondered. Or just an overall sense of discontent?

Her cheeks pinkened, she chewed the inside of her cheek and her embarrassed gaze tangled with his. "You're going to bring this up regularly, aren't you?"

Gareth resisted a smile. "Not regularly, I'd say. But often enough to enjoy seeing you squirm." He rocked back in his chair, lifting the front legs off the floor. "It's certainly made the news circuit. I caught a glimpse of it on late-night TV last night as well. And my sister had actually e-mailed me the link Saturday, right before you got here." His gaze found hers once more. "Weird timing, eh?"

She rolled her eyes. "I think I'd call it more 'bad luck,'" she said, tucking a stray strand of hair behind her ear.

Gareth chuckled and passed a hand over his face. "I know that you're probably sick of it, but it's damned funny."

Her lips twitched and she gave him a long-suffering look. "It's funny to you because you're not the one who made a fool of yourself. Nor are you living with the consequences. And if those other two girls—one's from Louisiana and the other's from Texas, I think—are having the same sort of trouble I am…" She shrugged. "I've had to change my home number, I'm getting inundated with calls through my business line and I've been contacted by no less than *three* Internet dating sites which promise results." She rested her chin in her hand and stared at him. "Evidently successfully helping me find my perfect match would be a public relations coup."

Gareth felt his chest shake with silent laughter. "I wouldn't say that you made a fool of yourself, precisely. You were—" he felt his mouth quiver "—certainly…vehement," he decided, looking for the right word.

She snorted indelicately and leaned back. "I came across as a thwarted, miserable harpy on a lunatic rampage against love."

"I wouldn't say that. Besides those other women weren't any more opinionated than you were."

She quirked a pointed brow.

"Really," Gareth insisted. "You were all equally thwarted, miserable harpies on a lunatic rampage against love." He grinned. "Telling Cupid to kiss your ass was a classic moment."

Another smile shaped her lips. "A fine moment my mother was proud of."

Gareth remembered her mother. A true Southern belle with a soft lilting accent and perfectly coifed pale-blond hair. The woman undoubtedly bled sweet tea. *No,* he thought, silently agreeing with her.

Her mother probably wasn't thrilled with the clip. "I'm sure it'll blow over," he said.

"I hope you're right. It can't happen soon enough to suit me, I can assure you."

He should really get back to work, but he was reluctant to leave her. She was easy company, Gareth decided, enjoying being with her more than he'd expected. "So, have you always hated Valentine's Day or did something precipitate your, er…*strong* opinion?"

She considered him for a minute, as though not quite sure what to make of this line of questioning. He knew he was prying, but he had to confess intense curiosity all the same. He wanted to know why she hated it so much. Had someone hurt her? Did she really believe that she was an ugly duckling, never destined for romance?

It wasn't true, Gareth decided, feeling that strange snake of heat she inspired coil in his loins and slither up his dick, readying it for action. He shifted, trying to ease a bit of the pressure.

"It's never been my favorite holiday," Juliet finally said. "Relationships don't come easy for me." She exhaled loudly, as though reluctant to share the rest. Then obviously deciding to get it over with she continued. "But that particular day I'd been on a bad blind-date—trolling for a Valentine date so I wouldn't be alone again this year—and I just…snapped. Honestly, I didn't have any idea it all sounded so terrible until Bianca called me and told me to check my e-mail. She'd sent me the link to kissmyasscupid.com," she explained. "And there I was, in all my bitter glory."

"Well, if it makes you feel any better, I probably would have done the same thing, had that happened to me."

"I find it difficult to believe that you'd ever have a hard time getting a date," she said, taking a sip of her water.

"Not necessarily getting a date," he admitted, unwilling to lie. "But that doesn't mean relationships are easy. Hell, I found my last so-called girlfriend under my Christmas tree with my business partner a couple of months ago."

She choked on her drink.

A hard smile turned his lips. "She was wrapping his present, so to speak."

She winced. "I'm sorry, Gareth. That had to be tough."

He looked away, stared at a chickadee bathing in one of the

water features outside. "Well, it wasn't the best thing I got for Christmas, that was for sure. But I was well rid of her. The relationship had flat-lined. We'd stayed together more out of habit than any affection." He looked back at Juliet and felt a shadow of a smile cross his lips. "To tell you the truth, I miss my business partner more." He jerked his head toward the pool. "I could sure use his help right now."

She didn't look surprised. Merely curious. "You could forgive him?"

Gareth lifted a shoulder. "Alcohol was involved. He'd just come off a bad break-up. She admitted that she'd initiated things." He was thoughtful for a moment. "Yeah, I think I could. I'd like to."

She grinned and the rest of the room seemed to shrink away. A long strand of dark hair hung against her pale cheek, emphasizing the creamy perfection of her skin. "Congratulations, Mr. Harper," she said. "A rational, well-thought-out, testosterone-free conclusion. I'm impressed."

Gareth chuckled. "Let me get this straight. I impressed you with my ability to reason? With my small Neanderthal-sized male brain?"

She shook her head, pretending she could scarcely believe it herself. "That's why it's so impressive."

A hearty laugh broke from his throat. "Ouch," he said, rubbing his jaw as though she'd struck him. "Excuse me while I recover from that backhanded compliment."

"I can tell you're wounded."

He shook his head. "No, but I will be if Highgrove sees I'm still on lunch." He paused. "This has been nice," he said, meaning it. "What do you say? Same time tomorrow?"

She hesitated.

"Or not," he countered, hiding his disappointment.

"Portia's seeing someone," she blurted out.

Gareth blinked, confused. "What?"

"Portia's s-seeing someone," she repeated. "So if that's why you're, you know…" She trailed off, gesturing helplessly.

Understanding suddenly dawned. She thought he was hanging out with her to covertly pump her for information about her sister. Best to clear that up right away.

"Are *you?*" he asked pointedly.

She looked so startled, it was almost heartbreaking. "Er…no."

"Good," he said. "Because you're the one I'd like to have lunch with."

She nodded, letting out small breath. "Okay."

And just to make absolutely certain she understood—and because he was powerless to stop himself—Gareth leaned over and pressed a lingering kiss to her cheek. An electric current zipped down his spine at the first touch of her skin, making him inhale her scent, something fruity and clean and intensely tantalizing, then to his surprise, his lips moved of their own volition to her mouth.

She tasted like ginger and oranges and a spicy flavor all her own. His body quickened and a strange sensation took root in his chest— and more familiar ones further south—as she tentatively touched her tongue to his.

He quaked.

Then he breathed her in, relishing the pleasure of her lush mouth beneath his, her soft moaning sighs as she moved closer to him, bracketing her hands on his face, then pushing them into his hair. A shiver worked its way through him at her touch.

He fed at her mouth, deepened the kiss and aligned her body more tightly against his. She was tall and her surprisingly full breasts pressed against his chest, soft and womanly. Gareth slipped his palms over her cheeks, mapping the slopes, testing the hollows of her cheekbones against his hand. Silken threads of her hair slid over his knuckles, making him long to feel more of it against his naked skin.

The strange attraction morphed into something else, something much stronger. Need chugged hotly through his veins and desire took on a whole new meaning. He'd wanted a woman before, but this was different. Threads of emotion tangled through it, making it much more potent. Much more terrifying.

Shaken, Gareth brought the kiss to a close while he still could. "I'll see you tomorrow," he said, his voice sounding rough and strangled to his own ears.

Juliet nodded, making a little nonsensical little sound in her throat that kept a smile on his face the rest of the day.

5

HE'D KISSED her.

Juliet didn't remember walking out of the kitchen, going back to work, actually *doing* any work, or getting into her car at the end of the day to drive to her favorite art supply store, but somehow she must have done it. Otherwise she wouldn't be standing in the aisle, holding a bottle of Verdant Grass #512 in her hand. Strictly speaking she didn't have time to be mooning around like this. She needed to get back to work, but…

She still couldn't quite believe it. When she'd told him that Portia was seeing someone and he'd come back with a very direct *Are you?*, it was a miracle that she hadn't keeled over in shock. Her poor heart had actually skipped a beat, then raced into a rhythm that made her knees almost buckle. She still hadn't recovered from the shock when he'd kissed her.

First her cheek, which had been heartbreakingly perfect, then, as if he simply couldn't help himself…her mouth.

And sweet mercy, if anything had ever been more wonderful in her life, Juliet couldn't recall it. The feel of his tongue sliding over hers, his lips tasting hers, his big hard body pressed boldly against hers. He was warm and dark and thrillingly male and she'd never, *never* wanted anything as much as she'd wanted him in her life. Gareth was funny and charming and, wonder of wonders, seemed to find her attractive. That significant bulge she'd felt pressed against her belly had left little doubt about that.

It was mind-boggling.

Other than a couple of clumsy experiences in college which had been fueled by too much alcohol, low self-esteem and a bit of curiosity, Juliet's sexual education was sadly lacking. Sure, she could have trolled the local bars and snagged a string of one-night stands.

But that wasn't her style. She'd found her niche in the art world, had discovered a sense of self-worth which had always eluded her and that little boost to her ego had bolstered her pride and prevented her from lowering her standards. She wanted to meet a guy, date, then take things to the next level. She wanted to follow the natural order of things, not jump ahead to the main event out of some misguided sense of sexual urgency. It didn't mean she didn't *want*— she did. It just meant she refused to settle.

And for the first time in her life, she actually didn't think she would have to. If she was reading things correctly—and she didn't see how she couldn't be—Gareth Harper *liked* her.

Juliet basked in the warm glow of that thought as she paid for her purchases and stepped out onto the sidewalk. The puffy Valentine hearts and pink streamers advertising the coming holiday didn't scream "Failure!" at her quite so loudly.

"It's her!" a confident male voice shouted.

Startled, Juliet turned and found a bleached-blond, dark-browed, dark-eyed, tanned, stocky man in a white linen shirt and khaki trousers pointing at her. A pair of black designer sunglasses were resting on his forehead and a silver angel-wing earring dangled from his right lobe. A small camera crew trailed after him.

Oh, hell. They'd found her. And once again, they'd brought cameras.

"Good evening, darling," the man said, staring at her hair with a critical eye. "What's your name?"

"Why?" she asked suspiciously. Was this some sort of trick?

He chuckled. "Because I'm Eros Amore with Channel Six's *Makeover Madness* and you have been chosen for a random makeover."

So he wasn't with the local news? Or related to the kissmyasscupid thing?

He leaned in and fingered a strand of her hair. "I can make that guy you're into really sit up and take notice," he whispered in her ear. Then he leaned back. "Are you a fan of the show?"

He could make the guy she was into sit up and take notice? How did *he* know she was into someone? Of course, it could just be a line to convince her to play along, but the comment hit a little too close to home. Very strange, Juliet thought.

She cleared her throat. "I've never heard of it."

Laughing, Eros rounded and faced his entourage. "A virgin!" he said, before turning back to her. "Oh, this is going to be fun. Here's how it works. You turn yourself over to me and my crew for the next two hours and we're going to make you over. New 'do, new makeup—" his gaze slid over her outfit "—and a few fashion tips. Are you free?"

"Free," she admitted, which wasn't altogether true. She really needed to log in a few more hours at Highgrove's mansion. "But not interested, thank you." She turned and started to walk away.

Eros tsked loudly. "No room for improvement, eh? That's awfully arrogant."

Arrogant? *Her?* Was the guy on crack? Juliet stopped and turned around. Eros wore a patronizing smile and blithely polished his nails against his shirt. "I didn't say there wasn't room for improvement. I merely said I wasn't interested. There's a difference."

"So you don't care how you look?"

"I'm happy with myself," Juliet lied, releasing a silent sigh of relief when a bolt of lightning didn't strike her down.

He frowned, seemingly puzzled. "Are you a woman?"

She could feel her blood pressure rising. For some reason she was getting the distinct impression that Eros whatshisname was purposely baiting her. Her lips twisted into a humorless smile. "Last time I checked, yes."

"Then you're an anomaly. I've been in this business a long time, sister, and I can tell you, I've never met a woman yet who was completely satisfied with her appearance." He took a step forward and lowered his voice. "Let us work our magic with you. I promise, you won't regret it."

Juliet felt herself waver. Of course he was right. Who wouldn't want to look better? And he'd unwittingly struck her Achilles' heel. Still, she'd been to dozens of stylists over the years and had never been happy with the end result. And makeup… She hated it. Aside from not liking the way it felt on her skin, she wasn't altogether certain she'd be able to apply it.

"Look," she said, giving her head a small shake. "I appreciate the offer, but this—" she gestured to her hair "—is as good at it gets and make-up isn't my thing. It's just too much trouble."

He glanced down at the bag in her hand. "You're an artist, right?"
She nodded.

"Then you know that the proper tools make all the difference in the world. Gimme a chance," he implored, as if it were almost personal for him. He jerked his head over his shoulder, indicating the people behind him. "You're killing me here. What have you got to lose?" He smiled engagingly. "Hair grows back and makeup washes off."

He was right, Juliet decided. What could it hurt? A secret part of her thrilled at the idea of reinventing herself. At showing up tomorrow morning at Highgrove's house looking better than she'd left it. She didn't expect Eros and his crew to work a miracle on her, but he was right. There was definitely room for improvement.

Juliet nodded. "Fine," she said. "I'll do it. But nothing too radical with my hair."

TWO HOURS later, after much cutting and blow-drying, waxing, moisturizing and applying of makeup, Eros looked at her and beamed. The little salon next to the art supply store had provided the room and necessary equipment for her makeover and he'd sent one of his minions down the street to a local boutique to pick out a new outfit. Juliet had been ushered into a room without a mirror and instructed to change. The brown cowl-necked sweater was a soft delight against her skin and the matching tweed pants would never have been anything she'd chosen for herself, but she had to admit they felt nice and fit well.

"Are you ready?" Eros asked.

Juliet released a shaky breath and felt a nervous smile shape her lips. "I don't know. Am I?"

Eros leaned in closer, as though he were about to impart something important. She'd actually come to like the impertinent little man quite a lot over the past couple of hours. "Listen, I don't say this often because I think the term gets tossed around a little too lightly these days, but you're beautiful."

Her breath caught. Before she could protest or utter a single word, he whirled the chair around to the mirror. Dimly she noted the cameras zooming in, presumably to catch her reaction.

She barely recognized the woman staring back at her.

It was her body, her face, but they were…different. Her hand flew to her hair and she tentatively touched a strand. She smiled, stunned, and her heart began to race.

"You have great hair," Eros said. "It just needed a better cut. And it will be amazingly simple to take care of. Just blow it dry and everything will fall into place. No curling necessary."

It was still long, but no longer all one length. The stylist had angled the sides to swing toward her face, starting just below her jaw. The effect was nothing short of amazing. It opened up her face and rather than hide the sharp angle of her jaw, seemed to highlight it.

As for makeup, he'd used a mineral-based sort that didn't feel the least bit sticky. His artist had applied a light dusting of a deep-rose-colored blush on her cheeks, emphasizing the hollows, a pale shimmering gold on her lids and just the smallest amount of mascara. Her lips were colored in a soft gleaming shade just a hint darker than her own color. Small changes, but ones that had a dramatic effect. As an artist, she could certainly appreciate them. She didn't necessarily agree that she was beautiful, but pretty?

Yes, she thought, blinking back tears. She laughed, amazed at the change, and turned to Eros. "I don't know what to say."

He rocked back on his heels, pleased with himself. "What do you think of the outfit?"

Juliet had been so busy staring at her head, she'd neglected to look at the rest of her body. She stood and did a half turn, inspecting herself in the mirror. The sweater was a great color on her—not too dark, but definitely a complimentary shade—and hugged the curve of her breasts in a very flattering style. And the pants were particularly nice. Very slimming.

"I adore it," she said. "It's lovely."

"*You're* lovely," Eros told her. "We've arranged for a complimentary wardrobe at Jenny's Boutique where this came from. See her and she'll outfit you." He explained the makeup, which ultimately consisted of five little things—hardly the arsenal of supplies she'd imagined—and how to use them. "You'll need to keep the brows waxed. It's tedious, I know, but necessary. Your hair will need a trim every six weeks. Lisa here at A Cut Above will take care of that for you." He handed her two cards. "Your next appointment has already been scheduled. Don't miss it," he warned. "And here's my card if you need me. I do special occasions as well."

Juliet smiled, overwhelmed. "I don't know that I'll—"

"You will," he said, sounding so certain she was inclined to believe him. "Good night, Juliet," he said. "And good luck."

"With what?"

Another enigmatic smile turned his lips and the angel-wing earring caught a particularly bright flash of light. "Love. It's in the air this time of year, after all."

And with that parting comment, he ushered her out of the door of the salon.

For the first time in her life, she was actually optimistic about Valentine's Day.

6

GARETH WALKED into the boudoir where Juliet was working and drew up short, unprepared for the sight that met him.

"Wow," he breathed before he could stop himself.

Juliet turned and smiled, her dark eyes highlighted by the faintest hint of a gold shadow, a sheer rosy color painted on her mouth. But it was her hair which had undergone the biggest change. Instead of the ponytail, her long straight locks hung in a tapered curtain around her face, particularly along her jaw, emphasizing its unique shape.

He'd dreamed about licking it last night. Again, in the grotto.

She fingered a lone strand. "I got a haircut last night."

"I see that," he said, knowing that he was gawking at her but unable to make himself stop. The difference was...breathtaking.

She looked...sexy. Gorgeous.

Smiling, he released a shaky breath and sidled forward for a closer view. "Juliet, you look great," he said. "Not that you didn't look great before," he added hastily. "But—"

"There's always a little room for improvement," she said, her eyes twinkling. "It's okay. I know what you mean."

"I'm just surprised at the difference," he said. He slid his finger along the line of her jaw. "I love the way it hugs your jaw." His gaze dropped to her lips. "It's very sexy."

"Th-thank you," she said, a bit breathlessly, an embarrassed tinge of color washing over her creamy skin. She blinked, seemingly confused. "Is it lunch time already?"

He chuckled, remembering why he'd sought her out. "No," he said. "It's only nine, but I wanted to ask you something and didn't want to wait. I hope you don't mind the interruption." He glanced around the room, taking note of the scenes she'd sketched.

So far, the Beast, whom she'd managed to make attractive, and Beauty were locked in a passionate embrace. Beauty was rocking some serious cleavage and didn't look the least bit terrified. On the other wall, Little Red Riding Hood's cloak was slipping off a bare shoulder and she was looking behind her at the Big Bad Wolf with a come-hither grin. Rather than draw an actual wolf or beast, she'd painted men with those qualities. Beast was a large, muscled man with a strong jaw and big hands. The wolf had been drawn with sharp eyes and a lean frame. She'd done a beautiful job on the sketching, but hadn't applied the first bit of paint yet.

"It's fine," she said. "I've still got to finish up the Ugly Duckling scene and—" she pointed to the wall which held the door "—I'm putting a Secret Garden scene over there."

He nodded, impressed. "Nice," he said, then paused. "You know, I actually have a Juliet Swan original," he told her.

Shock registered on her face, then morphed into a slow pleased smile. "Really?"

Trying to ignore the bed in the background and how she would look sprawled naked across it, Gareth struggled to focus. "I do. I bought it for myself last Christmas," he said. "From Linda's Gallery on Broad Street, downtown." His gaze tangled with hers. "It's the one called 'Reflection.' It's…haunting," he said, for lack of a better description. "I get a weird feeling in my chest every time I look at it."

Almost identical to the one he got every time he looked at her, Gareth realized. Breathless. In perpetual anticipation.

A surprised chuckle bubbled up her throat and her expression took on a wondering look. "I love that painting," she admitted. "In fact, I was reluctant to part with it, but Linda was adamant. She insisted on including it with the others." Her gaze searched his and a ghost of a smile touched her ripe mouth. "I'm glad that you've got it and that you're enjoying it. That means a lot."

"You're very talented, Juliet," he said, meaning it.

"Thank you." She paused, the moment lingering between them. "Oh, you said you wanted to ask me something."

"Right," Gareth said, starting. Incredibly, he felt a burst of nerves shoot through his belly. He smiled sheepishly. "It's been about twelve years since I've asked a girl this, so forgive me if I'm rusty."

He let out a loud breath ."I was wondering if you'd like to go to the prom with me."

Gareth waited, holding his breath.

JULIET BLINKED, certain she'd misunderstood him. Her heartbeat thundered in her ears, making her momentarily deaf. "The prom?" she squeaked. She cleared her throat, hoping to bring a little bit of moisture back into her suddenly dry mouth.

"Yeah," he said, looking adorably nervous. "I know it's short notice, but I just agreed to chaperone for my nephew's prom yesterday and I'd love for you to be my date. It's next Friday."

The day before Valentine's Day, Juliet realized, the closest thing to a real Valentine she'd ever had. And a prom. She couldn't believe it. A do-over. For some inexplicable reason, an image of Eros's angel-wing earring suddenly flashed through her mind.

"Of course, if you've already got plans—"

"No," she said hastily. "I don't. I'm just a little surprised. Typically, people our age don't go to the prom."

Gareth grinned and rolled his eyes. "Tell me about it. But my sister, who teaches at my nephew's school, insists that it will mortify my nephew if she's there as a chaperone and that it's my duty, as his uncle, to prevent that from happening."

Juliet poked her tongue in her cheek and crossed her arms over her chest. "In this case, I would have to agree. Having his mother at the prom would certainly cramp your nephew's style."

He quirked a hopeful brow. "So you'll go?"

Warmth bubbled through her middle and she resisted the adolescent urge to squeal. "I'd love to."

Seemingly relieved, Gareth rocked back on his heels. "Excellent. It starts at eight. I thought I'd pick you up around five-thirty and we could do dinner first."

"Sounds nice."

He waited expectedly. "I'll need your address."

Right now? Juliet wondered, startled. "Er…sure." She rattled it off. "You can't miss it. I've got a Swan painted on my mailbox."

Gareth chuckled. "That would definitely tip me off."

"Yeah, it's cheesy," she said. "But appropriate."

Gareth released a pent-up breath. "I'd better get back to work before Highgrove sees me in here and thinks he's not getting his money's worth." He paused, as though a thought had struck him. "Oh, by the way, I'm sure he'll tell you himself, but he's going to be out of town next week on business. He'll be back next Friday night. He's going to give you a key and has offered his house in the final days before completion in the event you or I want to stay here and put the finishing touches on our work." He grimaced. "I don't know about you, but it might come to that for me. We're moving along, but not nearly as fast we need to."

Actually Juliet was making pretty good time on her own project and hoped that when she actually started applying some paint it would go faster. Still, the idea of having a reason to stay here and hang out with Gareth was intensely appealing.

She'd thought of little else but Gareth since she'd run into him again. And had barely gotten a wink of sleep thanks to that heart-breakingly perfect mind-scorching bone-melting kiss yesterday. In fact, after she'd finally managed to doze off, her fertile imagination had taken that whole scene to a completely different level last night.

She'd had her first ever wet dream.

Curiously, though she hadn't gone out and looked at the grotto, that's where her mind had put them. Hot, wet, naked skin. His wicked mouth feeding at her breasts, those talented fingers tangled in her curls, stroking her. Then the feel of him, hot, hard and male pushing into her while the waterfall sang in the distance and the water lapped over her open thighs. A dark fantasy where the ugly duckling turned into a sensual swan in the most thrilling way.

It could happen, Juliet thought, staring at Gareth's sinfully crafted mouth now. He'd kissed her. He'd asked her to a prom, a dream she'd fully given up on. And he'd just put her on notice that he would be staying here at some point over the coming week. A hint? she wondered.

"What about you?" he asked. "How's your schedule looking?"

He was fishing, she decided, inwardly pleased. Juliet feigned a wince, glanced around pretending to mull it over. "It's going to be tight." This was her chance to grab the brass ring. She couldn't hold on to it forever—it wouldn't last, she knew. She wasn't lucky like that. But…

"If Highgrove offers, I'll probably camp out here next Thursday night and try to finish up." She grinned at him. "Friday's shot now, you know. I'll be too busy getting ready for the prom."

His smile was pure sin. "All you've got to do is show up, Juliet, and I'll be happy."

It was quite possibly one of the nicest things anyone had ever said to her. An unexpected rush of warmth blanketed her heart, then moved like a tidal wide to her furthermost extremities.

His gaze tangled with hers and unspoken innuendo hung between them. "Thursday could turn into an all-nighter for me, too," he said. His voice lowered an octave. "We could keep each other company."

He bent forward and pressed a long, hot kiss against her lips. His arm banded her waist, dragging her up against him where that bulge she'd felt yesterday made another brand against her belly, sending a depraved thrill whipping through her.

Her limbs quaked, her nipples budded and an achy throb commenced between her legs. He tangled her tongue around his, probed the soft inner recess of her mouth, mimicking sex. His big hands slid down her back, over her rump and squeezed, setting off another little pleasure bomb of sensation.

She wanted to crawl out of her skin and into his.

She wanted to feel his hot flesh against her own, naked and warm and wonderful.

She made a little sound in her throat and wrapped her arms around him, sliding her hands over his back. Muscles bunched at her touch, giving her a heady start. He rocked against her, looking for that same desperate release she craved so badly. She squirmed frantically, trying to put that hardest part of him against the softest part of her. His hand slid up and over her ribcage, sending gooseflesh racing over her back, then cupped her heavy breast. She mewled as her pouting nipple pebbled against his palm. He gave a gentle squeeze and she felt her panties grow damp.

"Damn, Juliet," Gareth panted hoarsely, tearing his mouth away from hers. "You're killing me." He chuckled softly and rested his forehead against hers.

"You started it," she said.

"I know." He grinned down at her. "And I never start anything I don't intend to finish."

Oy. Her toes actually curled. "So you're goal-oriented. That's an admirable quality in a man."

"And just think. I haven't been trying to impress you." He winked at her and her foolish heart gave a little leap. *"Yet."*

7

MOMENT OF TRUTH time, Gareth thought as he flipped the final switch, sending power to all the various lights and fountains throughout the finished grotto and pool area. He'd been checking each one individually all along, but this was the first time the entire system had been tested as a whole. The fountains burbled to life, cascading over fieldstone and granite, bits of moss and fern, and the lights danced beneath the mist-covered waters, giving off an almost other-worldly glow.

It was just past eight o'clock on Thursday night—a bolt of anticipation quickened his pulse, thinking about what was to come—and his weary crew gave a whoop of joy when everything worked as planned.

Gareth grinned. "Congratulations on another job well done, guys," he said, rubbing the back of his neck as they picked up their equipment and started to leave. He'd promised them a share in his expected bonus and given them the next day off. Lord knows they deserved it. He and his crew had logged in sixteen-plus-hour days to get to this point and, though it had been to meet Highgrove's deadline, Gareth had imposed a secret one that had increasingly become more important than his actual client's.

He'd wanted to get finished at a decent hour so that he could celebrate with Juliet. On the pretense of making sure everything worked right, he'd brought his overnight bag and bathing suit—and had told her to do the same. It was time to give the sex grotto a test run.

Tonight. With Juliet.

In fact, ever since last Thursday when they'd planned this so called camp out at Highgrove's, Gareth could honestly say that the only things that had saved his sanity were the long hours, and the back-breaking, exhausting work he'd put into this project. If he'd spent too long thinking about this evening with Juliet, he wasn't altogether certain his body could have withstood the stress of the anticipation.

He thought he'd wanted before, thought he'd known true desire. He'd been wrong.

This past week, sitting across a table from Juliet, feeling his body quicken with need every time he looked at her—the smooth slope of her cheek, the way those ripe lips closed around her fork, those keen dark eyes perpetually sparkling with humor—had taught him that, until her, he hadn't known a thing about true desire. In the past, that sexual pull had been a purely physical sensation, concentrated below his waist.

This was different.

This was a hammering need in his blood which pounded against his heart, letting loose with every blow an emotion he dared not name, making it all the more intense, yet all the more desperate.

He didn't just want her—he had to have her. To keep her. He felt as if his very life depended on making her his. And of course, since he was a man, nothing would make him feel more as though he'd succeeded than burying himself as quickly as possible between her thighs. But he knew that wasn't enough. Still, his physical need was the only damned part of this newfound attraction and desperate desire which made any sense at all.

Simply looking at Juliet made something in his chest swell and tighten and his fingers twitched with the perpetual urge to touch her. She was smart and funny, insightful and heartbreakingly insecure. He hated that for her. Hated that she couldn't see how truly beautiful she was. Of course, though he'd been attracted to her, he hadn't seen it as plainly as he did now, so it was no wonder she was confused over what she saw in the mirror every morning.

He wanted to fix that for her, Gareth thought. He wanted to make her see what he did. Because to him, she was utterly perfect.

Gareth's gaze slid to the French doors leading into the boudoir, where Juliet was framed in the paneled glass, and something in his chest gave a little squeeze. She stood in the middle of the room, apparently inspecting her work, her ripe lips closed around the end of a paintbrush. How many times this past week had he caught her like that and wished her mouth was wrapped around something else?

he wondered, his dick twitching in his pants. With her hair pulled up in a clip, a paint smudge on her cheek, she was in full-on artist mode.

Because he hadn't been able to help himself, he'd taken a look during various stages of her work throughout the past week. He'd actually been afraid that she would finish early and ruin their spend-the-night plans. But thankfully—at least for him because he was a selfish bastard—she'd stumbled a bit at the end.

The "Beauty and the Beast," "Little Red Riding Hood" and the lush garden scenes had all come together without a hitch, but "The Ugly Duckling" had presented a problem. "I can't seem to get a grasp on it," she'd told him yesterday, a worried frown lining her otherwise smooth brow.

Gareth had assured her that she would. But given the critical expression she now wore, it didn't appear as if that had happened yet. He sidled to the doors and gently rapped on the glass. Maybe a new set of eyes could offer some fresh perspective.

STILL AGONIZING over "The Ugly Duckling" mural—something was off, but she'd be damned if she could figure out exactly what—Juliet started and her gaze flew to the French doors, where one obviously tired but endearingly sexy Gareth stood. Her heart gave a little leap and an instant smile spread over her lips.

God help her, she was so far gone.

This couldn't possibly end well.

She knew that, knew that it was a miracle that she'd ever caught his attention to start with. But keeping it up on a permanent basis? It was utterly out of the question. She didn't dare even let herself think about it.

But she wasn't going to think about that tonight, or even tomorrow when they went to the prom. Another little jolt of glee shot through her. She'd think about it all later, after she'd selfishly basked in the anomaly of his interest and had her wicked way with him. She'd brought her overnight bag and her bathing suit, as he'd instructed, and was prepared to fully embrace a single night of unrepentant passion. She deserved it, dammit. Furthermore, she didn't think she could stop herself even if she'd wanted to. And she didn't, but…

Mercy, the man did something that made her insides turn to total goo. Better still, *tingly* goo. A mere quirk of that lopsided smile, a lone look from those beautifully sexy green eyes and she became a moaning, panting puddle of lust. Every minute she spent with him left her all the more enchanted, all the more attached and all the more desperate. Each lingering look—and Lord knows he'd given her more than a few of those over the past week—each long kiss, every second spent wrapped in his arms had made her anticipate this evening with him all the more.

Unfortunately, while she was technically finished with the room, she wasn't satisfied with "The Ugly Duckling."

Gareth came up behind her and massaged her tense shoulders, his big hands warm and wonderful. "Problem?"

She winced. "I'm finished," she said, "just not altogether happy with this wall."

Gareth stared at the painting for a minute, then glanced around the room at the other walls. "It looks great," he said hesitantly.

"But?" Juliet prodded, glad that he hadn't tried to gloss over her concern with some sort of generic platitude. She knew he had a good eye. After all, he was an artist of sorts as well.

He cocked his head, studying it more thoroughly, then shook his head and gave her an uncertain smile. "But…I don't know. The execution is perfect. The whole mirror and reflection element is very evocative. I love the way you've painted her reflection in the water, with her hero over her shoulder so that you know you're seeing her through his eyes. She's this beautiful swan-like creature. Very sensual. Very lovely." He gave his head a small shake. "But something about her doesn't feel right. I don't know what it is exactly. It's almost like she doesn't buy it. She doesn't believe that she's gorgeous, sexy even." He chuckled softly and sent her an apologetic smile. "That probably didn't make a bit of sense. Sorry."

Juliet stilled and studied the woman she'd painted. It was in her eyes, just the slightest hint of doubt. Gareth was right, she realized. "Actually, I think you might be onto something." She wasn't entirely sure how to fix it, but she did believe that he'd discovered the problem. Her swan needed an attitude adjustment. And it was because she suffered from it herself. Despite every evidence to the contrary, she still couldn't quite make herself believe that Gareth truly wanted her, that she was anything less than the ugly duckling she'd always been.

"Glad I could help," he said. "I'm going to go take a quick shower." He pressed a kiss against her neck, sending a flurry of gooseflesh down her back. "Let me know when you're finished."

Her heart was finished the day he'd kissed her, Juliet realized, her belly becoming a muddled mass of jittery heat. She watched him stroll from the room, his big shoulders draped with a confidence that she envied.

With a sigh, Juliet looked back at the painting and tried to think of some way to make her duckling-turned-swan appreciate her own appeal. When none came, she signed her name in an inconspicuous corner and deemed her day complete. The sound of the shower reached her ears.

Warm, wet naked skin. Broad, muscled shoulders, fluted spine. Bare chest, dusted with auburn curls…

Juliet released a shuddering breath, snagged her bathing suit from her bag and made for the pool.

Her day might be finished, but it was *far* from over.

8

HIS SWAN was in the pool.

Gareth stood at the door and watched her for a moment a tight feeling crowding into his chest as she glided effortlessly through the water. She wore a modest white two-piece bathing suit, one of those that covered her middle, but left her back bare. Her legs were long, toned and strong and it was obvious that she was truly in her element in the water. Utterly graceful. Not that she wasn't all the time, but something about the way she moved through the pool was eerily reminiscent of her last name. She swam beautifully. Desire stirred in his loins as she flipped over onto her back and floated in the warm water. Her full breasts thrust up and she lazily swung her arms back and forth over her head, then along her side. She barely made a splash. Just floated along an invisible current all her own.

Unable to stand there any longer, Gareth ventured outside and dove in to join her, the heated water cool against his skin. He opened his eyes and surfaced right in front her and without waiting, without the slightest bit of hesitation, he did what he'd been dying to do all day. He bracketed her face with his hands and slanted his lips over hers. He kissed her long and deep, slowly backing her beneath the cascading waterfall and into the grotto. He'd been patient. He'd waited.

Waiting was no longer an option.

With a soft eager groan her arms came up and wrapped around his neck, her legs around his waist. His dick jutted against her, instinctively recognizing the unspoken act for what it was—an invitation to come inside her body.

And he fully intended to. As swiftly as possible.

The grotto was warm and welcoming, a hedonistic cave he'd built with his own two hands. Better that he should enjoy it first, Gareth thought. After all, Highgrove would have it to himself every night afterwards. He was testing it, Gareth told himself. Making sure it would live up to Highgrove's expectations.

He backed Juliet into one of the small seating areas and rocked hard against her. "Do you have any idea how desperately I want you?" he asked her, his voice as tortured as the rest of his body.

Juliet slid her hands over his chest, gently abrading his nipples with her fingernails. "I h-hope it's as much as I w-want you," she said, a hint of nervousness in her breathy voice. She licked a path down the side of his neck, then kissed the underside of his jaw, making his flesh prickle and burn. A hiss slipped from between his clenched teeth. He bent his head, nudged the cup of her bathing suit aside and suckled the perfect tip of her rosy breast. The taste of her danced over his tongue, making him groan with pleasure.

Juliet gasped, a sound of delight that resonated directly in his loins. He reached up and carefully, slowly pulled the tie of her bathing suit from behind her neck, then smiled against her nipple as the fabric came free. "Lovely," he murmured thickly as her creamy skin came into view. "So damned beautiful."

She tensed. "You don't have to say those things," Juliet said. "Really."

Gareth paused. He looked up and his gaze caught hers. "I know I don't have to say them," he told her. "I want to say them. Because they're true." He didn't touch her, merely pinned her with a sincere gaze, laying bare how he felt about her. "You are the most beautiful woman I've ever seen, Juliet." He bent forward and kissed the tip of her nose. "To me, you are perfect."

A soft melting look came into her eyes, twin pools of dark emotion and a slow wavering smile slid over her lips. "Thank you," she said, her voice a bit shaky. "I think you're pretty damned perfect as well."

Gareth grinned at her. "You know what else I think is going to be perfect?" he asked, sliding a finger determinedly down her belly.

"Wh-what?"

"Us. Together."

He trailed a finger over her mound and smiled at the immediate catch in her breathing. Then he lifted her up over the side of the pool, where she landed on the oversized beach towel he'd placed there earlier today. Smiling at him, Juliet rolled over, making room for him as he quickly slid out of the water as well.

Rather than jump immediately onto her, Gareth allowed his gaze to drift over her, a slow, lengthy perusal, drinking her in. Telling her she was beautiful was one thing—proving it to her was going to take much more attention to detail.

Starting now.

He bent and slid his tongue over her collarbone, tasting the beads of moisture which had collected in the delicate hollow, then tasted a path over her shoulder, up the side of her neck, and found her mouth. She was open and ready, rolling into him, her hot wet flesh branding him where it touched. Want sizzled along his nerve endings, heat flared in an instant, burning up good intentions, charring anything remotely resembling restraint. Her hands were suddenly all over him. Sliding over his shoulders and down his back, tugging at the waist of his trunks, then slipping beneath to where his eager dick practically leapt into her waiting palm.

Gareth bit back a groan as she slid her hand up and down over his slippery skin. He hardened to the point of pain, felt his balls draw up, the impending orgasm gather in the back of his loins.

Not now, dammit. Not before he'd been inside her.

Gareth snagged a condom from the edge of the blanket, stripped off his trunks and carefully slid the protection into place. Juliet had slithered out of her bikini bottoms and kicked them to the side.

Concave belly, long graceful limbs, plump rosy-tipped breasts, and a dark thatch of curls that dared him to try and take it slowly.

A shudder worked its way through him and he swallowed hard as he positioned himself between her thighs. She arched her hips in welcome, her dark eyes heavy-lidded and desperate, yet still just the slightest bit unsure. Bare, but scared, he realized.

He bent forward and kissed her, twined his fingers through hers, then pushed slowly into her. Lights burst behind his lids and a feeling of utter contentment washed through him as he seated himself firmly inside her. He drew back, shaken, then plunged once again.

"You—"

He thrust again, rocking forward, watched her mouth open in silent pleasure.

"—are—"

He pushed again, tightening his fingers around hers, desperate to stem the flow of heat pounding through his veins.

"—beautiful," he finished. Then, unable to control himself for another minute, he grabbed her hips and plunged in and out of her, back and forth, harder and deeper. He couldn't get close enough, couldn't bury himself far enough into her. He had to— He needed—

JULIET LOCKED her legs around Gareth's waist, bent forward and licked a male nipple. He pounded harder, pushing her closer and closer to the edge of mindlessness. She could feel her body tightening, readying for release and the knowledge that they could actually get there together made her buck determinedly beneath him.

She clamped her feminine muscles around him, desperate to keep that wonderful draw and drag between their joined bodies. Her breath came in short, faltering puffs. Her breasts bounced, absorbing the force of his manic thrusts, and with every push of him deep inside her, her nipples tingled and pouted, wishing for one more kiss from his hot, wonderful mouth. Sweat slickened the small of her back and she bit her lip as another bolt of pleasure lanced through her.

"Gareth," she gasped, begging for more. She drew her legs back even further, allowing him to go deeper and he took it greedily, hammering into her. Harder and faster, then deeper and faster still. The corded muscles of his throat bunched and the look of determined delight on his face was enough to make her preen with pleasure.

She'd done this to him.

Her.

You are beautiful, he'd said, punctuating each word with a determined thrust into her body. And for a moment—in this very instant—she could believe him.

Juliet drew his head down for a kiss, pulling his tongue deep into her mouth. He groaned against her lips, a masculine sound that was one of the best things she'd ever tasted in her life.

"Juliet," he murmured, his voice anguished with need. "Do you have any idea what you're doing to me?"

She rocked hard beneath him, leaned forward and nipped his shoulder. "I hope it's as fabulous as what you're doing to me." She giggled. "I'm almost impressed."

He drew back. "Almost?" he asked suspiciously.

She chuckled at him, then tightened around him once more. "I'll let you know when I'm *really* impressed," she said.

A knowing smile slid over that wonderfully carnal mouth. "Clearly I'm not trying hard enough." He reached down between their joined bodies and knuckled her clit, tearing an unexpected gasp from her throat. "But that's easily rectified."

Three strokes later her mouth opened in a silent scream, her back bowed so hard off the beach towel she feared it would break, a dizzying array of color flashed behind her closed lids and every nerve ending in her sex sang with unprecedented joy. She couldn't catch her breath, and every muscle tensed with the long-awaited release.

A masculine smile of approval clinging to his lips, Gareth stared down at her, mossy eyes twinkling. "Are you impressed now?"

She couldn't talk, couldn't form a single word. Instead, though every pulse made her tingle with unbearable delight, she lifted her hips and begged for more.

Gareth's smile promptly fled and, having satisfied her, he seemed to release a bit of his rigid control. He pushed into her, sliding her back across the towel. From the dimmest recesses of her mind, she heard the water falling in the distance, saw the steam rising up. Gareth pushed again, harder and deeper, and she met him thrust for thrust, determined that she wouldn't be the only person here who left impressed.

She bent forward and licked his chest, his neck, slid her hands over his hot flesh. Warm supple muscle beneath her greedy palms. She made a little noise in her throat and a second later, she felt Gareth go rigid above her. He drove into her, angling deep and held, his big body quaking above hers. She felt him tremble and shudder inside her and a rush of warmth gathered near her womb as it pooled in the end of the condom. Another sparkler of heat detonated in her belly and she held him close, enjoying the contact.

Gareth drew back and smiled down at her, then pressed a tender kiss against her lips. "I was right," he murmured, a strange look in his eyes, one that was tender and curiously unreadable.

"About what?" Juliet asked, feeling oddly nervous.

"Us. We're perfect together." He carefully withdrew, disposed of the condom, then rolled her toward him and wrapped them in the beach blanket.

Heartbreakingly so, she silently agreed, snuggling into his side. Pity she couldn't bring herself to believe that it would last. This single

night would have to be good enough, Juliet decided, knowing that
the end had to come. And soon, because she didn't want the mess of
an awkward official brush-off or break-up to ruin her memory.

For the first time in her life, Juliet Swan felt beautiful and sexy
and wanted. This was a memory she would protect at all costs. Ir-
rational? Yes. But self-preservation didn't always follow logical
thought....

9

GARETH KNEW he was supposed to be a chaperone, but when his date looked as good as Juliet did, admittedly he was having trouble focusing on his responsibilities. Particularly not when all he wanted was to find a deserted room and have his wicked way with her. Preferably against a wall.

"Mom didn't say you were bringing a date," his nephew said. Jeremy nodded, seemingly impressed. "She's pretty hot."

Gareth grinned, watching Juliet return from the ladies' room. "Thank you. I think so, of course."

"Is it a secret that you brought a date, or can I tell her?"

"Keep it under your hat, if you don't mind. I want to keep Juliet to myself for a little while before your mother gets hold of her."

His sister, intuitive wench that she was, would undoubtedly recognize what Gareth wasn't quite ready to admit to himself—that he'd fallen head over heels in love with Juliet Swan. Then they'd have to talk about it and his sister would press him for plans, and at the moment, other than spending as much time with Juliet as he possibly could, he didn't have any. And given that she'd been a bit…distant since he'd picked her up, he wasn't altogether sure how long that would be. He suspected she was spooked. *Welcome to the club, sweetheart,* Gareth thought.

He was freaking terrified.

Jeremy snorted. "Can't blame you for that." He clapped Gareth on the back, then with a muttered "cool," strolled onto the dance floor where he reclaimed his date from a group of gyrating young girls.

Looking absolutely stunning in a long Grecian-style white gown, Juliet walked over toward him. "Thank you so much for bringing me here tonight," she said. "I skipped my own prom, so this is an unexpected treat."

He frowned. "You skipped your prom?"

She shrugged. "I didn't have a date and I didn't want to go alone."

That was perfectly understandable. But it tugged at his heart-strings to think of her home alone in her room, missing what should have been a memorable milestone in her life. The guys in her class must all have been morons. Then again, would he have recognized what a beauty she truly was at seventeen? He'd like to think so, but he wasn't certain.

"Well, I'm glad that you're with me tonight." He paused, searched her face. "In fact, I was hoping that you'd spend the night with me." He nuzzled her ear. "We'll bring in Valentine's Day in style."

Juliet's eyes took on a guarded quality and she shook her head. His stomach turned to lead. He knew—*knew*—before she said another word what was coming. He'd been feeling it all evening, her slowly but surely distancing herself. He couldn't imagine why, nor could be understand how he'd read things so terribly wrong last night.

"Sorry, I can't. I've actually got a pretty busy morning."

"More work at Highgrove's?" he asked, knowing that it was impossible. He'd awakened alone in the grotto and had found her back in the boudoir putting the final touches on "The Ugly Duckling." Whereas the swan had been uncertain of her beauty before, Juliet had repainted her with a small sensual smile which bespoke intimate confidence.

The change was subtle but significant, and he recognized it in her as well. He'd told her she was beautiful last night and he knew she'd believed him. So why then was she pulling away? What possible reason could she have for backing off when things were going so well between them?

"No," she said, giving her head a small shake. "Just studio work. Then, of course, lunch at my parents."

He waited, hoping she'd invite him. He swallowed a sigh when the invitation didn't come and ignored the uncomfortable prick in his chest.

"Dinner tomorrow night, then?" he pressed. If she was going to cut him loose, then he would *make* her do it. He wouldn't let her take the easy way out. Frankly, he thought he deserved better than that.

Again, she shook her head. "I'm going to keep things low-key. Stay at home and gorge myself on chocolate."

"And conversation hearts?" he asked.

She smiled wanly. "Of course."

"Would you like some company?" Or was she already having company? Gareth wondered, remembering the bleached-blond guy with the dark tan he'd seen pull out of her driveway just as he was pulling in. She'd said he was her stylist, but now Gareth wasn't so sure.

"You know, Gareth, I think we need to slow things down a bit."

He felt his temper flare. "That wasn't the impression I got last night. Do you want to slow things down, Juliet, or end them altogether? I think after the past couple of weeks, you owe me the courtesy of the truth."

Gauntlet thrown down, Gareth stared at her and waited.

JULIET'S STOMACH twisted into a knot of dread. She'd really wanted to avoid this. But apparently Gareth had sensed the change and wasn't going to allow it. Juliet had absolutely no experience in breaking up with someone and decided that it wasn't to her liking, particularly when she suspected she'd fallen in love with the man she was attempting to end things with.

Which was all the more reason she'd decided she had to break things off with him. She had to beat him to the punch, to insulate her heart to the best of her ability. This was—he was—quite simply, too good to be true. Guys like Gareth didn't fall for girls like her. Makeover or no, it just simply didn't happen. Hoping for it, wishing for it wouldn't make it so. She was smart. She was practical. And her smart, practical mind told her this could not last. She'd be better off to take what she'd gotten—wonderful memories of the most wonderful sex of her entire life—and be done with it.

And though it was really tempting to savor a Valentine memory with Gareth, Juliet just couldn't bring herself to do it. Every year would mark the anniversary of something she'd loved and lost. She didn't care what Tennyson had said, she didn't want that. Didn't think she could bear it.

But Gareth was right. After the past two weeks—and particularly last night—she did owe him the truth. "Are you sure you want to talk about this now?" she asked.

"My shift is over at midnight," Gareth said. "That's five minutes away, so I guess now is as good a time as any."

She'd been afraid he'd say that. Juliet released a shaky breath. "I actually think we should quit while we're ahead," she finally admitted. "What we've shared has been great," she admitted, cursing the crack in her voice. "But, as I said, things are moving a little too fast for me." *And I have a wonderful memory I want to savor. I don't want it spoiled with a broken heart later.*

He stared at her, his mossy green eyes in torment. "Are you saying you don't want to see me anymore?"

Damn, this was much harder than she'd thought it would be, and she hadn't counted on it being easy. She couldn't bring herself to say the words, essentially to break her own heart, so instead she merely nodded, just the slightest jerk of her head in affirmation.

Ironically the intro to Journey's "Faithfully"—one of her all-time favorite ballads—suddenly played through the speakers, the last dance of the night. Rather than say a word, looking defeated and hurt, Gareth merely took her hand and led her out onto the dance floor. He held her close, his big warm hand at the small of her back, the scent of his aftershave in her nostrils. She breathed him in, imprinting this moment in her memory.

And above the music, a sound only she could hear, she could have sworn she heard her own heart break.

10

VALENTINE'S DAY and Cupid, the chubby winged bastard, had screwed him again, Gareth thought as he sat in his recliner and watched the sun peep through the blinds. Sleep would have offered an escape, he knew, but he hadn't even tried. Instead, he'd come right in, opened a bottle of Scotch and had nursed it off and on all night while staring at his painting.

His gaze zeroed in on her signature in the corner and he felt the back of his throat burn. What the hell was wrong with her? Couldn't she tell that they had something special? That this wasn't just some damned harmless going-nowhere fling?

Evidently not. Because, according to her, she had very little experience with relationships. He snorted. For someone who had so little experience, she'd certainly mastered the breaking-up part pretty damned well. Because he'd wanted to retain the smallest portion of his pride, he hadn't argued with her last night. He'd wanted to, but…couldn't.

A knock at his front door sounded, momentarily disrupting his morose thoughts. Juliet? he wondered, his heart giving a pathetic jolt. He bolted up from his chair and hurried to the door.

Keith, his former business partner, stood on his front porch. "Last person you expected to see, eh?" his old friend asked.

"Yes," Gareth admitted, taken aback. Obviously, Keith had come here for a reason, so rather than press him, Gareth just waited.

Keith shifted uncomfortably. "Listen, man, I just wanted to tell you again how sorry I am about what happened with Courtney. I was a total ass, and a worse friend, and I just—" He smiled awkwardly. "I just wanted you to know that."

Gareth nodded. "You still seeing her?"

"Er…no. Haven't seen her in months." He looked relieved about that, Gareth noted, feeling a bit vindicated.

"Look, this isn't about me getting my job back," he said. "I'm working. I just miss hanging out and talking football, shooting the shit, ya know?"

Gareth did know. He and Keith had always been close. A guy needed friends. Particularly when he'd just been so thoroughly dumped.

Keith's gaze slid over him and he winced. "I know that I came here to apologize, and, well, this isn't exactly in the right spirit of things...but you look like hell, man. You been hitting the Scotch?"

"I've had a drink or two," Gareth admitted, opening the door wider to allow Keith inside. A silent gesture, one that indicated he was accepting the olive branch. Keith grinned. "You only break out the hard stuff when you're having woman trouble," he said, taking his usual seat in the other recliner. "Anyone I know?"

"Hell, no," Gareth said, "And stay the hell away from her."

Keith grimaced. "Is this going to become a frequent warning?"

Gareth glared at him.

"Because it's cool if it is—I deserve it. I'd just like to know."

"Not a frequent warning, no. I can't warn you away from someone who's ditched me, can I?"

Keith made a face. "Damn, man. That bites. What are you going to do?"

Gareth frowned. "What do you mean?"

"Look, I know that we haven't spoken in a few months, but I can read the signs here." He gestured to the liquor. "You've polished off almost a full bottle of Scotch, you haven't gone to bed and you haven't bothered to turn on the television for any sports therapy." He shrugged and helped himself to a swig from Gareth's bottle. "That tells me all I need to know about this girl." He grinned. "She's done what no other woman has managed to do."

"Really?" Gareth replied sarcastically, surprised at how easily they'd fallen back into their old routine. "And what the hell is that?"

Keith grinned. "She's caught you."

Gareth remained silent.

"Then thrown you back." He shrugged, picked up the remote control and surfed channels until he found a college basketball game. "The old Gareth I knew wouldn't have stood for that."

Gareth sat there for a minute, absorbing Keith's assessment. He blinked, stunned, and looked at his friend. Sweet God, he was right. What the hell was wrong with him? Why was he sitting here like a pathetic lump? The woman he loved was sitting down at her parents' table today—once again, without a date on Valentine's Day—and he was here, halfway across town.

Hadn't he just remembered she didn't have any experience when it came to relationships? He was the one with the so-called Master's degree. Letting her call the shots was the height of stupidity. She didn't know that the hell she was doing.

Luckily for her, she had him to point out the flaw in her logic, Gareth decided.

He abruptly stood. "You're right, Keith."

His friend sighed happily. "I usually am."

Gareth quirked a pointed brow.

"But not all the time," Keith replied quickly.

"I'll see you later," Gareth said, heading for the shower. "I've got to go get caught again." And if she wouldn't listen to reason, then he'd just have to *impress* her again.

"JULIET, you've barely touched your chicken divan. What's wrong? Are you ill? Are those infernal people at the Internet dating sites still bugging you?"

Juliet offered a wan smile to her mother. "I'm fine, Mom. I'm just not hungry."

"But chicken divan is your favorite," her mother persisted, unwilling to let it go.

"Leave her alone, Cecilia," her father admonished. "She's an adult. She's allowed not to be hungry."

"I know she's allowed," her mother replied. "I just don't like it. It makes me worry."

"I can't get over the difference that hairstyle makes on you, Juliet," Portia said. "You look fabulous."

"Thanks," Juliet murmured, because a response was called for. If this is what doing the right thing felt like, then she would have been much happier being wrong.

If she'd ever been more miserable in her life, she couldn't recall. What had she been thinking? Why had she thought breaking up with

Gareth now rather than later would be better, when breaking up at all was still going to make her wretched?

She was an idiot.

He was the greatest thing that had ever happened to her and she should have had sense enough to hang onto him and make more memories before he broke things off with her. Would he do that? Certainly. But at least she could have enjoyed his company and that lopsided smile and those haunting green eyes a little longer. She could have made love to him over and over again, enjoying every second of his touch.

Remembered heat stole through her limbs and settled in her sex and her lips tingled from that sweet, desperate kiss—one he'd hoped would change her mind, she realized now—last night when he'd walked her to her door.

A gentleman to the end.

Because that was just the sort of man he was. One who could make her laugh until her sides hurt, make her toes curl, make her want things she'd never dared to hope for before. One who would forgive a friend the greatest insult and chaperone a nephew's prom to save the kid embarrassment.

A good one, Juliet realized, tears burning the backs of her eyes.

The doorbell chimed, announcing a visitor. Excellent, Juliet thought. She'd give up her chair and go home.

"I wonder who that could be," her father mused. "Are we expecting anyone?" Her father's gaze slid to her.

Both Portia and Bianca's dates were present and accounted for. Juliet shook her head. "I'm not."

Frowning, her mother stood and hurried to the door. She heard her mother's startled hello, followed by a muffled greeting. "Er, yes, she's here. Juliet, you say?"

Juliet's head jerked up and her gaze darted to the dining-room door where Gareth suddenly appeared. Portia gasped and a look of confusion crossed her face. "Gareth?"

Juliet stood. "Er…what are you doing here?

Portia's gaze darted to Juliet, then back to Gareth. Suddenly, her eyes widened and a huge smile split her face. "Oh," she said significantly.

Her parents and Bianca looked suitably stunned.

"I wanted to talk to you," Gareth said. "I didn't like how things ended last night at the prom and—"

Her father's bushy eyebrows rose. "The prom? But—"

"Hush, Warren," her mother said. "Why don't you and Gareth talk about this in the parlor, dear?" Cecilia suggested.

"Please, Juliet," Gareth said.

Her heart hammering so loudly in her ears she was almost deaf, Juliet stood on virtually numb legs and made her way into the parlor. She turned and faced Gareth, wondering what on earth could have brought him here.

His woefully familiar gaze traced her face. "I've been thinking about what you said last night and I've decided that I don't agree."

"What?"

"Look, Juliet, you've admitted that you don't have a lot of experience with relationships, so I think you probably shouldn't be the one making decisions about this one for us."

She blinked, trying to decide whether she should be annoyed or overjoyed. "Are you saying that I shouldn't have any say-so?"

"No, I'm saying that you apparently don't recognize that we are perfect for each other and that I'm hopelessly in love with you. I can only chalk that up to your inexperience." He sidled closer. "But don't worry. I'm going to take charge now and fix everything."

Warmth bubbled through her middle and again, that strange vision of Eros's angel-wing earring flashed through her mind. "You're going to fix everything?"

He nodded. "I am. And I'm going to start by refusing to let you dump me like yesterday's garbage and ruin Valentine's Day for both of us." He withdrew something from his pocket and placed it in her palm. "Here," he said. "I've got something for you."

Tears blurring her vision, Juliet looked down and found two conversations hearts resting in her hand. *Be Mine* and *I Love You*.

A strangled laugh broke out of her throat and she threw her arms around him. "I'm s-sorry," she sobbed. "I was just scared. I didn't want to get hurt. Things like this don't happen to me. Things like *you* don't happen to me."

Gareth drew back and stared down at her, his green eyes bright and sincere. "Juliet, things like *you* never happen to me. And I'm not letting you go without a fight."

Her chest bursting with joy, Juliet twined her arms around his neck and offered her lips up for a kiss. "I surrender," she said.

A whoop of delight sounded from just beyond the doorway and she heard her mother's feet retreating down the hall, muttering something about setting another plate.

"Do you have a grotto at your place?" Juliet asked, warmth rushing to her core.

He chuckled. "Not yet. But I've got a bed."

That would do, Juliet thought. "I think I need you to impress me," she murmured, sliding a kiss along his jaw. "And the sooner the better."

And They Lived Happily Ever After...

AND SO IT WENT *that Juliet and Gareth married on a bright June morning. The bride, no longer laboring under the misapprehension that she was an ugly duckling, glided with swan-like grace down the aisle in a simple white dress. The groom, resplendent in a black tux, waited impatiently in front of the minister.*

They built a beautiful house on a lovely little parcel of land which overlooked a small lake. On moonlit nights they could be seen walking along its shore or paddling quietly across its smooth surface in a cozy little canoe. Occasionally, Juliet would peer over the side and study her own reflection. The confident woman who smiled contentedly back at her never failed to make her heart swell with an inner, private joy.

Though life would never be entirely pretty, dear Juliet had learned a very valuable lesson—true beauty comes from within and true love deserves respect.

Juliet painted, and word of Gareth's talent with sex grottos spread throughout the South like kudzu. He made his fortune creating other private paradises like Highgrove's, but never one so special—or so used—as the one he built for them.

Because it's not a happy ending without a lot of great sex!

Epilogue

February 15

LB KICKED his feet up onto his desk, laced his fingers behind his head and happily puffed on a Cuban cigar. The first fingers of dawn rose in beautiful pink and amber hues over the Chicago skyline, and from his vantage point in the sleek downtown high-rise, the world was looking pretty damned good.

The preliminary numbers were in and they *rocked*.

His office space and his ass were both safe.

Another peek at the spreadsheet confirmed that Love, while technically not running neck and neck with Sex, was at least on the rise. Baby steps, LB, told himself. Steady growth. That's what they needed. And if he had to put a more personal hand into things—he mentally patted himself on the back for bringing about Shay, Scarlett and Juliet's changes of heart—then so be it. Hell it had been fun. He'd spent so much time stuck behind this damned desk, he'd forgotten how great it could be to be back in the trenches, so to speak.

Without bothering to knock—as if she'd ever need to—Venus strolled into his office. LB scrambled to put his feet on the floor and hurriedly extinguished the cigar. His mother didn't approve of the habit.

"You need to e-mail those haters at that Web site and tell them to update their homepage," his mother said. "I hope they'll be as quick with the new information as they were with the old, unflattering variety."

LB nodded. "Of course."

"I've taken a look at the new numbers." To his vast relief, she nodded approvingly and the faintest hint of a smile shaped her mouth. "Well done."

Relief washed through him. "Thanks, I—"

"I liked your initiative, darling. I think you're finally beginning to understand how significant love truly is. That's what it's all about." She jerked her head toward the door. "Pack your things. You're moving up. Corner unit, fourteenth floor."

LB felt his eyes widen. The fourteenth floor? The Holy Grail of Office Space? Finally? "Seriously?"

Venus grinned. "Seriously."

Hot damn, LB thought. Love was on the rise. And it looked as if he was, too.

CELEBRATE
60 YEARS
OF PURE READING PLEASURE
WITH HARLEQUIN®!

We'll be spotlighting a different series
every month throughout 2009
to celebrate our 60th anniversary.

Look for Harlequin® Blaze™ in March!

0-60

*After all, a lot can happen in 60 years,
or 60 minutes...or 60 seconds!*

Find out what's going down in Blaze's
heart-stopping new miniseries *0-60!*
Getting from "Hello" to "How was it?"
can happen fast....

Look for the brand-new 0-60 miniseries in March 2009!

DIAMOND IN THE ROUGH

John Callister is a millionaire rancher, yet when he meets
lovely Sassy Peale and she thinks he's a cowboy, he goes along
with her misconception. He's had enough of gold diggers,
and this is a chance to be valued for himself, not his money.
But when Sassy finds out the truth, she feels John was merely
playing with her. John will have to convince her that he's truly
the man she fell in love with—a diamond in the rough.

THE MEN OF MEDICINE RIDGE—a brand-new miniseries
set in the wilds of Montana!

Available April 2009 wherever you buy books.

www.eHarlequin.com   HR17577

HARLEQUIN® *Romance*®

This February the Harlequin® Romance series
will feature six Diamond Brides stories featuring
diamond proposals and gorgeous grooms.

Share your dream wedding proposal and you could WIN!

The most romantic entry will win a diamond
necklace and will inspire a proposal in one of
our upcoming Diamond Grooms books in 2010.

In 100 words or less, tell us the most romantic
way that you dream of being proposed to.

For more information, and to enter
the Diamond Brides Proposal contest, please visit
www.DiamondBridesProposal.com

Or mail your entry to us at:
IN THE U.S.: 3010 Walden Ave., P.O. Box 9069, Buffalo, NY 14269-9069
IN CANADA: 225 Duncan Mill Road, Don Mills, ON M3B 3K9

REQUEST YOUR FREE BOOKS!

2 FREE NOVELS PLUS 2 FREE GIFTS!

HARLEQUIN®

Blaze™

Red-hot reads!

YES! Please send me 2 FREE Harlequin® Blaze™ novels and my 2 FREE gifts (gifts are worth about $10). After receiving them, if I don't wish to receive any more books, I can return the shipping statement marked "cancel." If I don't cancel, I will receive 6 brand-new novels every month and be billed just $4.24 per book in the U.S. or $4.71 per book in Canada, plus 25¢ shipping and handling per book and applicable taxes, if any*. That's a savings of 15% or more off the cover price! I understand that accepting the 2 free books and gifts places me under no obligation to buy anything. I can always return a shipment and cancel at any time. Even if I never buy another book, the two free books and gifts are mine to keep forever.

151 HDN ERVA 351 HDN ERUX

Name	(PLEASE PRINT)	
Address		Apt. #
City	State/Prov.	Zip/Postal Code

Signature (if under 18, a parent or guardian must sign)

Mail to the Harlequin Reader Service:
IN U.S.A.: P.O. Box 1867, Buffalo, NY 14240-1867
IN CANADA: P.O. Box 609, Fort Erie, Ontario L2A 5X3

Not valid to current subscribers of Harlequin Blaze books.

Want to try two free books from another line?
Call 1-800-873-8635 or visit www.morefreebooks.com.

* Terms and prices subject to change without notice. N.Y. residents add applicable sales tax. Canadian residents will be charged applicable provincial taxes and GST. Offer not valid in Quebec. This offer is limited to one order per household. All orders subject to approval. Credit or debit balances in a customer's account(s) may be offset by any other outstanding balance owed by or to the customer. Please allow 4 to 6 weeks for delivery. Offer available while quantities last.

Your Privacy: Harlequin Books is committed to protecting your privacy. Our Privacy Policy is available online at www.eHarlequin.com or upon request from the Reader Service. From time to time we make our lists of customers available to reputable third parties who may have a product or service of interest to you. If you would prefer we not share your name and address, please check here. ☐

Harlequin® Historical
Historical Romantic Adventure!

The Aikenhead Honours

HIS CAVALRY LADY
Joanna Maitland

Dominic Aikenhead, spy against
the Russians, takes a young soldier
under his wing. "Alex" is actually
Alexandra, a cavalry maiden who
also has been tasked to spy on the
Russians. When Alexandra unveils
herself as a lady, will Dominic flee,
or embrace the woman he has
come to love?

Available March 2009
wherever books are sold.

The Inside Romance newsletter has a NEW look for the new year!

Same great content, brand-new look!

The Inside Romance newsletter is a FREE quarterly newsletter highlighting our upcoming series releases and promotions!

Click on the Inside Romance link on the front page of **www.eHarlequin.com** or e-mail us at insideromance@harlequin.ca to sign up to receive your FREE newsletter today!

You can also subscribe by writing to us at: HARLEQUIN BOOKS Attention: Customer Service Department P.O. Box 9057, Buffalo, NY 14269-9057

Please allow 4-6 weeks for delivery of the first issue by mail.

IRNNEW09

HARLEQUIN Blaze

COMING NEXT MONTH
Available February 10, 2009

#453 A LONG, HARD RIDE Alison Kent
From 0–60
All Cardin Worth wants is to put her broken family together again. And if that means seducing Trey Davis, her first love, well, a girl's got to do what a girl's got to do. Only, she never expected to enjoy it quite so much....

#454 UP CLOSE AND DANGEROUSLY SEXY Karen Anders
Drew Miller's mission: train a fellow agent's twin sister to replace her in a sting op. Expect the unexpected is his mantra, but he never anticipated that his trainee, Allie Carpenter, would be teaching him a thing or twelve in the bedroom!

#455 ONCE AN OUTLAW Debbi Rawlins
Stolen from Time, Bk. 1
Sam Watkins has a past he's trying to forget. Reese Winslow is desperate to remember a way home. Caught in the Old West, they share an intensely passionate affair that has them joining forces. But does that mean they'll be together forever?

#456 STILL IRRESISTIBLE Dawn Atkins
Years ago Callie Cummings and Declan O'Neill had an unforgettable fling. And now she's back in town. He's still tempting, still irresistible, and she can't get images of him and tangled sheets out of her mind. The only solution? An unforgettable fling, round two.

#457 ALWAYS READY Joanne Rock
Uniformly Hot!
Lieutenant Damon Craig has always tried to live up to the Coast Guard motto: Always Ready. But when sexy sociologist Lacey Sutherland stumbles into a stakeout, alerting his suspects—and his libido—Damon knows he doesn't stand a chance....

#458 BODY CHECK Elle Kennedy
When sexually frustrated professor Hayden Houston meets hot hockey star Brody Croft in a bar, she's ready for a one-night stand. But can Brody convince Hayden that he's good for more than just a body check?

HBCNMBPA0209